D1289518

PHANTOM VIRUS

A BOMBER HANSON MYSTERY

DAVID CHAMPION

ALLEN A. KNOLL, PUBLISHERS
SANTA BARBARA, CA

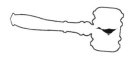

Allen A. Knoll, Publishers, 200 West Victoria Street, Santa Barbara, CA 93101

First Edition

05   04   03   02   01   00   99   5   4   3   2   1

Author's Note:

In this novel, several fictional terms are used: R4 is a virus, Wanns is a condition which shatters the immune system, and JCD is a drug given to Wanns patients. These letters and this number have no meaning, were not derived from anything and are not acronyms. Some readers may find it convenient to substitute these terms for words in medical currency. If so, it would be well to remember, this is foremost a work of fiction.

—D.C.

Library of Congress Cataloging-in-Publication Data

Champion, David.
    Phantom virus : a Bomber Hanson mystery / David Champion. -- 1st ed.
        p. cm.   🗷
        ISBN: 1-888310-93-6 (alk. paper)
        I. Title.
    PS3553.H2649P47   1999
    813'.54--dc21   98-48992
                                                     CIP

Text typeface is Caslon Old Face, 12 point
printed on 60-pound Lakewood white, acid free paper
Case bound with Kivar 9, Smyth sewn

Also By David Champion

Celebrity Trouble
Nobody Roots for Goliath
The Mountain Massacres
The Snatch

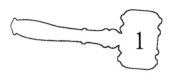

I heard the screaming when I turned into the parking lot in front of the Victorian house that held the law offices of Bomber Hanson, his flea-brained secretary, Bonnie Doone, and his beleaguered son, Tod—that's me.

I parked my clunker next to the shiny Chinese-red Bentley that belonged to you-know-who. Hint: not the secretary. On the other side of the Bentley sat a nondescript rental car with an inferiority complex.

The screaming continued unabated as I made my way tremulously up the steps to the porch and front door. There I recognized the voice of a distraught and angry male. Inside the office the shouting was deafening—and it wasn't coming from Bomber.

Bonnie Doone was shaking her empty head and rolling her vibrant eyes—two gestures she had honed to a fine art. Today she had wrapped herself in something clingy and lime green and apricot and it put me in immediate mind of a luscious fruit salad. For it cannot be denied Bonnie Doone was miraculously constructed and had a marvelous penchant for adorning herself in a fashion that continually reminded you of the peerless proportions underneath the fabrics. I give her all that, just don't ask her to think.

"Bomber's fit to be tied," she said, on seeing me. "If you ever came to work on time, you might have stopped this," she said with a quaint mixture of tenses, and she tossed her floppy hair in the direction of Bomber's turbulent office.

"Who is it?"

"Some Italian guy, and he's about to burst a blood vessel. That's if Bomber doesn't murder him first." she said. "He was planted on the doorstep with the missus when Bomber came in. Bomber told him you did all the screening, but the guy wouldn't hear of it. *Especially* since you weren't here to run interference."

A draught of air, a stiffening of the backbone and a hoist of the petard and I made my pseudo-macho way to the rescue of my helpless father, who could hold his own in any courtroom in the country but was apparently having some difficulty in this circumstance.

I entered the room, with the floor-to-ceiling photos plus written tributes to the great Bomber, without knocking. I always knocked, but this time it would not be heard above the roar.

I had expected to find some mean mountain bruiser. Instead there was this tiny Popsicle stick man, red in the face from ranting.

He was short and wiry and his whole life was right there on his sleeve. His wife was subservient—short and *sympatico*. I almost got the idea she was somehow turning him on by remote control—like operating one of those toy boats on the water from the shore. But it was an afterthought. I didn't think it at the time.

"Good!" Bomber boomed, "here is my son now, he will handle this." Bomber rose to his feet but made no inroads.

"He will not!" the little man said. "I will not be foisted off on the second team. You be a man enough to listen to me. I am man just like you are. No better, no worse."

"I don't argue that, Mr. Scioria. Tod screens all my cases, I—"

"Good! You listen then. You want boy Bomber to listen too, it's a no problem."

"Not too—*only*—" Bomber shook his head in frustration. He looked at me with an uncharacteristic sense of hopelessness. "Boy," he said, "meet Angelo and Regina Scioria; you're welcome to them." Bomber started to move from behind his desk. Incredibly, Angelo blocked him.

"No!" he shouted. "My child is dead. It was a no accident."

"That is what you say."

"That is what I *know!* There must be vengeance. Vengeance is mine, sayeth the Lord."

"Yeah, well that's where you should turn then."

"Don't you smart mouth me, big lawyer," Angelo said, "we little people, we come to you alla way from Jersey, but you too important to talk to us—too big—"

"I don't care if you came from Afghanistan, I am not breaking my rules for you."

"Rules?" he seemed startled. "What are these rules? You talk like you the U. S. government or something. Well, I want to tell you something, you maybe don't know—you just a man, like I just a man. The pants go on the same in the morning an off da same at night. You might be bigshot in court, it don't give you no call to talk to me and my missus like you was better than us, cause we got the same heart and liver and big toes—alla same. My daughter—my little girl too," he said, choking up. "But she is no more.

"A big wrong done her, Mr. Lawyer—an you is known as a man who rights wrongs. So why you afraid a this one? Huh? Why?" He was so insistent, he was so absorbed in his pitch, he didn't grasp that Bomber was about to explode. I couldn't blame him—he didn't know Bomber—he couldn't interpret that reddening face, the narrowing eyes, the tensed lips. Angelo was so intent on his pitch, he wasn't even looking at Bomber—and when their eyes did meet, nothing registered on the immigrant.

I heard him say, "We come here with all our hopes and dreams for our baby—in Regina's womb. Then Regina—she has a miscarriage. Then two years later, she have our beloved Merilee. We are so happy, I cannot tell you. We have lots a love for big family. Want many children—but we get only one. God's plan and we don't a argue. So we pour alla love on this one baby." And he actually poked his finger in Bomber's chest, which caused an instant, instinctive recoil. Bomber didn't like to be touched. "You have son—you must understand." He looked at me. "How you like it, somebody take him from you?"

3

"That's it!" Bomber blew. "Get out!"

Bomber must have seen this as a threat. I didn't, but I wasn't as hot to get rid of the little couple.

It is said an elephant has no chance with a mouse. Obviously an elephant could stamp a mouse to death in seconds. But the mouse doesn't give him seconds. The mouse is too quick and agile for the big guy.

I've no doubt, if the rules of the courtroom were in force, Bomber would have Angelo under the witness chair in short order. But this was a free-for-all, and Bomber was not coping at all well.

"Sir," I said, thinking a new voice might calm the waters, "my experience here tells me you and your cause would be better served by going through the hoops Bomber set up."

"Hoops? I don't jump through hoops—I no a trained dog."

"Then just jump the Sam Hill out of here," Bomber said, kicking up the decibel level.

"Wait a minute," I interjected. "Start from the beginning."

"He no wants to hear my story. I tried, he don't listen."

"I'm listening." I said. "Tell me."

Angelo closed his mouth and looked at me, then at Bomber, who sat back down mute but glaring, then back at me. I stole a glance at Angelo's wife. She sat mute too, but somehow she showed agitation with her silence. Like she was the undertow that pulled her husband adrift.

"My girl—my baby, she's a dead."

"When?"

"Two years, four months, three days," he sniffled. "Murdered."

"Did you go to the police?"

"Police? They laugh at me."

"Oh, I don't think..."

"You? What do you know?"

"I know the police don't laugh when you report a murder."

"Their kind a murder. This is a different."

"How?"

"I'm a just find out. This a murder not wid a gun or a knife. This with medicines."

"You mean poison?"

"'Zactly! Only by prescription."

I scrunched my eyebrows. This little man was talking in riddles. "Who did it?"

"Doctors," he said, "drug companies—my little girl— pure—never had a chance to know a man." He shook his head so hard I thought it would fall off. "And what's a her fate? To die of a sex disease! She was a trooper, that one. She done what the doctor told her—an' she died. Taken from us like she didn't deserve nothing better. Well, we sued that dentist. We sued his estate because he was already dead o' the same thing. An' we got a two million dollars. Two million! Two hundred million would not a been enough, but we took a the blood money as our daughter's due. An' we never spent a penny of it. An' a we're not a gonnto neither. Not unless we can make a meaningful memorial to her. An what is that? A statue? A donation? *Nothing*," he screamed. "There is nothing because now it is all a mistake. We got that money false."

"What do—"

"False!" Angelo reiterated. "She died not a from the disease, but from the cure."

"How do you know that?"

"I just found out. We are killers. *We* told her to take the medicine. This JCD drug. Thirty years ago when they tried it on rats they all died. It was too dangerous for people. We hear about this doctor at your Berkeley college—Walter Daimler. JCD is toxic, he says. Now it is killing the Wanns patients who take it."

Bomber started to speak, doubtless in protest, but I shot him a glance that said, let me handle it, and he closed his lips.

"That's an interesting view," I said. "What did you want from us?"

"I want the Bomber to sue the pants off a them—the doctor, the drug company who made JCD without testing it right. I want to make statement so nobody else has to lose their darling child to big medicine egos and phony science."

I nodded sympathetically. My goal was to get rid of him. That's what I divined Bomber wanted, and he signed my checks. Personally, I felt sorry for Angelo, but his story sounded crackpot. I didn't know anything about Wanns disease or the JCD drug, but I was not about to sign on any crackpot conspiracy theories. So I said, "Why don't you let us check on this information," Bomber was giving me the negative signal, "we'll let you know if we think we can do you any good."

Angelo shook his head, tightening his lips in the process. "I know the brush-off when I see it—" He was running down. He was approaching the desperation stage.

"I'll spend the two million suing *you* for malpractice," he sputtered.

"Very nice," Bomber said, in command again, "but you'd have to have been a client of mine—and you won't be, not the least because of that threat!"

It sobered Angelo. His wife stepped into the breech, speaking for the first time. "Mr. Bomber," she said, holding her head up with dignity and perhaps reaching five feet in the process. "You cannot realize the pain we have suffered. Our lives are already over. You could restore to us—and Merilee, a measure of dignity."

"No, Mrs. Scioria, I am sorry, but blaming doctors and drug companies for death is not my line. And lawyers aren't much for restoring dignity either. You have it or you don't. If your daughter had it, no doctor could take it from her."

"Yes, that is easily said," she said, "but not by us. Come, Angelo, we are not welcome here."

It is usually the women we turn to for wisdom.

"I won't give up," Angelo said, with a quiet intense force that seemed to hit us harder than any of his shouting did. Somehow she got him out of there, muttering all the way to their rental car which was infortuitously parked beside Bomber's red Bentley. I saw Angelo look at the extravagant car and read his mind. He wanted nothing so much as to drive his little rental into that big Bentley. It was as if that were all that was left to empower him. I was about to run out to save the day—how, I had no idea. I wouldn't have thrown myself in between the cars—when Mrs. Scioria put her hand on Angelo's arm and that seemed to break the spell. He climbed into the driver's seat and they left the small parking lot without incident.

As Bomber saw the last of them, he sank back and abandoned a sigh too long pent up. "Phew," he said. "That is some piece of work. Did good, Boy," he said, passing a reluctant, understated compliment. "And you didn't stutter once," he said, breaking new ground. He had never commented on my stutter before.

"That's b-b-because I wasn't t-t-talking t-to you."

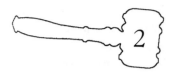

2

The next day was a day like most other days in Angelton, California: idyllic. The sun was shining, the air was clear and balmy. You didn't get much air pollution from the breath of tourists.

Our enterprise—Bomber Hanson, Attorney-at-law—was removed from the wiles of those transient spenders. In fact we rarely saw them from our Victorian house cum office on Albert Street (Queen Victoria's Albert, of course). It was a modest edifice for a man of Bomber's accomplishments, but out front he parked his red Bentley automobile that I lusted to drive. I wouldn't dream of telling Bomber that, of course. Some things you didn't tell your father. Most things.

The office was beginning to look a little down at the heel, and when I suggested it might benefit from a paint job, Bomber grunted. For Bomber was not adroit at spending money, only making it. And that was really a sideline. What consumed him, set his heart a-racing, was winning cases—the more difficult the better. All kinds of cases—murders to lawsuits. He didn't much go in for class action work—a lot of faceless plaintiffs who would settle out of court for a pittance and the lawyers would make millions. "Shyster work," he called it. For to Bomber, the law was not about large settlements, it was about trying cases, about winning the hearts and minds of jurors to his way of thinking. And he was justly famous for his startling successes.

Myself, I wonder sometimes at the lusts of man for glory and the challenge of the game. I, myself, am a guy who devotes his earthly efforts to writing music that perhaps nobody will hear. Which is better? Maybe there is no better, perhaps there are only choices.

I've heard all the clichés. The view is better when you're the lead dog. He who dies with the most toys wins (but he also dies).

There is this bloodlust which I cannot fathom. Does it throw back to the kill-or-be killed era? Sometimes I watch Bomber in action and try to picture him on the plain, surrounded by savage beasts closing in on him, and he, rather than digging in, bares his teeth, flexes his arms and attacks.

But I can't complain. I've thrown my bedroll in with an attack dog, and he keeps me eating to write my symphonies. So I get used to the barking.

Whether you consider it a watershed or a Waterloo, that night we reached a turning point in our dealings with Angelo and Regina Scioria.

I went to dinner at Mom and Bomber's house. By invitation, of course, which I often construed as a command performance. But tonight Mother made my favorite spaghetti sauce— a process which takes her hours—and I never in memory have had the strength of character to reject it.

Mom was an old-fashioned wife and mother. She didn't work outside her position as domestic scientist at her husband's beck and call. If she'd ever wanted to have a career of her own, she subverted those longings to her marriage. Though I think she was satisfied, even content, to do so. Happy? With volatile Bomber Hanson, that might be a stretch. She was a duty-directed person, duty-motivated and duty-bound. And, I expect, doing her duty fulfilled her.

She and I were taller than Bomber. We had that in common. Tonight Mother seemed subdued. Bomber asked cursorily how her day was and she said, "Okay." He did not pick up on the nuance. She usually said, "Lovely" or if she was not feeling so hot, "Fine." I noticed, but held my tongue.

Throughout dinner Mom seemed polite but glum. When she'd cleared the dishes, I was about to sail out of there when she said, "Tod, I have something to tell you and your father."

"Oh?" I said, not thinking too much about it.

"Let's sit in the living room, shall we?"

"Oh, just come out with it," Bomber said. "Tod wants to go home."

"It will only take a minute," she said, striding into the living room, giving us no choice but to follow. She sat on the striped love seat, Bomber in his favorite wing chair with the ottoman, and I in the lone seat facing Mom with Bomber perpendicular between us.

"Thank you," Mom said softly when we were seated. "I got a call today from Anne Gibbs."

"*Anne!*" Bomber said. "Well, how is she? God it's been what since they moved East? Must be going on five years."

"Seven," I said. I knew because I had entertained notions of forming an alliance with the beautiful, smart-as-a-whip daughter of the family, Wyma Gibbs, but Wyma went East to college and married someone else. A career Marine I understood, though, of course, I could never understand it. She was delicate and graceful and not the type you would picture with a macho Marine.

My sister had been Wyma Gibbs's best friend—before Sis packed it all in driving her car off the pier without saying a word to anyone. Sis'd had polio and it withered her some, and I expect she despaired of ever snatching one of the Gibbs boys—or anyone else. It was tough on Mom and Dad, and I bore the brunt of the details—the only thing I ever did better than my father. But then I developed this aggravating stutter—only when I talked to him. Anyway, the point is, we were very close to the Gibbs family—they lived just down the street and we'd had a lot of good times together. Even Bomber liked them in his reticent way. He wasn't one to rave about anyone's kids—not even his own. But you could tell he liked the Gibbs family. Especially the youngest boy, Alden. He was like a third child around our house.

Sis and Wyma were the same age, and Wyatt and I were were a year apart. Spunky Alden came maybe six years later, and he was like a mascot at our place—the child Mom and Dad might have had, had they not ceased having them.

"Seven is exactly right," Mom was saying.

"So, what's up with them? Coming to see us?"

"Nnnooo."

"Well, why did she call?"

"Alden just died."

"Alden? What?" Dad and I said together.

"An accident?" I asked.

Mom shook her head. "Wanns," she said.

"I don't believe it," Bomber said at last. "Don't tell me he was queer. I refuse to believe it."

"Not the way Anne tells it," Mom said. "She says he got a blood transfusion. Apparently, he was in a car accident and lost a lot of blood. He mended all right, but it turned out the blood he got was R4 positive. They went into a panic. Their doctor was alarmed. He checked with Wanns specialists who told him to take JCD. He was not feeling bad, no diseases seemed to have taken hold, but when he took the drug he started developing all these symptoms of Wanns. He begged to stop taking it, but the doctor said it was his only hope—so the parents pushed it—and he died a miserable death," she hung her head and tears built up in her eyes.

Bomber and I looked at each other. We didn't have to say anything.

I hadn't seen Mom and Dad so glum since Sis died. I wasn't feeling so hot myself, so I retreated to the sanctity of my modest home above a nice old woman's garage on the beach. My first thought was to write a musical composition in memory of Alden. A requiem would be ideal, but the chance of performance would be slim. That was the thing about composing. You had to have a performance and an audience to communicate. Perhaps for unaccompanied solo instrument. Something plaintive like an oboe or viola. Picking out melodic lines on my battered spinet helped me finally go to sleep.

* * *

Bomber didn't come to my "office" door often. I can't

11

remember when he did last. His usual method of communication with me was through Bonnie Doone, our airhead secretary; Bonnie, who was an exercise freak and a person who claimed to actually *like* yogurt. She did the gym routine in the (as yet) vain hope of finding a man. I kept telling her she should put something in her head if she wanted a man, but she was satisfied to put her major effort downstairs.

But there was my dad, coming to *me*, and though he would never admit it and tried to hide it, I detected a slice of humble pie in the offing.

"Son," he said, and I didn't jump up, or bow and scrape or anything, I just said, "Hmm?" I wasn't consciously playing hard-to-get, I just was so astonished to see him standing in my doorway, leaning on the door frame in the most bogus of casual ways that I didn't want to spoil the effect of him in this posture of supplication.

"What do you know about Wanns?" he asked, as though he were passing along an invitation to dinner.

"Nothing."

"Think there could be some truth in what old Angelo said?"

"I don't know. Seemed pretty hysterical to me."

Bomber nodded.

"Lot of people glom onto these c-conspiracy theories. Especially people prone to hysteria."

He nodded again, but I didn't follow up. Letting one nod pass for an answer was my limit.

There was a long pause before he spoke again. This time he was looking over my head. "I called Anne Gibbs," he said. "Most difficult call I ever made." I realized that could be true because *I* made all the calls about Sis when she went off the pier.

"I didn't realize she was a religious woman," he said.

"Maybe she wasn't," I offered. "Calamities have a way of b-bringing those mystical feelings within to the s-surface."

He didn't acknowledge my answer, but spoke as though I wasn't there—like it was a soul-cleansing soliloquy. "Said she couldn't handle Alden's death so she just turned it over to the Lord." He paused again. "Remarkable," he said, at last, "this turning to a higher being in times of crisis."

"Perhaps that's what He or She is f-for."

"Yes," he said, drawing it out. "Perhaps." Was he thinking of Sis? It was something I knew I could never ask him.

"So, I g-guess we know how Angelo feels," I said, but he only nodded. I decided I had contributed all I had to on the subject. At times like this I got the impression Bomber wasn't listening that closely to his sounding board.

"What do you say to doing a little investigation into this Wanns business? See if there is any basis for Angelo's beef."

"And a case?" I asked.

Bomber gave a slight lift to his shoulders, with one of his why-that-never-crossed-my-mind looks.

"You pay the bills," I said, hoping to impart my lack of faith in the cause, yet not wishing to discourage further visits to my broom-closet office.

"Yeah, well, talk to this guy he mentioned, will you? This Ph.D. up north. See what you make of him."

"Okay."

"And get the other side too. Let's see if there's any truth there."

That was it. More marching orders for the reluctant soldier. It was amazing what personalizing these tragedies could do to the old cynic. Alden Gibbs had been one lovable kid.

I didn't venture to ask if Bomber was thinking of the case in terms of Angelo and Regina Scioria or Anne Gibbs. Or both.

He didn't so much leave my doorway as he just seemed to vaporize. One moment he was there, the next, pftt!

I called the University of California to get in touch with the man whose name was Dr. Walter Daimler.

3

The University of California at Berkeley was in a charming, picturesque community. But the campus itself seemed to be largely constructed of indestructible concrete. I first thought using concrete was a natural instinct of the bureaucrats who made it possible to squeeze the maximum life out of the buildings. Then I speculated it was to vaccinate the structures against the attacks of the students. After talking to Walter Daimler, I decided the concrete structures were necessary to withstand the constant onslaughts of faculty politics, which are said to be the most vicious of all interpersonal conflicts.

It seemed fitting that my first sighting of Walter Daimler should be through the myriad of vials and test-tubes of fluids on shelves. It was like one of those puzzles where you get only parts of a person sliced and obscured in horizontal sections like a seven-layer sandwich. Beside him in his lab stood a young woman, also sliced.

Before either of them saw me approaching, I realized how indicative this partial view was of personal relationships. We only knew of people the parts that were revealed, never the whole person. And often the revelations were arbitrary, like the relative height of the shelves of test-tubes.

Dr. Daimler looked my way and saw a similarly truncated version of myself. We were both around six feet, so he must have viewed the same slices of me as I had of him. He came to greet me with his hand extended. "You must be Tod Hanson," he said. "I'm Walter Daimler. Pleased to meet you." And he actually seemed pleased. When I shook his hand, I was so grateful that no disappointment was expressed at my paltry stature substituting for my famous father.

Walter Daimler was athletic and wiry—I could visualize him darting in and out of rooms and conversations like a welterweight prizefighter feinting and jabbing his way to the knockout punch.

He had curly graying hair close to the scalp with just enough of the original color to keep him from looking really old. He wore a white smock, as did the other person in the room—the dark-haired (also unruly) young woman who looked like a real plugger.

He introduced me to her as his lab assistant, then added sheepishly she was also his new wife. If she was more than half his age, it was not by much.

"It's the only way I can afford to experiment," he said, and I think he meant in cellular biology rather than amorous pursuits. "Emily Wentz was one of my last graduate students. They have me teaching undergraduates now." He smiled wryly, "Can't make many inroads on the minds of young scientists in introductory courses," he explained. "Science used to be about questioning—about doubt," he pursed his lips. "Now it is all about conformity. It used to be you could have a hundred studies supporting a hypothesis and if you had one legitimate study that got contrary results the original work would go out the window."

He spoke with a German accent though he had been in the U.S. for more than thirty years. His mind was on science, not on native pronunciation.

Emily Wentz was nodding her approval as he spoke, and I knew, if nothing else he had one convert. I had a soft spot for mavericks, as Bomber did in spades, but I also knew the majority—especially such a lopsided one—was often right. I mentioned that to Dr. Daimler.

He shook his head. "Less and less as time goes on," he said. "We are living in conformist times. I expect that can be understood when you are dealing with teenagers, wardrobes, or television—but science is not about conformity. It can't be or it is no longer science."

He suggested we retreat to his office—a small room that in most municipalities wouldn't meet the square footage threshold for a bedroom. The chairs were government issue metal as was his desk, which was inundated with papers of every stripe.

I had, of course, little basis for judging this scientist, but I couldn't see any strain of the charlatan in him. He wasn't a wild-eyed crazy who had the cure for cancer in his coat pocket— he was a Ph.D. in molecular-biology, an expert on viruses, and he was shouting from the rooftops that Wanns disease was not caused by a virus, specifically the R4 virus. Neither was cancer, neither was Legionnaire's disease, neither were a host of other diseases the group he called "the phantom virus hunters," initially claimed were caused and transmitted by a virus.

He had evidence on his walls of former glory: citations, awards, testimonials from all the prestigious academies of science, governmental agencies and academic bodies. All predated his theory that there was no connection between the R4 virus and Wanns disease. It was as though he needed a reminder of what life was like before he had been ostracized by the scientific community for his contrary theories.

He attempted to give me a condensed, layman's view of his thesis. "Wanns is the only disease diagnosed and proclaimed by press conference," he said. "Dr. Carl Valentine, a man of painfully limited scientific abilities, but a genius for media-manipulation, rose to the top of the phantom virus hunters. This should not be surprising in light of his background as a plagiarist who not only borrowed ideas, but stole entire experiments in his shameless pursuit of glory. He announced the connection between Wanns and R4 at a press conference without *any* studies to prove it."

"Why would he?"

"For power and prestige and for bucks. Big, big money has gone into this fallacious theory. Billions of dollars has been heaped on the virus hunters by the federal government."

"Have you ever heard of Merilee Scioria?"

"Oh, yes," he said. "This man called me from New Jersey. His daughter died of Wanns, he said. That celebrated dentist case. Said he read my book, and he starts out challenging everything I said in the book. A combative guy. I didn't argue. I waited until he wore down, then I said, quietly, 'These are my opinions, based on my research. Unfortunately you can't get the same response from the other side. The only studies they quote are not relevant to any connection between R4 and Wanns.

"I sent him some more material, and I haven't heard from him since."

Dr. Daimler talked long and energetically, giving me a ton of debating points on the phantom virus, as he called it. He said flatly the R4 virus did not cause Wanns and the scientific community was marching in erroneous lock step. "A million people have the R4 virus in them. Only five percent develop Wanns.

"It is a disease where the cure causes the disease." Then he looked me directly in the eye and added, "And kills the patient."

I left Dr. Daimler an exhausted skeptic. I couldn't conceive of virtually the entire scientific community marching down the wrong path with no studies to back them up. I thought Daimler must be a crackpot.

He didn't seem that way, but I knew next to nothing about science.

Because of our lack of expertise and my inability to fathom the truth, I was going to tell Bomber to forget this one.

The motels I get to stay in on the road are interchangeable. They could each be called "no-frills motel." Four walls, a roof, a bed, dresser and chair, ancient TV and what passed for indoor plumbing in an earlier era. Though I would prefer a room without a telephone, that is one amenity Bomber insists on; so he can bug me.

I was sound asleep when the phone rang. I don't know how often it had rung until I answered, groggily. "Hullo…"

"What the Sam Hill is going on up there? You on some kind of a holiday or something? Weren't you supposed to call me after you saw Daimler? Jesus Jenny, Boy, am I wasting my money on you?"

It was Bomber. Who else?

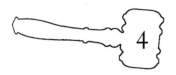

4

You didn't have to be clairvoyant to guess that Bomber wanted me to go to Washington.

"You don't get anywhere with half measures," he said.

I groaned. So I was off to Washington to look in on the Wanns establishment, then on to New Jersey to verify the Scioria story about their perfect child.

When I questioned Bomber about snooping on the dead girl before we took the case, he said, "Makes a big difference what kind of person the victim was. Give the defense a thread, they'll pull on it until your pants are gone."

"They said she was pretty innocent—"

"Yeah," he said, "but don't forget, there's one perfect child and every mother has it."

"But, d-don't you think w-we should ch-ch-check with Angelo? I m-mean, he may have gotten another lawyer."

"Boy, if we agree to take the case, he'll drop the other lawyer like a hot potato."

Modesty was not one of Bomber's stronger points.

In the capital, I was greeted at the Wanns headquarters by a functionary who had been sent to "brief" me. The word brief in this context had always set me wondering. I really didn't want to be briefed, I wanted to be depthed.

Finally, I was ushered in to see the big man himself—Dr. Carl Valentine.

His office was a stark contrast to Daimler's. If the size and decor were any indication of the relative merits of their arguments, Daimler should have thrown in the sponge.

Though I had never seen the office of the president of General Motors, I didn't think Valentine's would suffer from comparison. It was large enough to park all of GM's car models in.

In addition to the *de rigueur* aircraft-carrier desk, there was a generous seating area larger than Bomber's living room. The whole thing was gotten up like an upper-eastside-Manhattan luxury apartment.

Dr. Valentine pointed a palm toward the chair facing him across the aircraft carrier. I realized right away this was not going to be a friendly, cozy, sitting-room chat. Instead, it was going to be all business, and for Valentine, the shorter the better.

Cordial but cool was my take on Dr. Carl Valentine. He was going bald on top and an effort was being made to disguise that fresh, taut skin—side hair grown to an absurd length and plastered with grease across the top to join compatriot hair on the other side.

"I feel sorry for Dr. Daimler," he shook his head to show me how miserable the whole thing made him feel. "I know him, he had a good reputation before this."

It was Dr. Valentine who had diagnosed the R4/Wanns connection at a press conference. I asked him about it.

He shook his head again. "Daimler makes it seem like I just pulled that out of the air. Not so; not so at all. We had done our homework, believe me. Oh, perhaps the disease doesn't fit all of Daimler's rigid criteria. That doesn't make it less deadly, unfortunately. But this is a new virus with new criteria. He doesn't want to understand that."

"He says R4 is not new, only newly discovered."

"In science if you live in the past, you are lost. Daimler is living in the past. Look, I have told him, come up with a cure. You will be a hero. Nobel Prize, no question. Instead, all he does is criticize those of us who are laboring to find a cure."

"He is apparently unable to get funding for his research."

"Does that tell you something? Oh, I know how para-noid he is about it. Says all his fellow scientists have ganged up on him. But now *you* answer a question. Do you think virtually the whole scientific community would be against him if they thought he had anything close to a solution?"

"He says you are looking in the wrong place for it."

"I know what he says," Dr. Valentine said, icily, losing some of his initial cordiality. Before it was completely gone, I tried to put to him some of Dr. Daimler's questions. He sighed and shook his head like you do when you are exasperated with the ignorance of some inferior being. "I can see you really have no grounding in the sciences yourself. You two should make a good pair, because Walter Daimler seems to have lost the brilliance he once had and is babbling like a first-year 'D' student in areas he knows nothing about. I can't discuss it with you because you wouldn't understand the language of science or the concepts themselves.

"Since the beginning, Daimler has been a burr in my saddle and I have tried to tolerate him." He stood up. "I do appreciate your interest in our cause. Please put your energies to positive use. Any ignorant child can criticize. Why don't you contribute something instead? Good day," he said, and saw me out with a cool, curt nod.

I wasn't batting very high in the numbers behind the decimal point. I called Bomber from my hotel, which must have been the inspiration for the Motel 6 chain.

"So," he boomed after I said hello, "I suppose they badmouthed the Kraut pretty good."

"Yes," I said. "It's a muddle," I tried to discourage Bomber. "The expert talked down to me b-because I don't understand science."

"Good! Let them talk down to the jury. Rotten salesmanship."

"Yes, b-but I don't see…I mean, how are you going t-to make a jury understand these c-concepts? High falutin."

"That's the beauty of it, Boy. Where reason strays, emotion takes hold. We got a nineteen-year-old virgin and against her, big science, big medicine and some doctor who probably has a reputation for not keeping up and over charging."

"That's if everything goes p-perfectly. And it never does."

"Challenge, my boy—challenge and response. Get the lowdown on the girl, Maria something, isn't it? Start with the opposing lawyer in their suit against that dentist. He'll have the dirt." Then as if an afterthought, he said, "Oh, and talk to her doctor."

* * *

When I got to New Jersey I called the Sciorias, and Angelo was delighted we were doing some work toward possibly taking his case. He was not so delighted when I asked for the name and number of the attorney who represented the dentist. "Whudda ya want with that? I give you my attorney. That's a better."

So, I called his attorney and asked for the name and number of the dentist's lawyer, which he gave me, saving me, as I pointed out to him, the trouble of going to the courthouse to look it up.

Vernon St. John, the dentist's attorney, was one of those lawyers who always seemed to be considering some other line of work. Perhaps it was the lawyer jokes.

I met him by appointment at his office in Birchwood, New Jersey on the second floor of a tenant-starved building. And from the look of the premises (down at heel) and the advocate himself (ditto) I suspected the landlord of being patient about the rent.

Vernon was a guy who was often, *too* often, on the losing side. This for a combination of reasons. 1. He was willing to take hopeless cases. 2. People with good cases attracted good lawyers, and 3. Vernon was constitutionally unable to go for the jugular. The killer instinct was not in him, and a lawyer without the killer instinct is like a bull without horns.

His breathing was labored, his skin was red and flaky and he wheezed a lot.

"Girl made such a PR stink out of it we were lucky to get out of there with our skin," he said. "The poor dentist had no insurance. Premium was so high he decided to go bare. Good thing for him he died before they came after him. His estate was wiped out. We gave essentially everything to the Sciorias. When the other four patients heard about it, they wanted some pie too, but the cupboard was bare. Now they are after the Sciorias and their attorney. That's where the money is. This well is bone dry."

I could see that, but I didn't comment. "Did you fight the action for the dentist at all?"

"In the beginning, I gave it a good college try. But the hysteria was unbearable for his family. The media made it seem like he was single-handedly responsible for the black plague."

"It *was* a heartrending thing," I said. "Young, pure girl gets fatal sex disease from going to the dentist—something all us innocents do."

He nodded. "That's the way they made it look," he said, reliving a distasteful memory. "The thing you have to remember is journalists are lazy."

"What did you want them to do?"

"Check the story for starters," he said. "It was pure fantasy."

"What?"

He nodded as resolutely as he could make it in his condition. "First of all, she didn't get any R4 from the dentist. Those people wear gloves and masks and who knows what else while they are messing in your mouth. Nobody gave her an R4 test *before* she saw the dentist."

"You aren't suggesting she got it somewhere else?"

"Why not? The dentist discovered he had it, and did the noble thing—told all his patients, in effect, to run out and get an R4 test. She did," he threw out his hands, "and the rest is history."

"She's dead and your client paid off a couple million."

With a short nod, he said, "And he didn't have to."

"No?"

"I could have won the case."

Now he startled me. He didn't look like a man who had

any basis for such an assertion. I didn't suspect his won-lost record was anything that might provoke envy.

"How can you be so sure? I asked, my skepticism unhidden. "A pure young virgin and a dentist who dies of a sex disease…?"

He shook his head and wheezed. "The girl was neither pure nor virginal. In her tender years, she had slept in many beds not her own and taken enough controlled substances to kill an elephant."

5

Having heard the lament of the Sciorias', I found it hard to accept Vernon St. John's thesis. But he gave me chapter and verse and enough names and phone numbers to convince me.

A grunt followed by silence was what I got from the great Bomber when I called from Motel 5. What could you expect from a man who took his grownup name from a youthful experience—as a bombardier in Korea, called back from his first combat flight because the war was over. A guy with a towering intellect who wore elevator shoes, and he still wasn't as tall as I was. With the right pair of shoes and brand-new heels I was within tiptoe range of six feet.

When he regained his equilibrium, Bomber and I had a battle royal over who should confront the Sciorias about this lapse of the full-disclosure ethic. Each of us came down strongly in favor of the other: he, because he was a cream puff about that kind of stuff; I, because I knew they would take it better from him, and if I wasn't a cream puff, I was a marshmallow. The resolution of the disagreement will not come as a surprise to anyone who knows us.

I went to see the Sciorias armed with complete marching orders.

Angelo and Regina Scioria lived on a hill in Birchwood, New Jersey in a house that looked in front like a plantation. There were houses on either side, but Angelo was proud of the little extra space between them. He had worked hard to give his wife and daughter a nice home. In Italy, he'd worked in a restaurant, first as a dishwasher, then waiter, then maître d', and saved lots of money. In New Jersey, he was able to buy his own restaurant after just working one year as a cook. He opened his own diner in downtown Birchwood. He and Regina had worked long hours seven days a week making it a success. When the baby was born, Regina took care of her. But as the restaurant grew more successful, she felt she was needed there to oversee the cash register to cut down on thievery.

So Merilee grew up with a series of nannies. Her parents overcompensated for their long hours at the restaurant by lavishing unconditional love on their daughter. They had neither the time nor the inclination for disciplining the child.

The Sciorias made me feel welcome instantly. We retired to the living room, and there was something about the way they led me to it that made me feel it was something special. When we got in, I could see why. The Scioria's living room was decked out like a narthex in one of those landmark cathedrals. There were pictures of Merilee everywhere with votive candles, crucifixes, plain crosses and relics that no doubt purported to be the real shroud, the true cross or whatever.

The furniture was covered with plastic as if to preserve it for the ages. There were plastic runners on the floor crisscrossing in the traffic patterns.

When we were seated on the plastic, I made a modicum of small talk amid Angelo's confident declarations that we would take his case. "I knew you would," he said, excitedly in his Italian accent, "even when your dad was making big about throwing us out of his office."

"How did you know?" I asked.

"Because you are reasonable people. Because he has a son like you, and he had a daughter like we had and he lost her just like we did."

I didn't ask him how he had come into that bit of information. It wasn't exactly a secret, but neither was Angelo exactly local—he was almost three thousand miles away. Bad news travels fast and far, I guess.

"Angelo," I said, "I have spoken to Vernon St. John…"

"I told you not to talk to that shyster," he sputtered his anger across the plastic carpet. Perhaps *that* was the reason for the plastic coverings—a protective raincoat. "I told you to no listen to him. Why you no listen to me?"

"Bomber doesn't take orders from his clients," I said. "If you want him for your lawyer, you have to play his game—and that is not playing games. He must know everything. If the other side surprises him, it will be to your detriment. And it looks like we might have a problem here."

"Problem?" he put up a good show about being surprised. "What problem?"

I knew I had to be careful, I just hadn't thought out *how* I would be careful. He was staring at me accusingly, challenging me, and I realized I had to get it out somehow. The trouble was there was a tremendous gap between 'somehow' and 'how.'

"There seems to have been another, ah, opinion about your daughter's, ah, innocence," I started badly, but I couldn't retract the words. Predictably he blew his cork.

"Those are lies!" he screamed. "Lies, lies, *lies!*" he sputtered, and I realized I had not given him any specifics to refute, yet refuting he was with a vengeance. But more important perhaps than the truth or falsity of the claims of his daughter's character was the emotionally explosive temper Angelo was showing. Could Bomber control this loose cannon? I wondered. Would he want to try?

"Angelo, I can appreciate your feelings," I said. "But it would be unfair—even cruel to you—to not make it clear that someone else's perception of your daughter's character will be an issue if we go to trial with your case."

"Let them pay without a trial," he said. "The dentist's family did that."

"That was a very nice break for you. Their attorney, Vernon St. John, did not want to settle. He thought he had enough information on your daughter to win the case."

"*LIES!*"

"But the family had been put through the ringer and wanted no more. That will not happen with a doctor or a drug company that is making billions a year off the drug in question.

They will fight tooth and nail to the bitter end. Your daughter's reputation will become a huge issue in the trial."

"You mustn't let it," he said, reaching a hand out to me in desperation.

"Bomber would fight it, of course, but in these trials it is *de rigueur* to make the victim the criminal. It's what lawyers turn to when all else fails. Even if we can stop some of it from going on record, the word will be out to the media, and that is delicious grist for their sensation mills. A young girl, pretty, advantages, hardworking parents..." I shook my head, leaving the rest to Angelo's imagination.

"But those lies have no relevance," he said, passionately raising his voice again.

"Certainly true. Whether Merilee was a saint or a sinner or a blend of both, as most of us are, is immaterial. Bomber would attempt to show the drug JCD killed your daughter, and the doctor was guilty of malpractice in prescribing it and the drug company was negligent in manufacturing it and selling it without proper testing. But before we decide if we will take the case, we have to make certain determinations. Bomber *must* know everything or he won't take the case. It is that simple. Did Merilee have any friends I can talk to?"

"No!"

I nodded, I thought sympathetically, and looked from Angelo to Regina and back again. Angelo was trying to keep his upper lip stiff, Regina was not making any pretenses—her face sagged in worry. I stood up. "Then I guess it's goodbye," I said.

"Wait," Angelo put out his hand as though keeping me from falling off a precipice. "You don't tell me you come alla this way and do alla this work and not take the case?"

"I'm afraid that is exactly what I am telling you. If I can't talk to her friends, there is nothing more for me to do here."

"Impossible!"

"Possible," I assured him. Angelo was watching me, I could see the gears grinding, maybe even stripping, in his strenuous effort to calculate if he had made a miscalculation, and if so, what he could do about it without losing face.

"Thank you for talking to me," I said. "Whatever happens, I do wish you the best of everything," and I walked out the door, leaving Angelo and Regina sitting and stewing.

I took my time moseying to my rental car. I opened the door and slid in behind the wheel. I'd heard the footsteps, and I didn't want to make her work too hard.

She was pale and breathless when I looked up at her standing by the car door. Casually I lowered the window.

Mrs. Scioria gave me the name and phone number of Merilee's best friend.

6

If you can picture a plum-shaped face with a baby-acorn chin, you have an idea of the face of Evelyn Welsh, Merilee Scioria's best friend.

She was, she said, twenty-two years old, just what Merilee would have been had she lived. I met Evelyn at her place of employment—Eggsception in downtown Birchwood. From my observation, her world seemed one of overeasy, scrambled, and sunny-side-up.

Evelyn was just getting off, and I had to wait only twenty minutes or so until she finished taking care of her customers. She served the counter and also the handful of tables the Eggsception sported by the front window. It was one of those quick food kind of places that lent itself so nicely to the television culture. If Darwin was right, I see the evolution of these places into drive-through restaurants where you simply roll down the window and open your mouth and the food comes down a pipe and slides, already chewed into your mouth. With all the saved time, national television viewing averages could easily shoot up from seven hours a day to eight or nine.

The question that came first to mind was had Evelyn ever considered working for the Sciorias?

"Oh, no," she said, "they don't approve of me."

"Why not?" I asked.

She wrinkled her nose. "Not good enough," she said. "But then *no*body was ever good enough for their darling Merilee."

She said I didn't have to buy her the cup of coffee she had before her. "It's on the house. One of the fringe benefits of working here," she said, smiling a face full of curiously placed dimples. Her face seemed adrift in those dimples. She herself had been adrift, she said in other words, until she moored herself in this job. Like many children of middle-class virtue, Evelyn was working somewhat below her capabilities and was getting through life without any major calamities. She held her head so straight I thought it must be in a neckbrace. I found her easy enough to talk to, with copious opinions on her late best friend and family.

"It's an old story," she said. "Spoiled only child, parents always working," she shrugged.

"Can you give me any specifics," I asked, "about her relationship with her family?"

"It was kinda strange in a way. They seemed to dote on her one minute and ignore her the next. I mean, like, they were working all the time to make money so Merilee would always have anything she wanted. Like when she turned sixteen, they bought her this neat red Mustang."

I raised an eyebrow.

"Yeah, she wanted a Miata, but the Sciorias were hundred percent American. They wouldn't dream of buying a foreign car. So, Merilee pouted for a while. When they were looking, she wouldn't drive it. It was one of the few battles Merilee didn't win. They were hung up on this All-American stuff. I mean, look at the name they gave her—Merilee, like she was some modern Southern belle or something. Has a funny ring with Scioria, don't you think? Should have been Maria or Sophia or one of those ee-ah names. But they wanted a with-it American name and Merilee is what they came up with." She smiled at the insanity of it all.

"What did you like about her?" I asked.

"Merilee? She was fun. She was a happy-go-lucky kid, once she got out of the house."

"How did she get so happy? Anything to do with controlled substances?"

Evelyn shrugged again and turned her head toward the window. "We were young. We experimented."

"Hard stuff?"

"Nothing came along we wouldn't give a try."

"Addicted?"

"Nah," her eyes shifted away from me. "We could take it or leave it."

"Anything unusual happen when you were under the influence...?"

"Hey, what a neat way to put it. Like a drunk on booze—"

"Did you?"

"Booze?" she shrugged, "Sure."

"Have any boyfriends?"

"Me or Merilee?"

"Merilee."

"Sure. She was a good-looking chick."

I was a little surprised at her characterization, but I was after information, not language niceties. "Did she, ah, sleep around any?" I asked, trying to keep to the niceties.

"She was active," she nodded without judgment.

"Did her parents know?"

"Ha! Her parents saw only a halo around her head. Or so they would make you believe. Some of the guys she got it on with were not the type you'd take home to daddy. So they didn't see any of that personally, not that I know of. But they ragged on her for staying out late—or not coming home at all."

"How many guys was she with?"

"Pff—I don't think Merilee knew. You lose track when you're high."

"So, I guess it's a good bet they weren't all close friends."

"You could say that."

"So, some of these, ah, men might have been diseased?"

She shrugged her shoulders again as though that were of little consequence, and if we were speaking of contemporary reality, I suppose she was technically correct. Merilee was dead. We could speculate all we wanted to about the cause.

"Did you ever discuss, ah, disease with her?"

"You mean Wanns and stuff?"

"Yeah."

"Well, of course," Evelyn said, as thought I had just fallen off the turnip truck. "And she didn't seem to care. Not while we were in high school anyway. I think after the dentist thing, she got worried enough to have a test."

"Was it her first R4 test?"

"Far as I know."

"You ever have one?"

"I've had a few," she admitted.

"And?"

"Nothing."

"May I assume you were also, ah, active?"

"Sexually? You might say that. Not like Merilee though. She was driven. I was more like, accommodating."

"You have any reason to suspect Merilee might have gotten Wanns from someone other than the dentist?"

"How would I know? That lawyer—that St. John guy—he went through all this. He was convinced she did."

"Do you know the difference between R4 and Wanns?"

"*Is* there a difference?"

"Yeah. Apparently about three percent of the R4 people get Wanns every year; Ninety-seven percent don't."

"No kidding." She didn't say 'kidding,' but something, well, saltier.

I nodded. "What I'm told. Did you ever talk to her about it?"

"Well, sure—she was scared after the test. I don't think she knew anything about that ninety-seven percent stuff." Again "stuff" was not the exact terminology she utilized.

"So, what did she do after the test?"

"Panicked. Like, I guess, everyone does. And she went to her doctor. He didn't know too much about it—he asked around, I guess. It's what she told me anyway. I mean, she didn't feel bad or anything—it was like business as usual as far as she was concerned. But everyone thought she was gonna die unless she did something. And something turned out to be this medicine with a bunch of initials. Merilee wasn't exactly opposed to popping pills. She'd gotten some real highs in her time, so she took the stuff."

"Then what?"

Evelyn shrugged. "She had trouble. Got real sick. She got this hard core yeast infection you just wouldn't believe. She was getting weaker and madder all the time. Throwing up, skin going to pot. It was a terrible sight, and, as I say, she was pissed. The thing about Merilee is she was a fighter, you know. So, she just got on the old soap box. Even went to congress before some committee or something and spilled her guts trying to get them to do something, I guess."

"You know they have spent billions every year trying to do something?"

"Nah, I don't pay that much attention. Anyway, if it was billions, Merilee wanted trillions. Whatever it took to make a cure. And the media ate her up—with all the people who had Wanns they really glommed on Merilee."

"Do you think that could be because most of the Wanns victims are homosexual men, and the Wanns establishment was anxious to include women? Viruses, I'm told, do not discriminate in the population. Wanns seems to."

"I never thought about it that way."

"And women are so vulnerable, we reach out to protect them…"

"Hah! *Who* reaches out?"

"Men."

"Gimme a break! You know different men than I do. The guys I know are out for number-one. If they are doing any reaching out, it is to grab something for themselves before anyone else gets it."

"Was that Merilee's experience?"

"It's *every* girl's experience," she said, fixing me in a stare meant to make an impression.

"Did she have a special boyfriend—?"

"Yeah, I guess."

"What can you tell me about him?"

"I could tell you he was tall, dark and handsome. In great shape, rich—a doctor, in fact, who always considered her every wish."

"Wow—I thought you said men were out for themselves?"

"Yeah—I said I *could* tell you all that, but none of it would be true. He was, rather, self-indulgent, abusive, crude, coarse and I'll never know what she saw in him. A real loser as far as I could see."

"Work?"

"Did some pharmaceutical work from time to time," she said. "I think he was in distribution. Name was Buck Rogers, believe it or not. At least, that's what he said," she said, rolling her eyes.

"Any idea where I could find him?"

She shook her head. "Ask around in any of those joints you see a lot of glassy eyes," and she gave me the name of a handful. I thanked her, and we went through the motions of exchanging phone numbers and the ritual promises of keeping in touch. Evelyn Welsh would make a good witness at our trial, but not for our side.

I called Bomber who was not encouraged at the news of the character of our Joan of Arc. He told me to run it all by Daimler and report back.

I reached Walter Daimler by phone.

"Ach," he said, in his German accent. "the classic case. Drugs and sex, and when you have both, the virus hunters and the media want to blame sex. It's more dramatic, more frightening. Well, sex isn't new. Wanns is new and these designer drugs are new."

"Isn't it true most people think Wanns is a sexually transmitted disease?"

"From the media, sure. But homosexuals take these nitrites to relax them for their kind of sex. It breaks down the immune system."

"What's the best way to argue our case?"

"With the facts."

Easy for him to say. Unfortunately, the facts, as they say, were in dispute.

7

The inquiries I made into the whereabouts of one Buck Rogers led to blind alleys and dead ends. Buck Rogers lived, to put the best face on it, a shadowy existence. Blind alleys and dead ends was about it. I knew if he came anywhere near these parts I would smoke him out eventually. But in the meantime, I turned my attention to Merilee's doctor.

Getting a meeting with Dr. Bill Bern proved to be a piece of cake. He almost seemed eager to see me.

"Anytime," he said on the phone when I made my request.

"Surely you have patients scheduled."

"Nobody I can't move," he said with affable good nature.

"No, please," I said. "I wouldn't want to do that—isn't there a time that you wouldn't have to inconvenience anybody? The end of the day, perhaps?"

"That's fine," he said. "You name it."

We agreed on 4:30 that afternoon, though he told me a doctor's day never ended.

Dr. Bill Bern's waiting room was borderline plush, like a guy who was showing he had dough and enough taste and sense not to flaunt it, but not to hide it either.

There were high-backed chairs with muted fabrics and gentle stripes, Tony magazines on the glass-topped side tables and a plush beige carpet that could take you in to your ankles.

The doc came out to greet me. I always thought that showed a lot of style. And after we went through the smile and the handshake and his I'm-so-glad-to-meet-you act, we repaired to his office.

Dr. Bill Bern's P.R. could not be faulted. A ready, flashing smile, bespeaking a conscientious flosser, a firm handshake and a trim, if short, middle-aged body indicative of a guy who worked out.

My initial impression was I'd rather have him for us than against us.

In his private office, all pretense of modesty had flown. Instead of sinking into the carpet to my ankles, I almost made it to my knees. His desk, carved out of some rare, dark, exotic wood, might have been rejected by the White House as being too large.

The lighting in the office was borderline bizarre—pinkish-amber hues that shone on the doc just so to make him look like a movie star.

He sat on one side of his football-field desk, and I was the visiting team. I was dumbfounded at what the light did to his skin. Close up it looked waxy, like a cheap embalming job, but from a distance he was on the silver screen in its heyday.

He sat grinning at me as though I were some long-lost and beloved frat brother come home to let the good times roll. I always admired guys who could make you feel, at first meeting, they were just nuts about you.

His glimmering, toothy smile turned off for just a moment when I mentioned his late patient, Merilee Scioria.

He shook his head. "Terrible," he said, "a terrible tragedy. She was like a daughter to me."

I tried a shot in the dark. "I understand she was a model teenager."

Dr. Bern's face clouded. He bobbed his head with the negative spin you put on a positive action.

"Wasn't she?" I didn't let up.

He bobbed his head some more. "Normal," he said finally. "Ups and downs like most teenagers, I suppose." Then he brightened. "I thought she was adorable."

"Have any boyfriends you know of?"

He waved my question to obscurity with his hand. "Nothing serious I know about."

"You were the family doctor for twenty-some years, I understand."

"Yes, but I wasn't *personally* involved with any of them. So from boyfriends, I know nothing."

"Doctor," I said. "I'm going to ask you a tough question. The Sciorias are considering a suit against the drug company that manufactures JCD." I was careful to avoid any reference to any inclusion of him in the action.

"On what basis?" he asked.

"You may or may not know that there is a formidable section of the scientific community which has vocally pounced on JCD as a chain terminator—killing off the DNA chain while going after bad cells and getting the good ones with the bad and finally killing the patient. Do you know anything about that?"

"Oh, I've heard hysteria like that before. I think you exaggerate when you say formidable for those on the anti-JCD fringe. They are neither formidable nor sizable. It is what I rather consider a lunatic minority. JCD has been approved by the FDA. They are no slouches, and they are our final word on drugs. You want to sue someone, I suggest you go after the United States Government."

"You think that might be a winner?" I asked with a palsy-walsy slanted smile.

He laughed. "I hear they aren't hurting for lawyers or cash. Might be uphill." Then he shrugged his shoulders and threw out his hands. "Be my guest."

Ah, yes, I thought—just-stay-away-from-me seemed suggested by his attitude—and, of course, I wanted him to think I agreed.

"Well, I expect you're right," I said. "It may be a lost cause."

"Rather you than me," he agreed.

I decided against putting him on the spot. I'd let

Bomber ask the hard questions. He was so good at it. It wasn't until I stood to leave that I saw, on the shelf behind Dr. Bern, Dr. Walter Daimler's book, *Phantom Virus*. I thought it odd he had not mentioned it, so I didn't either.

When I made my report to Bomber later that night on the telephone, he was silent while I blubbered on, telling him what a delightful, concerned, gentleman the doctor was. I mentioned Daimler's book on Bern's shelf only casually, in a throwaway line.

When I wound down he said, "He's our pigeon."

"Excuse me?"

"He's a worm. Get the goods on him—"

"But, how d-do you know that? I told you only p-positive things."

But he had hung up.

As I flew home to Angelton, I cogitated a way to convince Bomber not to take this case.

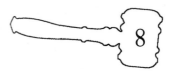

8

I should have been able to predict Bomber's course of action. Bomber, you see, is a sucker for a maverick. Dr. Walter Daimler seemed the quintessential maverick of the 20th century. He had gone against his colleagues and been ostracized as a result. Though I had never known my father to be big-hearted about those whose opinions differed from *his*, he took great joy in that fact pattern when others were involved. Now he was angry at science. How much of that was for the thing itself, and how much was the natural animus of one profession for another, (how many doctors speak well of lawyers and vice versa?) I don't know. And how much of his emotional investment was for the Sciorias and how much for our friend Alden, I don't know.

That doesn't mean I didn't push the devil's advocate sword into the hilt. We were sitting in his office after my return from the beleaguered East, where the underprivileged live in the delusion they are superior to the hicks out West.

My thoughts went something like this (though they were not expressed with exactly this precision): Sure, Daimler is persuasive, but we're not scientists. We don't have any idea who is right. They may all be wrong.

"So," he said, glaring at doubting Thomas, "we shouldn't take a murder case because we're not murderers?"

"B-b-but this case rests on science."

"Hogwash!" he boomed. "It rests on *sales*manship, just like every other case. *Selling* the jury, my boy."

"B-b-but you d-d-don't want to sell them on something you d-don't know is t-true."

He bore in on me with those eyes that could sink ships. "Discovery, my boy," he said. "We'll do the depos and find out what is true. You don't think a grasping drug company will risk a lawsuit, do you? The first thing we'll see when we file this case is the drug company's checkbook."

"You sure?"

He smiled ruefully. "Sure as God made little green apples."

I was not as sure. "You don't think they'll fight with all their billions—like the t-tobacco company? Can they afford to d-dump cash on anyone who dies after t-taking JCD? Precedent?"

"Can't say you've made an invalid point, my boy," he said, then looked up and down his walls of framed pictures of VIPs he'd known, or at least had his picture taken with. I suppose that was a subtle gesture to point up his worldly experience compared to mine. Just in case I might let my head swell up from his quasi-compliment.

"Here's the case we'll make," he said, returning to earth from his celebrity cruise. "That drug, what's it called?"

"JCD?"

"Yeah. I think we can prove it's a killer—and if it is it kills indiscriminately sick and well alike. It doesn't cure anything. Both sides agree on that. So what does arresting a disease mean? Give some poor bloke another couple months of misery. Big wow!"

"But they'll say all that was explained. They hope to g-gain a couple months until they f-find a cure for Wanns."

"Hogwash! We all know it. I think this Kraut is on the money. Dimler—What's his name?"

"Daimler."

"Yeah, but even if he's wrong about R4 not causing Wanns, we can make our case that JCD kills cells, is a chain terminator, and if taken long enough, kills all the patients—even well ones who started taking it without having any Wanns symptoms."

"Minefield," I muttered.

"What's that?"

"It's a m-m-minefield," I said, though Bomber often

said "What's that?" more as a challenge to the idea expressed than as a question.

"Then we'll just have to send in the minesweepers," he said. He loved military metaphors. He rubbed his hands together in what I thought was inappropriate glee. Then he waved one of the hands at me. "Ah, it's just a starting point," he said. "I've got more exciting things in mind, but I don't want to tip my hand." Of course, he wouldn't tell me what he meant. It was maddening.

So, we filed the papers. Bomber's secretary, Bonnie Doone, typed them. She was a young woman sublimely constructed with a fine head of air—and that's not a misprint.

"Blicky," she said when she saw what was up in the shop.

"Excuse me?" I said.

"Wanns," she said, "blicky," and she made a face. "I don't know why he wants to get involved in it."

"I don't either," I agreed. "Why don't you suggest he back off?"

She looked at me as only Bonnie can when she is trying to pass herself off as a being in possession of superior intellectual faculties. "Because I need to work," she said, then added a personal dig: "I don't have a lucrative future in musical composition to fall back on."

I, of course, had no lucrative musical-composition future to fall back on. I reminded her that musical composition in my chosen area of classical music was anything but lucrative.

"So, write rock or country," she shrugged, in a characteristic display of her naïveté.

I didn't dignify that stupidity with an answer. Bonnie knew full well why I was doing Bomber's legwork.

"No joke," she said, "how many symphonies would you have to write to make what you could bag with one rock hit?"

"I've no idea. The number would probably approach infinity."

"So," she shrugged again, bobbing that tantalizing hair

here and there. That was all she said—so— as though that were self-explanatory.

"The subject was Wanns," I reminded her.

"Blicky," she repeated. "I mean, it is so emotional— young people dying of this horrible disease. And you want to fight the company that makes the only drug—"

"There are others now. Not much better, however."

"But can you win a case like that? Isn't it like going against apple pie?"

"Not quite as easy," I admitted.

"Really Tod, don't you…? I mean, what do you think of the homosexual scene?"

"I don't think of it that much, I guess."

"Would you want some guy kissing you?" she asked.

"No, but I don't know if I mind if some guy kisses a guy who wants it—or whatever—"

"Yeah," she said, rolling her eyes, "whatever! Phew! I don't even know what they do. They aren't really built for it."

"They find options," I said.

"Sick," she said. "I can just see this place crawling all over with that kind of," she hesitated, "person."

I let her know my indifference with my shoulders. But, I had to ask myself if I really *was* that indifferent. I remember walking the streets of San Francisco one night and having a creepy guy follow me. I crossed the street, he crossed, I went back, he followed. I was eighteen or nineteen and I was terrified. Finally, I ducked into a liquor store for protection. He came in too. He cornered me and asked if he could buy me a drink.

"I don't drink," I answered—trying to be firm, but not rude.

"Coffee then," he said.

"I don't drink that, either," I said, and left the store. He had the good grace not to follow me farther.

There were other incidents more direct to which I gave tough-guy responses, like, "Get away from me or I'll bash your face in." This, I will admit, to a pathetic, emaciated, toothless beggar who looked like he could hardly move. So, I suppose, deep down I had some prejudices which I tried to keep deep down in deference to my aspirations to tolerance.

There was some fuss about gays in the military. If you were considering the military as a sexually sensitive service, it would seem since heterosexuals outnumber homosexuals by a wide margin, the bigger risk to sexual unrest rested with men and women in the same service.

"Do you think of Wanns as a homosexual disease?" I asked Bonnie.

"Well, isn't it?"

I shook my head. "According to our guru, that presents some problems. First, those who think Wanns is transmitted by the R4 virus are compelled to consider it a general disease because viruses do not discriminate between sexes, ages, sexual orientation. Wanns predominates in homosexual men between twenty-five and forty-nine."

"So, what about all the R4 people who aren't homosexuals?" she asked.

"Exactly," I said. "The only hookers who get Wanns seem to be the drug addicts. The virus groupies claim the virus is passed by contaminated needles. They overlook the damage the drug itself could do."

She gave herself over to an economical shudder. "If he takes this case," she said, "I see only trouble."

So? I thought. It would hardly be the first time.

*   *   *

It is always enlightening, not to say fascinating, to see our adversary for the first time. This one, Jude Carstairs by name, advocate for the drug company Brogger-Wexler, had the nerve, or naïveté, to call Bomber from New York, where he was the lynch pin of the mega-firm, Carstairs, Ballentine, Racine, Algonquin and Palmer, and suggest that Bomber might drop by for a chat.

I was in the room when Bomber guffawed at that idea.

The poor man on the other end, who was trying to be civil in the confines of his innate feeling of superiority, attempted to save the day by shilly-shallying that Bomber was such an important man he thought he might just be coming to New York for some other reason.

"I can't think of any reason to go to New York City," he said, "while still in possession of one or two of my marbles." He went on to say Angelton, California, where our office happened to be, was heaven here on earth, and if Mr. Jude Carstairs wanted to experience that, Bomber would be glad to see him.

I guess Mr. Carstairs thought that was an okay idea, for he hopped on the next plane.

9

Bomber was reading Dr. Daimler's book *Phantom Virus*. He barely acknowledged my presence when he said, "This is fascinating. Claims Wanns isn't caused by sex at all, but by drugs. I'm no scientist, but he sure makes a persuasive case."

I am somewhat embarrassed to say I can't see my father in a bookstore. I didn't ask, but I'm sure Bonnie Doone bought the book for him—quite a feat since getting Bonnie inside a bookstore would be one giant step for mankind.

While we awaited the arrival of Attorney Carstairs, the next day, Bomber asked me if I thought Carstairs would be gay. Before I could answer, he said, "God, what a sissy word. Queer was so much more descriptive. Gay used to mean lighthearted, happy; these guys often seem anything but."

"How did he sound on the phone?" I asked.

"Not too lightweight," he said. "Let's put him to the Bonnie test. See how he reacts to her."

I could see the front door over Bonnie's shoulder from my closet Bomber called an office, so I left my door slightly ajar to check the reaction of our visitor to Miss Bonnie Doone, Miss Dunderhead of nineteen ninety-something. He passed with flying colors. The way his eyebrows bounced, his cheek twitched and his head jerked, I had the impression if I had been a mind reader I would have been embarrassed.

When she stood to lead Mr. Carstairs to Bomber's door, I saw she was taller than he was.

I came out of my closet and Bonnie introduced me. "This is Tod, Mr. Carstairs—he's Bomber's associate. He'll be joining you for your meeting."

He stuck out his hand and I took it. He had a bone-crushing handshake of which I could see he was very proud. It was as if he had only two big things about him: his handshake and his smile. The latter was all over his face, and it was always standing by to be pressed into service at a moment's notice. And it came at you like a bullet from a high-velocity assault rifle. It was good advice to be always defensively armed around Jude Carstairs. The only other guy I ever met with such a dazzling smile was Dr. Bill Bern.

Bomber coped with being short by wearing elevator shoes (a secret) and his bombast (hardly secret). Carstairs coped with his smile and handshake.

After Bonnie made the introductions, she left the three of us alone. Jude Carstairs's eyes roamed the floor-to-ceiling photographs of presidents and kings, prime ministers and princes. "Most impressive," he said.

"Better not be too easily impressed," Bomber said.

"All right," he said, launching his smile from a Howitzer, "fair enough." He sat in the chair facing Bomber, who was behind his battle-station desk. I gravitated to the couch on the wall, among the celebrated creatures of civilization. "I'm here to ask you to drop your case against my client, Brogger-Wexler."

Now Bomber flashed a smile of his own. He had pretty good teeth, but his smile at its least sincere reminded me of the smile of a hammerhead shark.

"Would you like to know my reasons?" Carstairs asked.

"Not particularly," Bomber said, "but I expect you're going to tell me."

"Well, I came this far..." and he held out a pair of faux-hopeless, manicured hands.

"At your instigation," Bomber said.

"Yessss..." he let it fizz like a carbonated drink going flat. "Wanns is a catastrophic disease. Those who have it have very little hope. It was the victims of this disease who clamored for a cure."

"Then why didn't you give it to them?" Bomber interrupted.

"Because it doesn't exist. The best we had, and I mean the very best anybody had was our JCD."

And what did that do for the patient?"

"It gave him hope. It gave him the feeling that something was being done for him and his illness—that someone cared about him."

"But essentially," Bomber said, "it killed him."

"No," Carstairs said. "It killed the bad cells—"

"Along with the good ones."

"It would be far better, of course, if we had something that would retard only the bad cells—" he lifted a shoulder, "We're working on it."

"In the meantime, you're selling, at an enormous profit, a drug that kills people."

"You don't understand—"

"Under the guise of helping them."

"You don't know what it's like to have the feeling of utter hopelessness. If you had R4 and were dying of Wanns, would you want to take something that might prolong your life?"

"And might shorten it? I trust you have studies that show what a patient can expect if he takes your drug?"

"Of course."

"And the doctors who prescribe the drug are made aware of its effect?"

"Certainly."

"Then why would anyone prescribe it?"

"Hope, counselor."

"Then you are selling elixirs, amulets, superstition."

"Well, I wouldn't—"

"You wouldn't?" Bomber boomed, as though he were outraged. "Your precious drug is killing people—it is making well people sick, then killing them too."

"That's not the way it is—"

"No? Then perhaps you can produce some studies that support your position."

"I can."

"Good. I'll look forward to seeing them."

"Then will you drop your case?"

"Let me see the studies, first. We may place varying

interpretations on them."

"If you are convinced by the studies, then you will drop your case?"

"I expect if I am convinced, we will not press the case."

"Good!" Jude Carstairs said. "For please understand, Bomber, I am passionate about this cause."

"Why?"

"It is such a tragic disease. There is so much suffering, anguish, pain. And we seem so helpless against it."

"Oh yeah?" Bomber said. "Not the way I see it. Not at all. I don't mean I haven't enjoyed your hearts and flowers, but the amazing thing to me is how you have whipped up this hysteria. You know it is a disease that strikes drug users."

"Not only—"

"And the homosexual men who take these drugs—"

"They don't all—"

Bomber wasn't letting him get his two cents in. "Either way this is a disease *you* claim is caused by errant behavior—dirty drug needles, promiscuous sex. It kills less people worldwide than measles, malaria, TB even, and you got that fading movie star doing your bidding between perfume gigs. Billions of bucks of tax money goes into this sham. Billions of bucks goes to the drug company. It is a public relations masterpiece!"

"That's not my line. I'm a lawyer, not a public relations person."

"Pity."

"Why so?"

"The PR mavens have done your company some good. You are in for nothing but bad—" Bomber loved to intimidate, and big as they might have been in different milieus, Bomber's foes were usually intimidated. I was amazed at the confidence he expressed in his position. *I* didn't have that much confidence we were right.

The gargantuan smile of Jude Carstairs tightened. He was willing another train of thought. "You know," he said, at last, "we will fight with all we have, and we have endless resources."

Bomber nodded. "I suppose you have everything on your side..."

"I think so—"

"But right."

"Is that so? Well what do you know about science? What do you know about medicine? What do you know about the pain and suffering of forgotten people? Everyone who takes JCD does so by choice. They beg us for it."

"And with an astronomical price tag, you provide it."

"You know the outlandish amounts spent on research. Without ever knowing if you can recoup. Many projects are never recouped."

"This will recoup them all," Bomber said, "never fear. Here you have a real slot machine."

"It has been a success, yes, because of the demand. We would love to create demand for every product, but that is not the way of the world."

"Oh, I suspect there will always be a market for panaceas. Especially where the hysteria has built to boiling."

"We have not *caused* any of the hysteria," Carstairs said. Then he shifted gears. "Tell me, Bomber, is there anything you would take to drop the case?"

Bomber thought for only a moment. "Yes. Two million for my client, Angelo Scioria."

I watched Carstairs's face. It was impassive. The smile might have been ready to explode on the scene, but it didn't.

"And stop selling JCD until you have a study that shows it is good for something besides killing cells and killing people."

I could see Carstairs's brain cells bursting, but not with an answer. The process seemed one of suppressing any angry response.

"Very well," he said, "we will file our answer in a timely fashion."

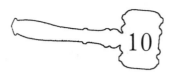

10

I must confess to a continuing weakness for the rare individual who not only says "very well" and "in a timely fashion;" but leaves you with the impression they are a perfectly natural part of his everyday speech.

And the answer we got to our filing validated my high regard. It was a masterpiece of the genre. I was worried.

Bomber wasn't. He knew the proof of the pudding was in the courtroom.

So, we flew from Los Angeles to Newark and rented a Cadillac for the rest of the journey.

"Piece of cheese," Bomber pronounced it as he drove me to Birchwood. Compared to his Bentley he was probably right. But the Bentley cost over five times as much as the Cadillac.

We checked into separate rooms at the Birchwood Inn, a pleasant place in a colonial mode this part of the country seemed to favor.

At 10 o'clock the next morning, we were seated in the office of a stenographic service in downtown Birchwood. Opposing counsel, Jude Carstairs, had offered his office in New York City, but Bomber thought it would serve us better to make him come to the suburbs instead. "I came all the way from California," he explained to me. To Carstairs, he said it would be more convenient for the witnesses who lived there. Besides, that was where the trial was to be so they might as well get used to it.

So, we were all in this Spartan room with a long table— the stenographer curled over her little typing machine on which she punched hieroglyphic symbols onto what looked like adding machine tape. It was an operation, both recording and reading, that was a mystery to me. There was a tape recorder at one end of the table, the witness was on her right—next to Jude Carstairs. Across from the witness sat Bomber, with me next to him. An attempt had been made to make the room homey with a picture of a sailing ship on the far wall.

Doctor Bill Bern was the witness giving his deposition. He was not tall, but he carried himself as though he were a man to be reckoned with. But in this stark, well-lit environment he looked less significant than he did in his office with the mile-high carpet and the theatrical lighting. Something about his dark hair in this bright light bothered me until Bomber put his finger on it. "It's a toupee," he whispered loud enough to embarrass Dr. Bern.

Bomber went over the basics—name, address, occupation. "Have you had your deposition taken before?"

"Yes."

"So, you know you testify under penalty of perjury?"

"Yes."

"Where did you go to college?"

"East Rutherford."

"And medical school?"

"Grant School of Medicine in Trenton."

"Where did you place in the class academically?"

The doctor showed his first discomfort. "I don't know."

"You don't know or you don't remember?"

"I didn't pay any attention to numerical ratings."

"So, is it safe to say, you were not near the top?"

The doctor's plastic face got a workout. He was in his early fifties and, in case you forgot, the toupee reminded you. "Not at the top, no."

"Nowhere near the top, Doctor?"

"I really couldn't say."

"If I refreshed your memory by reminding you your standing was 112th out of 115, would that be accurate?"

"I don't remember."

"Will you look it up for the trial, so you won't be embarrassed?"

"That's gratuitous, counselor," Jude Carstairs rang in with his first contribution to the proceedings.

These were Bomber's rattling tactics. I don't think he cared where the doctor ranked in his class. I was second last in mine—the Bomber was not near the top himself. But if he thought he could make the doctor look dumb, it would be a plus. And, with any luck, the doc would carry the fear to the trial. The fear of being belittled in front of his fellows. It could put him off his feed.

"Doctor, were you acquainted with Merilee Scioria?"

"Yes, I was."

"How did you become acquainted?"

"She came to me as a patient."

"How did she find you?"

"Her parents brought her."

"Are you a specialist?"

"I have a general practice."

"In the course of your general practice, do you have an opportunity to prescribe drugs?"

"I do."

"What kind of drugs?"

"Whatever kind I think will help the patient."

"Help in what way?"

"Cure a cold, stop pneumonia, kill pain."

"Ever prescribe a drug known as JCD?"

"Yes."

"How often?"

"Once."

"Only once?"

"Yes."

"How many Wanns patients have you had?"

"Just one."

"Who was that?"

"Merilee Scioria."

"How did you determine she had Wanns?"

"She tested R4 positive."

"Did you do the test?"

"I don't do those tests. I took the blood sample and sent it to the lab for testing."

"What was the result?"

"I just told you," the doctor said, "positive."

"What were her Wanns symptoms?"

"She had a yeast infection."

"A yeast infection? When did that become a Wanns disease?"

"I don't know. Around the time she got it."

"Did you discover the infection, or was that a subcontracted test also?"

"Yes. The lab. I diagnosed it, I believe. The lab confirmed it."

"What lab was that?"

"I don't remember. I use several."

Bomber pumped him for the names of his labs. He seemed to be reluctant to reveal them.

"Do you have records of these lab reports?"

"I believe I do."

"You *believe*? Are there circumstances where you destroy your records?"

Dr. Bern gave Bomber a fisheye. "I don't destroy records."

"So, you want to change your answer?"

"What answer?"

"You said you *believed* you had records. Do you mean to change that now to say you are *sure* you have the records?"

"Insofar as I am *sure* of anything."

"If you didn't have them, what would be the cause of that?"

"I don't know. Never got a copy. Lost. Misfiled."

Bomber was nodding happily. From the look on the doctor's face, he couldn't understand why.

"So, you prescribed JCD for Merilee Scioria?"

"Yes."

"The first and only patient for whom you did so?"

"Yes."

"Why did you prescribe JCD?"

"It's the only drug available to combat Wanns, or was at the time."

"How did you know that?"

He seemed startled. "I'm a doctor," he said. "I keep up."

"And what does keeping up on JCD entail?"

"I read the literature."

"What literature?"

"Written about JCD."

"Written by whom?"

"Brogger-Wexler."

"The drug company that manufactures JCD?"

"Yes."

"You consider that an objective source?"

"They've done the testing."

"What do the tests show?"

"The FDA approved the drug for Wanns patients."

"Did they point to any one person whose condition was reversed by JCD?"

"It is, I believe, an arresting drug, not a reversing one."

"What happened to Merilee Scioria after you prescribed the drug?"

"She continued to weaken."

"Did she recover?"

"No."

"She died?"

"Yes."

"What was her reaction to JCD?"

"She and her family were adamant about taking it when she'd received the results of the test."

"Did you try to talk her out of it?"

"Well—no."

"No?" Bomber said. "Ever hear of Dr. Walter Daimler?"

"Sounds vaguely familiar."

"Ever read any of his studies?"

"I don't believe so."

"How about his book, *Phantom Virus?*"

Dr. Bern scrunched his eyebrows. "I don't know it," he said. I had told Bomber I saw in on the doctor's shelf.

"Are you aware JCD was ruled too toxic for humans thirty years ago by the FDA?"

"I'd heard something," the doctor said. "But they approved it this time."

"You heard something? That was it, and you gave your patient this toxic drug?

"It is easy to second guess and speculate about drugs. But when people are sick, they want drugs."

"Don't you mean they want a cure?"

"Well—yes. But that usually means drugs."

"Does it, doctor? In the case of JCD, it seems to have the opposite effect, does it not?"

"I don't know about that. It was the only option."

"*Only* option?"

"Yes."

"What about doing nothing?"

"She might have died a lot sooner."

"Of a yeast infection?"

"Without an immune system to fight it, yes."

"Ever have a patient die of a yeast infection?"

"No. I never had one with R4."

"Do you know how many people in the U.S. have R4?"

"No."

"Were you aware of the million people with R4, only five percent of them develop Wanns symptoms?"

"Where are you getting your statistics?"

"I am the one asking the questions here, doctor. Perhaps the question should be, where are *you* getting your information?"

"Don't badger me."

"You ain't seen nothing yet, doctor."

"Bomber!" Jude Carstairs hit the table and it seemed to make his face red. "Restore some civility, please."

"Doctor, do you realize JCD is a chain terminator?"

"I'm sorry?"

"It kills cells. People can't live if you constantly kill their cells. JCD terminates the DNA chain in the human body."

"Don't lecture him," Jude Carstairs said. "Do you have a question?"

"The question is right there. The nature of JCD. Do you realize it is a chain terminator?"

"That doesn't discriminate? To kill a bad cell, a thousand good ones go with it. Yes. But a healthy body regenerates cells. So, the hope is if you kill the bad cells and get some good along with them there is a chance the good cells will regenerate."

"Did you ever see that happen?"

"Personally? I only had the one case."

"Ever hear of it happening?"

"As I said, I had only one case. I was not a Wanns specialist."

"Do you think, under those circumstances, you should have been treating a Wanns patient?"

"I consulted those who did specialize."

"Who were they?"

"I don't remember the names offhand."

"Do you have records?"

"I think I can find them."

"Good. Please do so, and give their names and numbers to Mr. Carstairs.

"Dr. Bern," Bomber asked, "in the course of your diagnosis of Merilee Scioria and her purported R4, did you seek a second opinion?"

Bern shifted slightly in his seat, then answered confidently. "Yes, I did."

"Tell us about that, please."

"After I got the results from the first lab, I sent a second sample to a different lab."

"But, doctor, isn't that a second opinion of the sample of blood you sent?"

"Yes."

"Wouldn't it have been sounder medical practice to have a second sample drawn from Merilee and sent to a second lab?"

"Well, that's what I did, of course."

"What about a second *physician?* Wouldn't that have been better practice?"

Dr. Bern shrugged. "Well, I neither analyze the blood nor make a conclusion. That is all done by the lab, so I don't know what purpose would be served by having another doctor draw the blood."

"You don't?" Bomber fixed him with drilling eyes—they were going for oil buried deep in the terrain.

"No." Dr. Bern was making a herculean effort not to squirm.

"Now, Doctor Bern, you said yours was a general practice?" It was another valley in Bomber's peaks-and-valleys show. Lull him, then lambaste him.

"Yes."

"What kind of medicine does that entail?"

"Everything from family medicine to minor surgeries."

"Ever do abortions?"

"A few. It's legal now, you know."

"I didn't question that. But thank you for illuminating your answer. Let us return to Merilee Scioria. What kinds of things did you treat her for?"

"She came to me as a young girl. Childhood diseases at first. Chicken pox, measles, as I recall. Strep throat. Acne. Things like that—at first."

"Later?"

Dr. Bern looked at his attorney. "I'm concerned about confidentiality," he said.

"You may answer him. If it isn't admissible in court, I'll keep it out of the testimony."

Dr. Bern nodded, unconvinced. He seemed reluctant to

part with the information. "She came to me in the early stages of pregnancy—for, ah, a termination."

"And did you perform it?"

"Yes."

"Did you ask who the father was?"

"Yes."

"What did she say?"

"She didn't know."

"She didn't know or she couldn't remember or it was a stranger who she didn't know?"

"I can only tell you what she told me. That she didn't know."

"And you accepted that?"

"Yes."

"You inform her parents of her condition?"

"I asked her if she had told them. She said they would die, and she would rather die than tell them."

"So, you didn't tell them?"

"No."

"Was that the only abortion you performed on her?"

"No. There was one other."

"When?"

"A year later."

"How old was she for these, ah, I believe you call them 'procedures'?"

"Fifteen and sixteen."

I'll say this for Bomber, he just kept questioning as though he weren't the least bit surprised at this bombshell. "Did you counsel her on birth control?" There, he aptly threw the responsibility back on the shoulders of the family doctor.

"Yes."

"Wasn't very effective, was it?"

"Apparently not."

"What other professional association did you have with Merilee Scioria?" Bomber asked the question to implicate the doctor by inference in possible quasi-medical associations.

"I treated her for drug dependency."

"What kind of drugs was she taking?"

"You name it; she tried it."

"Where did she get these drugs?"

The doctor smiled a crooked, know-it-all smile. "You can get them on any street corner."

"Did she get any of them from you?"

"Of course not!" Dr. Bern shot back, indignantly.

"She never got any drugs from you?"

"Never!"

"But doctor, didn't you just admit giving her the lethal drug, JCD?"

"That's not the same!" he snapped. "That's a prescription medication for a disease. That is not a recreational drug."

"How do you define recreational drugs?"

"Drugs taken only for recreation."

"Uppers and downers included?"

"Those can be prescribed for medical conditions."

"Such as?"

"Depression, hypertension."

"Do you do a lot of prescribing in those areas?"

"Not a lot."

"What would you say—average for general practitioners, above average, or below average?"

The doc shrugged. "Average, I guess."

Bomber now read him a list of drugs and asked him to characterize his prescriptions of them each by heavy, medium, or light. The amazing thing was the doctor didn't seem to think we could get this information, so he characterized all his prescriptions as "average."

"Doctor," Bomber asked, after going through the list, "isn't it true you are known throughout the world for being an easy mark for prescribing recreational drugs for 'medicinal' purposes?"

"That's not true," the doctor bristled.

"Do you prescribe for drug dealers?"

"Of course not," he said. "That's an insult."

"Insult noted," Bomber said. "Did Merilee ever talk to you about how she got drugs?"

"No."

"Yet you say they are available on every corner."

"Nothing unusual in that," he shrugged.

"And you also treated her for drug abuse?"

"Yes."

"But you don't know where she got the drugs?"

"Correct."

"Wouldn't that information have helped in the cure?"

His face contorted in one of those 'why?' gestures. "Makes no difference where she got them. The damage was the same."

"How would you characterize her usage—and the effects from it?"

"She was, for a time, a heavy user. The damage to her nervous system was significant. You might say brutal."

"Did it impair any of her functions?"

"Yes. She lost bladder control, was subject to fainting spells and fuzzy thinking, plus a destruction of her self-esteem. Then there was the erratic behavior."

'What kind of behavior?"

"Oh, she would come two hours early for an appointment one day and two hours late the next time. Getting pregnant twice in her teens and not seeming to know the fathers. I suspect she became promiscuous."

"Suspect? Based on what?"

"I have no proof," he shrugged, "but when I read between the lines there was evidence of indiscrimination in sex partners."

"In between *what* lines?"

"I can't explain it exactly."

"Then perhaps you shouldn't say it."

Challenged, the doctor tried to come up with an answer.

"Her yeast infection for one," he said. "She had sores on

61

her genitals which were indicative of venereal disease. Occasionally, I noticed marks on her that came from abusive treatment."

"But you had no proof?"

"No."

"Did Merilee Scioria ever explain any of these marks?"

"No."

"Did you ask?"

"Yes, I did. Merilee was not a communicative person."

"But she *was* able to tell you she was pregnant?"

"Yes."

"Twice?"

"Yes."

"Wouldn't you consider that intimate information?"

Dr. Bern shrugged. "It was a necessity. She needed the procedures. But she absolutely stonewalled me on the details."

"Couldn't that have been because she didn't trust you?"

"I had no indication of that," the doctor said. "She trusted me enough to terminate her pregnancies."

"How many pregnancies do you terminate in a year?"

"I don't do terminations ordinarily."

"Five, ten, fifty?" Bomber pressed.

"Not any."

"But I thought you said you did *two* on Merilee Scioria?"

"Yes."

"Why?"

"Because I was her doctor. Because she was young and vulnerable and I didn't want her to go to some stranger. Her psyche was too frail."

Bomber was obviously trying to pile up enough rope to hang the doctor with later at the trial. The doctor was a tough customer to figure. I found something suspicious in his manner, but it was far from anything obvious. I was almost certain a jury would take to him.

"So you did these…'procedures' without any experience?"

"I had done some in medical school."

"How many?"

"A few."

"Two, six, twenty-five?"

"A few," he repeated.

"More than one?"

"Yes."

"More than five?"

"I don't think so. I don't remember exactly."

"Were these 'procedures' done under the auspices of your medical school?"

"Yes."

"As part of your training?"

"Yes."

Bomber looked at Jude Carstairs, opposing counsel, and said, "Let's take a break." And that was Bomber to a T. A proprietorial statement, not a question.

Attorney Carstairs nodded, curtly.

Bomber and I walked outside. The air was fresh and invigorating. As we stood in front of the low office building, Bomber said, "He's lying."

"How d-do you know?"

"Just look at him. He's a scumbag in movie-star's clothing. He's got this friendly, almost ingratiating way about him, but take my word for it, underneath, he's a worm."

"Look good to a jury, though," I said.

"That's why we'll have to destroy him," he said.

Bomber gave me a list of chores to do while he harassed a couple of employees of Brogger-Wexler, the drug colossus.

My toughest assignment? To take Regina Scioria to lunch without her domineering husband. Even getting her to answer the phone was a challenge. Angelo was an old-world authoritarian figure and Regina didn't sneeze without his permission. So, I had to be devious. I went to their restaurant where she perched on a stool like a bird on a telephone wire. The cash register stood like a protective shield in front of her.

When Angelo was hustling a young couple to a table, I whispered in her ear a time and place. "Come alone," I said, as though I were some sort of spook.

"But..." she stammered, "Angelo wouldn't let me do that."

"No option," I said. "You want us to take the case."

"I thought you already..."

I shook my head.

"I can't..." she said.

After I left, I realized I was so nervous I had no idea what the place looked like. Then I was sure Regina *never* left her stool at the cash register. It would take some doing for her to get away for lunch, and I had no idea if she had what it took.

*   *   *

The Birchwood, New Jersey, police headquarters was housed in a brick structure that owed its architectural heritage to the depression and the W.P.A.—famous for its bridges, highways, and government buildings.

In other words, the city hall, fire department and police

department were in a ponderous, clumpy building that put you in mind of a fat pack of ladyfingers standing on end.

To get to the cops, I had to go in the side door of this corner monument, up a half-dozen steps, like I was going up the back way of some schoolhouse.

I didn't have to suffer any bigshot wait. This was no big city force nor was it a Southern Faulkner hamlet Bubba force. The cops here seemed to be guys who could have just as easily taught school or made telephones.

In a minute, Officer Ham Trout came out to greet me, swinging his arm purposely in front of him in a fair imitation of a cop swagger.

He looked like one of those cops you didn't want to run into in a dark alley. He was built like a barrel, but there was no fat on him—it was all muscle and attitude.

"Mr. Hanson," he said, sticking out a friendly ham-hand. "Ham Trout. Come on back."

He had a little room of his own with a metal desk and a metal swivel chair and papers everywhere. He flopped down in the chair, leaned back and laced his fingers behind his head.

"Merilee Scioria," I said to his what-can-I-do-for-you pose.

He nodded. "Sadness," he said.

"Did you have any involvement?"

Ham flipped a shoulder. "Died of Wanns disease," he said. "Not much to engage us there."

"Did you have anything on Merilee?"

"Some anonymous tip 'bout drug dealing."

"Look into it?"

"Sure we investigated. Didn't come up with much. The girl had some crappy associations."

"How so?"

"Drug dealers for starters."

"Specifically?"

"There's a guy in town goes by the improbable name of Buck Rogers." He shrugged, as if to say "Believe that one and I

65

have a bridge you might be interested in."

I didn't blink. I didn't want him to know I'd heard the name before. You have to have a good deadpan in this business. "Any evidence she was dealing?" I asked.

He pursed his lips and shook his head. "Spent some time on Rogers and her, but we were never able to nail anything down. When the DEA boys moved in, we moved out."

"They investigating *her?*"

"So I'm told."

"Can you give me a name at the DEA I can talk to?"

He smiled one of those crooked, dream-on smiles. "Those boys and girls talk only to God."

"You know where I might find this Buck Rogers character?"

"There's a bar called The Three Bears down on Hickory Street. Hangs out there sometimes. Far as we know he lives in a gopher hole somewhere."

"What was their relationship?"

"Hung out together. Didn't make her father very happy."

"Do I understand it would not have made you happy either—had it been your daughter?"

He grinned ruefully. "That's a fair statement," he said.

"What's your gut feeling on the thing? Was Merilee Scioria a drug dealer or simply a good girl who fell for some bad boys?"

He shook his head—once. "Gut didn't feel much on this one. See a lot of tragedy in this line of work—but her tragedy was medical, and that's not my line."

Nice as he was, Ham Trout could contribute nothing more to my investigation.

Putting Ham's negativity aside, I paid a call on the Drug Enforcement Agency's field office in Newark, New Jersey. There Ham's negativity was validated. Some Joe Blow type almost went blind looking down his nose at me while he explained the facts of life to a pesty greenhorn.

All the turn-off words like confidentiality, government policy, department regulations peppered the air.

I countered with one word, "Subpoena."

He one-upped me with two, "Good luck."

All in all, it was a depressing experience and put me in mind of Franz Kafka.

I realized I would have to tread on more fertile ground.

*　　*　　*

Comparing women to birds is unfair. Not because some women aren't birdlike, but rather because there are so many different birds, from the slashing vulture to the flighty sparrow, the kinetic hummingbird to the wise old owl. Then, of course, there's the turkey.... My waitress was a turkey.

While I was hopefully waiting for Regina Scioria at Barney's Cafe, a chubby but oh-so-friendly waitress filled me in on the place.

The eatery had been decorated by the owner's girlfriend, Netty, who seemed to have an eye for kitsch. But then, talent for interior decoration was not in her job description, she being, reputedly, rather adroit at more intimate endeavors.

There were white tablecloths and clunky blue-rimmed glasses on the tables. So far, so good. But the chairs were ladder back and so uncomfortable it was said they had been employed to speed up the turnover rate, as it was humanly impossible to dawdle while your body was suffering that kind of abuse.

Netty loved two things in the world more than anything else (though she tried to make her boyfriend think otherwise): dogs and painting dogs. She kept seven dogs and did as many paintings of each and hung them willy-nilly about the place. You could tell they were dogs. Not much else could be said for them.

Coming into the restaurant at last, Regina Scioria didn't look like a bird, but she moved like one—dark, flitting motions so at any time you expected her to take off into the wild blue yonder as Bomber's old Air Force song would have it.

Mrs. Scioria, as I called her out of respect for her age and angst, had legs so short it took her twice as many steps as it took me to make the journey, but she moved them faster. She looked flustered. When she sat down, she let the wind out of her sails and filled my ear with the string of outrageous lies she'd had to tell to make our meeting. "Angelo will be fit to be tied if he ever finds out," she said. "But I tell myself it is for his own good. He gets so excited about things..."

I smiled indulgently.

Feeling red meat was in order, I had the burger and fries with a chocolate milkshake. Mrs. Scioria ordered the house salad with the dressing on the side, then failed to put any of the dressing on the lettuce that looked like it had seen better days. She picked at it with her fork, which was doing the duty of a bird's beak, without actually eating any of the food. She pushed the food around as she talked, then seemed to make little piles of it, then merged the little piles into one big pile like a child trying to avoid eating her spinach.

Getting anything meaningful out of Mrs. Scioria's mouth was no easier than it was for her to put food in her mouth. She chronically deferred to her husband's judgment, prejudices and conceptions. Angelo this and Angelo that. It all seemed like a waste of time until I was able (quite by accident) to chisel away a shred of information.

"But what kind of childhood did Merilee have with you both working so much? Did she have a nanny or babysitter or what?"

"Merilee and I stayed home until she was able to walk to get into things—Lord, was she an active child though! It seemed like we just couldn't wear her out no matter *how* hard we tried. Angelo had tried several replacements for me at the restaurant and they couldn't satisfy him. So, I went back to work. Angelo wouldn't hear of anyone but me watching his child, so I tried to do two jobs—mother and bookkeeper—and it was a handful, I'll tell you."

"How did you manage so much?" I asked.

"It wasn't easy, believe me. But everyone at the diner was so nice," she smiled contentedly at the memory. "Eldon was especially good. He took to Merilee like a grandfather."

"Eldon?"

"Eldon Shaker," she said. "He worked for Angelo."

"Past tense?"

"I'm afraid so—"

"Why?" I had to pry, she was a tight one.

"They had a fight about something."

"What?"

"Oh dear, I don't know. I was never in on those business decisions."

"Do you know where this Eldon Shaker lives or works?"

"I'm afraid he isn't working, the last I heard. But Angelo wouldn't want you talking to him, I'm sure of that."

"But if it were vital to our case...?" I let the question hang with a provocative hoist of an eyebrow.

"Oh, but I couldn't go against my husband."

"Sometimes we must do what seems against someone's wishes to help him," I said. "This is one of those times."

"Oh," she said, holding her heart as if to keep it from bouncing out of her chest. "But, I couldn't—and even if I wanted to I'd have no idea where Mr. Shaker lived. One of those Lime places it used to be, but that was so long ago, at least a month." She looked at me slyly. "The last I heard. I don't remember which Lime. Wasn't West Lime though, or North or South. Around the corner from the bank, it used to be. But as I said, that was *so* long ago," she sighed. "My how time flies! Oh dear, I guess you'll just have to ask my husband," she smiled.

"Mrs. Scioria," I began, "we've had a deposition with Dr. Bern, you know."

"Yesss."

"He said some very disconcerting things about Merilee."

"Well, why would he do that?"

"That was what I was going to ask you."

"Goodness," she said, flapping her innocent eyes—she was too good to be true, "I don't know. What did he say?"

I looked at her cherubic face, trying to gauge her capacity for taking it—I wasn't optimistic. "Dr. Bern says he was your family doctor—and you took Merilee to him as a child—"

"Yesss." She was confused. "Is there something wrong with that?"

"No, no, certainly not," I assured her. "But he, ah, that is Dr. Bern, ah, indicated in his deposition that Merilee may have come to see him on her own as a teenager. Did you know anything about that?"

"Nooo—what was the matter with her? I don't remember her ever telling us about it."

"She didn't tell you," I said, "neither did the doctor."

"Oh, why on earth not?"

"Can you guess?" I said, hoping she would supply the unpleasant part.

"Nooo," she said, not making it easy.

"Dr. Bern claims," I spoke slowly, "Merilee came to him when she was a teenager to…terminate a pregnancy."

"Why on earth would she do that?" she said. "She wasn't pregnant."

"You sure?"

"Of course, I'm sure. Who would the father have been?"

"She didn't tell him. Then the doctor says there was a second, a year later."

"Ridiculous! She said not a word about it."

"Would she?"

"Of course, we were very supportive parents."

"You don't think your husband might have been angry…?"

"Well, disappointed, certainly, but I don't think he would have been mad at her."

"Ever see an angry reaction from your husband?"

"Well, nooo. But he's never had news like that."

"Dr. Bern also said she was a drug user."

Mrs. Scioria shook her head in rapid response. "That man is slandering my little girl, and I don't know why."

"You may be right, Mrs. Scioria," I said, looking off at a particularly inept dog painting, as though there were a clue hidden there. There wasn't. "But if we're going to have any hope of winning the case, I'm going to have to find out."

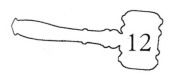

12

There was a grassy square in the heart of East Lime, and that was about it. If you stood in the middle of the grass and pivoted, you could see the bank, a pharmacy, a mom-and-pop grocery store, a dry goods emporium, and one of those places that sold secondhand clothes on consignment.

Eldon Shaker lived on the third floor of a three-story walk-up around the corner from this commercial paradise. His building predated elevators, and when Eldon answered the knock and let me inside, I was pretty winded—a grim testimony to the shape I was in.

At first glance, I saw that his housekeeping predated the vacuum cleaner and soap. There was the dead smell of cigarette smoke about the place and on Eldon himself. It was apparent social assistance from the federal government was keeping him alive. Barely.

He was a wimpy looking guy with a blond crew cut. He was in the Social Security range, with rounding shoulders that stooped forward when he walked, which was as seldom as possible.

He shuffled back to a threadbare brownish couch and sprawled across it as though he had reached a time in life where the conservation of energy was paramount.

"You can sit there if you want to talk," he said, nodding vaguely at the lone chair in the room.

I sat and glanced out the double-hung window at the backyards of the small shops along the main street. They were strewn with empty packing boxes, trash cans, snow shovels and scattered garden tools. There didn't seem a good housekeeper among them—though on my way to Eldon's I had noticed the fronts of the shops were immaculate. I looked back at Eldon

Shaker and decided the look on his face was not because he was unhappy to see me, but rather because he was just unhappy.

"Regina Scioria tells me you were a friend of her Merilee's," I said, as though we were talking about the weather.

His eyes glazed over and he lay there on the couch, his head on one couch arm, his feet on the other as if he were floating on his memories.

"Yuh," he said at last.

"Can you talk about it?"

He looked at the ceiling as if searching for the key to obliterate the memory. "Don't know where to begin," he said.

"How about the beginning? When you met the family—"

He considered that for a while, as though weighing the effort required against the results achieved. He closed his eyes and found the peace of Jesus or something, because he began as though he were in a trance.

"I started working for Angelo when Merilee was just a toddler." Eldon had a low, rumbly voice, like a steam engine, hissing and chugging. "You never saw a couple who doted more on their kid. I don't know why they didn't have a dozen—plumbing problems, I guess."

"What did you do for Angelo?"

"Best damn cook he ever had, if I do say so myself."

"But no longer?"

"No longer," he said, shaking his head in and twisting a gold wedding band on his finger.

"Why not?"

"In one word?—Merilee. Or is that two words? I never know."

"Angelo's daughter, Merilee? How so?"

"First you gotta understand what it's like working for Angelo. He's good to you, but he's a control freak. Do it his way or hit the highway."

"You didn't do it his way?"

"Sure I did—worked for him some twenty years, seven

days a week, ten hours a day. A day off was an eight-hour day. He'll tell you he never had no one better—told me so many times." He heaved a large sigh as though talking was a great effort for him. "You mind if I smoke?" he asked.

Of course I minded—but he was doing me a favor talking to me, and we *were* in his abode where the secondhand smoke was already coming at me from the woodwork. I tried to put this sentiment into words, but it didn't come out too well.

He lit up and drew the smoke deep down as if to cleanse his rusty soul. When the cigarette was in his mouth, his hand went absently to his wedding band. Eldon had a habit of twisting the gold ring, though I saw no evidence of a wifely touch about the place.

"I notice you're wearing a wedding ring—are you married?"

"Was."

"Oh," I said confused. "Still wear the ring?"

"Yeah. From my first wife."

"You had a second?"

"Yeah. Wore it then, too."

"Really? How did she like that?"

"Not much," he shrugged.

"Think that contributed to your divorce?"

His shoulders arose again. "Probably."

"Must have liked your first wife a lot."

"Did," he said.

"What happened?"

"Hell, how do I know? I was stupid, I guess. Working all the time. You're a cook, you're always working. She wanted a better time than I was giving her. She married again—a good-time Charlie. I still talk to her once in awhile."

"She know you're still wearing the ring?"

"She knows."

"How does she feel?"

"Gotta ask her, I reckon."

"Have any kids?"

"Only Merilee—"

"Merilee Scioria was *yours?*"

"Not biologically. Emotionally."

"How did her folks take to that?"

"Good at first," he said, spreading his hands. "Not so good later. When she grew up. Her father was a Hitler. I was someone she could spill her guts to."

"What did she spill?"

"Oh, the usual growing up stuff. Peer pressures, feelings of inadequacy—and..." he paused, "...the widest generation gap in history...with her father."

"She didn't get along with her parents?"

"You might say that."

"Not her mother either?"

"Her mother is a nonperson in that family. Angelo rules the roost."

"So, what was the conflict?"

"Hah!" he snorted. "What wasn't would be more like it."

"When did Merilee start coming to you?"

"She used to hang around me in the kitchen at the diner. When she was just a pup. We had a lot of fun whenever it got a little slack—which wasn't often. I'd let her lick the cookie batter dishes, the ice cream canisters. Later I'd let her stir stuff..."

"Her father approved?"

"Sure—anything that gave his little princess pleasure gave him pleasure."

"That stopped, apparently?"

"Did it ever. She grew up. The more she developed, the more paranoid Hitler became. He suspected her of all kinds of stuff you wouldn't believe—drugs, sex, theft—"

"Did she have any boyfriends?"

"Sure she did. She was a good-looking kid. Had the same feelings as her contemporaries."

"Get in any trouble?"

He shot me the fisheye. "What kind of trouble you have

in mind?"

I don't know why that made me blush. Perhaps because it was said as an accusation.

"Well, ah...like, ah, did she ever get...ah...pregnant?"

He shot me another withering glare. "You crazy or something? That girl was an angel."

"That's what her father thinks."

"He's right about that," Eldon said emphatically.

"So, why exactly did he fire you?"

"Meddling," he said, "with his daughter's head."

"But if she was so...pure and perfect...I don't get it."

"Join the club," he said, watching the cloud of smoke he sent toward the ceiling. He seemed proud of the result. "Paranoia," he said. "Pure paranoia."

"Lot of people saying otherwise," I said.

"They're liars," he snapped.

"Why are they so intent on badmouthing Merilee?"

He shook his head. "I got a lotta time to think, now I'm the guest of the federal social assistance system. What do I think? I think I don't know is what I think. I think, when I think at all, Merilee got mixed up with the wrong people, and those wrong people done her wrong. They used her for their purposes, then when the heat was on, they dumped her. Dumped *on* her while they were at it. Saved their own skins by skinning her."

It all sounded fanciful to me. I couldn't tell what, if anything, was behind the colorful language. "Could you be specific?" I asked.

Another cigarette was in the offing. Eldon Shaker made an elaborate show of sliding the cancer stick out of the pack, then rotating it with his fingers as though it were a delicately blended cigar. Suddenly the Zepf family from neighboring Pennsylvania came into my mind. It had been Bomber's big tobacco case. I thought of those adorable Zepf girls and wondered how they would look a year older. Would I have time to run over to Pennsylvania to see them? That was one of life's good intentions that wouldn't come off. The pressures of the present always seemed to take precedence over the pleasures of the past.

Eldon Shaker was thoughtfully coloring the air with clouds of his own making. They were gray, like rain clouds. There were storms ahead.

"You want specifics," he said in the haze. "For instance, that drug business. She was framed."

"By whom?"

"The big boys."

"What are their names?"

He shuddered. "No names," he said.

"You don't want to help clear her name?"

"I don't know them," he said. "She never talked names to me."

"All right. I was told she was dealing drugs."

"Lies," he said.

"She ever try drugs that you know of?"

He took a toke on his coffin nail just to keep the word drug in perspective, I supposed. Was he going to deny it? I wondered.

"She experimented some," he conceded. "Young kid in a big high school. Little marijuana perhaps—made her sleepy, is all."

"No hard stuff?"

"Nah. I'd never believe it," he said.

"She never told you anything about hard stuff?"

"Nah."

"Never anything about...pregnancies?" I added the 's' very slowly.

Eldon shot up his head from his prone position on the couch. "Where'd you hear that?"

"Around," I evaded—

"Crazy lies," he said. "I can tell you right now, that girl could do no wrong in my eyes. If you're here looking for dirt, you're at the wrong place."

"Well, I picked up a lot of dirt along the way—I can't

deny that."

"Well, I *can*," he said. "Whatever you heard is lies, lies, lies." He stood up, not without effort. "That's about all I have time for," he said "I got things to do."

I left without argument.

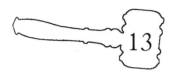

13

It was a part of town you didn't take the wife and kids to. Private investigators I read about seem to take this kind of atmosphere in stride. Not I.

The bar was called The Three Bears, for no reason I could discern. Personally I would have named it something like "The Queen's Latrine" in tribute to the smells that emanated therefrom. But not being a beer drinker, I never did develop a taste for the odor of saloons.

On entering this den of quasi-iniquity, the first thing I noticed was the battered upright piano against the far wall—out of harm's way.

There were only two guys at the bar facing the bartender, and they were at either end. Each sat silently—not to say morosely—staring into their glasses of suds. Both gave me the once-over and, seeing nothing of interest, went back to the inspection of beer foam, as though a doctoral dissertation on the subject was in the offing.

The bartender was a heavy man with "Sam" embroidered on his shirt. I wanted to make some crack about Sam being twice as easy on the embroiderer as Samuel, but thought better of it.

I sidled up to the bar as though I was an old hand there. No one was fooled. I realized right away I should say "Double scotch on the rocks" or something, but I wouldn't drink it and the barkeeper and his patrons would not take to that.

As the bartender lay the tiny paper napkin on the bar, he did so as though he were playing the winning card in a torrid game of Hearts. He brought his heavy eyes up to mine, stinging me with his silent question.

How do you explain being in a bar if you don't drink?

You don't. Better to get right to the point.

"I'm looking for a man named Buck Rogers," and even as I said it, I knew it sounded ridiculous.

"Are, are you?" he said, and for some inexplicable reason I was encouraged.

"You know where I could find him?"

"Who wants to know?" he asked.

"Tod Hanson," I said, extending my hand.

He just nodded. "What's it worth?"

I broke into my most innocent smile. "At my salary," I said, "I couldn't buy you a cigar—"

"Don't drink much either," he smirked, looking down at the lonely napkin on the bar between us.

"No," I said. "Sorry. I'm trying to help a couple—lost their daughter—maybe you heard about it on TV—Merilee Scioria?" He stared at me. "Ring a bell?"

He shrugged.

"You familiar with Angelo's Diner?"

"Heard of it."

"They've had a rough time of it," I said. "Girl may have gotten a bum-rap, reputationwise. Buck Rogers's name came up. He might help, that's all. I'm not looking to make trouble. Just want to talk to him. Heard he comes in here."

Big Sam shrugged again. I sighed to show him my patience was wearing thin, but I hoped his wasn't, because Big Sam did not look like he suffered fools at all.

"Mind if I play the piano?" I asked, and Sam the man's head darted up to a military posture. "You play?" he asked skeptically.

"Some," I said.

"Be my guest," he said, and I sidled over to the keyboard to observe keys with half of their ivory chipped off and the sustaining pedal completely gone. I sat down on the slab bench provided and ran my fingers over the keys. I thought I could play for hours until Buck Rogers showed up, or until Large Sam threw me out.

I started with Beethoven's "Turkish March" from *The Ruins of Athens*. I thought the beat and the drama made good barroom music. There was a silence after I finished which I would characterize as "stunned." I vowed to keep going until I got doused with beer.

Für Elise by the same composer was next. A nice melody and plenty of movement.

I stole a glance at the troops after the Beethoven, and I saw a curious grudging respect on Big Sam's face. The two customers seemed unmoved, as though my music were coming out of a speaker in a dentist's waiting room.

Next I experimented with Debussy's *Clair de Lune*, which wasn't really saloon music, but since Victor Borge, the comic pianist, calls it "Clear the Saloon," I plunged ahead.

My efforts, including Grieg, Bach, Rachmaninoff and even a little Tod Hanson (Piano Sonata no. 1, 1st movement), were met with stony silence. Though I noticed no discernible ill effects of the music on the clientele, and though I could play for hours and not know where the time went, I finally realized the folly of my logic that Buck Rogers would drop in on us while I was playing.

So, I got up to leave. A glance at the bar and I saw Big Sam's eyes were intent on me. If I'm not mistaken, I saw a drop of liquid in the corners. I gave him a weak smile.

"You play good piano," he said.

"Thanks," I said. I halted my progress out the door. Something in his tone led me to ask—"You play?" Since he had a piano in the place, I didn't think it was such a stupid question.

He shook his head. Then I felt the air being sucked into that large frame, "Daughter," he said at last.

"Oh," I said. "Your daughter plays?"

"Played," he said quietly. "Gone now."

"I'm sorry," I said. "Was she good?"

"The best," he said.

"Can you tell me what happened?"

"Car—drunk kid hit her head-on. He was passing in a

no-passing zone. She didn't have a chance."

The paradox of his still selling booze didn't escape me. One had to live, I supposed. We all do what we can.

"Nine o'clock," he said, and I didn't grasp the significance, until he added. "Buck comes through here 'bout nine o'clock at night."

It was almost six o'clock. I thanked Sam and told him I'd be back.

Then I went to Angelo's Diner for dinner.

The place was jumping. Mrs. Scioria was behind the cash register, and she seemed embarrassed to see me. Angelo was overseeing the operation like a kind of nervous floor walker, greeting patrons with a smile, doing odd jobs—filling water glasses, bussing dishes, ferrying credit cards and cash to his wife at the register.

It was an unpretentious place with scant thought given to the decor. Serviceable tables and chairs and thoughtfully prepared fresh food personally selected by Angelo. At the end of the meal, the check's bottom line wouldn't put you in the poor house. As a result, the place was jumping. The middle-aged hostess was no Merilee, if I can trust the pictures I had seen. The hostess told me it would be a twenty-minute wait. While I waited, standing in the tight waiting area, I was blissfully ignored by the busy Sciorias.

Twenty minutes to the minute the hostess seated me at a small table the size of a Mozart sonata—but how much space does a plate take?

It wasn't long before the proprietor himself came to the table. I could tell he was making an effort to control his anger in deference to the peace and well being of his establishment. But, looking in his eyes, so narrow for the occasion, there was no mistaking his feelings.

Even before he spoke, I could tell how his late daughter Merilee must have felt under that steely gaze of disapproval. The stare itself was enough to drive the stoutest heart to drugs.

"You listen here, young fella," he said with a quiet bite,

"I hire your father because my daughter she was murdered. Why you go around talking like Merilee was the criminal?"

I was sympathetic. "Mr. Scioria," I said, "I agree with you totally. But the reality is the opposition will base their defense on an offense, and the subject will be the character of the victim."

"But that's not right!" he protested.

"I agree. We *all* agree. But that's what they do, and I'm sorry to say it is often effective. So, we must anticipate everything they are going to spring on us and combat it if we can. Otherwise..." I threw up my arms in that universal gesture of hopelessness.

"I don't care," he said. "I don't want my Merilee dragged through the mud."

I nodded my understanding. "Only one way you can guarantee that," I said.

"What's that?" he asked.

"Drop the case."

He leaned over the tortilla-sized table and fixed me with that terrible stare. "You listen here, young fella. Merilee was all a the world to us. Everything! I will not a see her reputation destroyed because you are no competent. *You* see to it her reputation is a preserved through this horrible ordeal or I'll a see to you."

With that unsubtle, if obscure, threat, Mr. Scioria stalked off with the smile returned to his face for the more amenable customers.

After that happy confrontation, I felt I was eating at a funeral. I didn't feel like eating, but I knew I had to.

On my bill were printed the words:

Please pay cashier.

I left the tip on the table and made my way through the happy diners to Mrs. Scioria at the cash register. She was sitting birdlike, on a tall stool.

I proffered a twenty-dollar bill. She smiled sheepishly, rang up something on the cash machine, then handed me my twenty back.

"Your change," she said, with tight lips.

I looked at the twenty and at the tight lips. "But…" I stammered.

"Angelo says your money is no good here," she said, making what was often a gesture of good will sound like an insult.

"Thanks," I said, "I think." I smiled my own rueful smile and went back to the table to exchange the twenty for the tip. The tip was gone. I dropped the twenty anyway.

Expense account.

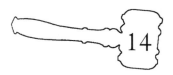

14

When I returned to The Three Bears bar, it was filling up and starting to smell like yesterday's vomit. Sam was at his work station polishing glasses and holding them up to the light to ferret out any errant smudges.

He looked through the glass at me, squinting. "You're messing with the wrong crowd, kid," he said. "You play good piano. I don't want to see you give up any of them talented fingers."

I tried to look nonchalant. I fear I failed. "What do you mean?" I sputtered.

The barkeeper's eyes shifted furtively. "I can't say any more," he said, *sotto voce.*

Then I noticed he was watching the front door open. He looked at me, then back at the door, but he didn't need to. I'd have known that visitor in the Colosseum.

His face was a showcase for scars, his arms a tattoo museum. He was not a guy who put you at ease with a sunny personality.

And, well-intended as the bartender's nod toward Buck seemed, it wasn't necessary; a small child could have told that this cartoon character was strictly from Hoodsville. I don't want to say he was built like the Empire State Building, but nothing else comes to mind.

Buck Rogers had a closely clipped beard and hair that played second fiddle tonsorially. He couldn't keep his hands off his facial hair. At first it led me to think he was craving some controlled substance that had been deprived him. Later I realized it was narcissism. Buck was one of a legion of dealers who was too smart to partake of his product—not intellectual or erudite maybe—if you asked him to whistle a few bars of a

Beethoven symphony, *any* Beethoven symphony, you'd observe a moment of silence. But *street* smart, he was that. I quickly realized he left me at the starting gate in that department.

Buck looked me up and down as though he were trying to place me in a pantheon of freaks.

He sat at the bar a few stools down and the bartender faithfully brought him one of those amber liquids without his asking. I whipped out a fiver to pay for it, and both the bartender and Buck Rogers looked at me with offense. I slid down the bar to sit beside him, then stuck out my hand. "Tod Hanson," I said.

He looked at my hand as though I were a leper. He didn't burden me with this name.

"I understand you might be Buck Rogers."

He didn't rouse himself to look at me.

"I also heard you might know something about the pharmaceutical market locally."

"You in the market?"

"Could be."

He nodded. "Look like a lousy cop to me."

"You flatter me," I said.

"No, I don't."

"Right," I said. "But if a guy had a knack for that sort of enterprise, where might he get the goods?"

"No idea."

"Dr. Bern, I understand, has been known to be generous with the prescriptions."

"I wouldn't know."

"Ever do any business with him?"

"Not so's you'd notice," he said, with that provocative smirk.

"You know Dr. Bern?"

"Yeah, I do. I went to him to have a couple warts removed."

That was hardly credible. I didn't know how anyone could tell a wart on Buck, he had so many pustules and bumps and crevices his face looked like the battlefield at Verdun.

"Do a good job?"

"What? Oh yeah, real swell."

"Give you any medicine?"

"Nah."

"Ever go back?"

"Nah—maybe a followup."

"When was that?"

Those hot eyes hit me again. "You doin' a movie on me or what?"

I'd say that comment was generational, but Buck Rogers was older than I was, and we used to say, "Are you writing a book?" I'm sure Buck Rogers had no idea what a book was. And if he ever sees this report of the events we spoke of, someone will have to read it to him. Perhaps Dr. Bern could do that. If he remembers how.

"So you know who Merilee Scioria was?"

"Maybe," he said.

"We're representing her parents. Her death shook them up some," I understated. "We have reason to believe her death may have been unnecessary."

"They're all unnecessary, but they're gonna happen to all of us sooner or later."

"Yeah, but this one may have been *too* soon."

"I get around, kid, I hear things, I see things, I can't help but put two and two together. She was bad news, and it was her old man's doing. He was looking for the second Virgin Mary and he got Typhoid Mary instead."

"Anything to do with drugs?"

"Yeah, drugs screw people up," he said, "but most people who take them are screwed up in the first place."

"How was Merilee screwed up?"

"Her father," he said with bleak emphasis.

"How's that?"

"I told you. He wanted the Virgin Mary and he got Mary Magdalene." Buck was good with the Marys. "He expected more than she could deliver. He wanted a valedictorian and prom queen all rolled into one, and she was the opposite. He blew."

I nodded. "So, how bad was she?"

"Bad," he said, turning his eyes on me. "Took anything she could into her mouth and arms. Screwed anything that wasn't nailed down. I saw her more than once laying somewhere stoned out of her mind. Needle marks up her arms to hell and gone." He shook his head and clucked his tongue. "Bad news," he muttered without taking his eyes off me.

I returned the stare—for a while. A short while. "If a person wanted to corroborate what you say, maybe get a different slant on it, where would you suggest he turn?"

"Nose's a little far from home isn't it?" he said, with an upward twitch of his own nose. "Maybe that nose got no business here," and he bent his forefinger behind his thumb pad then let it fly at my nose. It smarted. I flinched.

"Look," I said with more bravado than I felt, "I'm not here by choice. Just earning a living. Girl died of Wanns disease, they claim. There might have been foul play. There seems to be an effort here to besmirch her. They always go after the victim to make the accused look like a saint."

He shook his head. "*She* was no saint, that's for sure."

"You got any reason to badmouth her?"

"Listen kid, I'm gonna tell it to you like it is, like it or not. You do what you want with it. Then you get outta here and I never wanna see you again—alive."

Another threat that caught me wincing. His promised confession was not forthcoming, so I asked, "So, what do you do?"

"Do? I'm a good Samaritan," he said with a crooked smile. "I supply a need."

"Sort of altruism?"

"You might say that. Lot of people stumbling around in the dark. Can't afford a couple grand for some white coat to tell 'em they're screwed up and give 'em prescription pills."

"Like Dr. Bern?" I asked.

He shrugged.

"Can you give any leads? Any help at all?"

"You do what you want, kid, it's a free country. Just a friendly piece of advice: there's some people 'round here don't take kindly to people who ask stupid questions. Not that they particularly have anything against stupid questions, no, it's the people who ask stupid questions get 'em worked up. And I'm not talking kid stuff like shooting out a couple of knee caps; I'm talking going all the way. *Capisce?*"

"Kapish. So why all the fuss? What's anybody afraid of?"

He looked at me as though he wanted to laser a hole through my forehead. "Now that's a stupid question," he said.

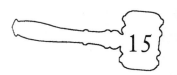

15

Early the next morning I hit the coroner's office, where I encountered a woman in midlife, sorely fatigued of her job. She was heavy and sighed heavily, as she hoisted herself and dragged herself into the chamber wherein were kept the sought-after records.

She probably had lunch while she was back there, and I noticed a patch of moss growing on my north side by the time she returned to the counter that separated the wheat (her) from the chaff (me).

With an unparalleled disdain on her lips, she set the folder down on the counter and found a checkout card for me to sign. This she slid across the counter as though lifting it might give her a hernia.

A few chairs were grudgingly provided along the wall for such meddlers as I to snoop in maximum discomfort.

I opened the folder, which seemed disappointingly thin. It was as though the death of Merilee Scioria was of no consequence, much as her life had been.

But there it was in the jargon of the trade—all the stuff inside Merilee when she stopped thinking about it. In the description of the body, there was the party-line note that the deceased had needle marks on both arms and traces of several drugs in her body, including heroin.

How, I wondered, did this intelligence get by the dentist's estate—the entity that paid Angelo Scioria and his spouse the two million for the wrongful death of their daughter?

The estate attorney had said the dentist's family didn't want to fight, but if Merilee Scioria was a hard drug user to the extent of needle marks up and down her arms, they certainly would have had a good case.

The signature of the coroner on the case was illegible. Underneath was typed the name Lander Zukerman, M.D.

I asked Miss Congeniality where I might find Dr. Zukerman. She pointed down the hall, saving all kinds of wear and tear on her vocal cords.

Dr. Zukerman was not in the small room that passed for his office. There was a straight-backed metal chair provided in the event he had a visitor. Everything in the coroner's offices seemed calculated to provide you unreachable pain, as if to say you'd be better off dead.

There were papers piled neatly on his desk and I had a yen to rifle them, but thought better of it. I returned to the main office and asked smiley where I might find Dr. Zukerman.

She pointed in the same direction. I shook my head. "Not there," I added.

"Autopsy room," she added. "Far end."

Unhappily, I saw him through a small window in the door. He was slicing off the top of the head of a pale-white cadaver. The doc was a slight man who looked like his product.

I retreated down the hall to the doctor's office and scanned some of the papers on his desk. They were coroner's autopsy reports, not unlike the one I'd read on Merilee Scioria.

I was safely back in the chair at the wall contemplating Dr. Zukerman's line of work when I heard a door open. I stood up, and peeked down the hall. I saw the doctor turn into his office. I followed. At his door I introduced myself. He nodded inquisitively. I told him what I was after, then surprised myself by asking, "What attracted you to this line of work?"

He shrugged and said, "Seemed easy. When I completed my internship, I had done a few autopsies, and I got interested in the whole procedure. It's like research—analysis—a puzzle really—putting bits and pieces of evidence together—come to a conclusion—something like the law, I imagine."

Dr. Zukerman was slick, his words flowed like mayonnaise from a liverwurst sandwich. All of this coming from a body that looked like death warmed over gave me an eerie feeling.

"Do you remember the Merilee Scioria, ah, case, do you call it?"

He frowned. "Not really. We have hundreds a year, you know. I can't say that stands out in my mind."

"She was the girl who died of Wanns disease. Do you get a lot of those here?"

"Some."

"Are you familiar with Dr. Daimler on the West Coast?"

His brows were furrowing in thought.

"Says there is no relation between Wanns disease and the R4 virus."

"Not my line," the coroner said.

"Do you test for R4?"

"We can, if we think it would help our findings."

"Did you test Merilee Scioria?"

"I don't remember...the case."

"Let me show you a copy of your report," I said, blushing at my sounding like a prosecuting attorney.

I handed him the copy. He frowned at it, then shook his head. "Sorry," he said, "I still can't picture her."

"It says her arms were covered with needle marks."

"I see that. Not unusual these days."

"What percentage?"

"Percentages don't mean much here. In raw numbers, I might see five or six pin cushions a week. Especially heavy in the case of violent deaths. The druggies have a way of dying by the sword."

"Could the needle marks be from something besides drugs—was she diabetic, for instance?"

"According to my report, no. As for other possibilities, if you stretch your imagination you can go anywhere. Maybe she was a mutilator and pins were her weapon of choice. I've seen crazier stuff."

"How likely in her case?"

"I wouldn't speculate," he began. Then he said, "I don't remember her."

"Anybody help you write these up?"

"No," he said. "I do them myself. Now if there's nothing else, I have a decedent calling me." He rose and left the room without shaking my hand.

*   *   *

Driving back to my motel, I passed Dr. Bern's office and saw a familiar figure going in. She moved with furtive steps and darting glances as though afraid someone would see her. I didn't connect her at first with our talk, but while I was waiting for the stoplight to change at the corner, I remembered who it was: Evelyn Welsh, Merilee's friend from high school.

I circled the block and parked across the street where I could observe the door of Dr. Bern's office. I checked the time. She was out in under ten minutes clutching a paper bag, again the eyes darting to and fro. I saw her duck into her car, and with hasty movements tear open the paper bag, take out a small bottle, open it and pop a pill in her mouth. She stared out of her windshield for a minute and let the pill do its work, while she seemed to be clearing her head.

When she started backing out of the parking space in front of Bern's office, I drove off wondering about all she had told me and how her "relationship" with Dr. Bern might have affected what she said about Merilee.

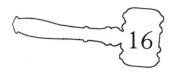

16

Bomber was grumpy when I called him from my motel room.

I laid it all out for him—trying to emphasize how bleak I thought the picture was. He listened without comment and let me wind down with my overkill redundancies.

"Okay," Bomber said at last. "Here's what you do. Lay it on Angelo and the missus. See what they're made of. Now's the time to find out. We don't want him tossing in the sponge in midtrial. Go to see him with this new evidence—what they're saying about his angel."

"I can't do that," I said. "He'll go to pieces."

"*Exactly!*" he said.

"B-but, I, I think, I'd rather you d-do it."

"Me!" he exploded. "*ME!?* You want *me* to fly across the country to do *your* job?"

"N-n-no. C-can you c-call him on the phone? He so prefers to t-talk to you."

"Hey! This is not a phone job. This is a personal thing—highly sensitive. Calling would be tacky. Go at it my boy."

"B-but he'll, he'll blow up. I can't take him going ballistic."

"Yeah," Bomber calmed down. "I'll share a secret with you," he said, "I can't either. Of the two of us," he said quietly, "you have the better chance of coming out of there intact."

"Oh," I groaned, but I was secretly flattered. In his own way, Bomber had just paid me a rare compliment. So I made an appointment to see the Sciorias under the pretext of bringing them up to date on the case.

They agreed to see me at their house at 3:00—between

the lunch and the dinner trade.

Angelo Scioria answered the door, though he looked like he didn't want to.

Angelo waved me to a chair, where the plastic covering had been removed and neatly folded underneath it. Mrs. Scioria was already seated, carefully out of the line of vision between where Angelo sat and me.

Angelo looked at me expectantly as if to say—"So?" but he remained silent.

I tried to make small talk, but it fell on deaf ears. So, I settled back for the nitty-gritty, belying my fears with my laid-back body language.

I went over everything I had learned, gently, patiently, always qualifying every incriminating statement with "In his opinion," or "That's what so-and-so said, I'm just repeating what he told me."

Angelo's mouth moved at the corners, like a man chomping at the bit to refute, but utilizing herculean restraint.

When I finished, the room fell silent. I expected to be assaulted with the sounds of little Angelo's big voice, but nothing materialized.

After what seemed like an interval long enough to play a Mahler symphony Angelo said, "What do *you* know? You are young! A child. An innocent. Who knows if you could ever get a job on your own. Carrying your father's water and you come here and dare to tell *me*—me, a man who has made it from *nothing* —about life. No, you don't do that. Not with me!" He was shouting now, in his inimitable Italian accent, and I was silent. Mrs. Scioria was silent too, and more than a little embarrassed, which manifested itself in fidgeting and darting looks between man and boy.

"I am a man who has lived! I have struggled. I have overcome obstacles. I have made success. You have your father's success to make you. I make my own. I learn when I live. Certain things I feel deep inside of me. I know Merilee—she's not a bad girl."

"No, Mr. Scioria. I am not making judgments. I never met Merilee. I am telling you what others are saying…"

"They lie!"

"And what they will say in court. Bomber insisted that I tell you what to expect, so you could plan accordingly."

"Plan? What's to plan?"

"They will be vicious. They will try to destroy your spirit so you will give up."

"Nobody destroy *my* spirit," he said with his head high—and I believed him—"And I no give up."

I looked at him with admiration. For such a slightly built man, he had a lot of fight in him.

"These people," he said, with steely eyes, "they are murderers!"

"If they are, they will stop at nothing."

Angelo Scioria looked at me as though he were putting an end to it. "I don't stop either," he said.

I looked again at Angelo, hoping to find a surrender that wasn't there.

"You find the truth," he said.

I nodded slowly. "Can you tell me where to look?" I asked gently.

In that moment I saw in the bleak pallor in his face a lifetime of accumulated suffering doubt.

"You ever have a child, Mr. Tod Hanson?"

"No."

"You celebrate Christmas when you were little?"

"With my parents, yes."

He nodded as though I were giving him the answers he wanted to hear. "You try and get through a Christmas sometime—after you lost a child. You relive every Christmas you ever had with her. The room is worse than empty, it is all day sorrow. That is truth. You experience that, you know truth. No need to find it. Already *found* it."

In that moment I saw how relative truth was. And how pliable, and how ambiguous and even questionable. For

Angelo's truth seemed at odds with reality, but is reality necessarily truth? At this juncture, what would reality serve him? Reality is heartless and cold. Truth can be a security blanket if it is your truth. Warm and fuzzy—comforting. We believe what we want to believe, and who can fault that? I certainly couldn't change it. All I could do was prepare Angelo for the worst. And as sure as God made those little green apples Bomber was always talking about, the worst was on its way.

I heard Angelo sniffle before I realized what was happening. Then it came at me like a hot Santa Ana wind—vicious, and dehydrating and in our Angelton, California, bringing with it the danger of terminal conflagration.

His body was shaking like a child who was not only hurt, but scared to death.

"My *baby*," he wailed. "She was my only baby! I wanted so much—" He drew a few quaking breaths, then added, "*Too* much. And all so stupid! She didn't have to be the queen of the May or the valedictorian or a basketball hero. She was my baby and I loved her—oh, I loved her so much and I didn't tell her—always expecting too much, always pushing and scolding. I ruined her. It is all my fault."

His sobbing was out of control and he couldn't speak now. Regina stood and came shakily toward him. She stood beside him and cradled his head to her belly.

"Now, Angelo," she said, soothingly. "You did what you thought was right. We are not saints, we are mere mortals. You loved our Merilee—I know it. She knew it. Everybody knows it."

I was inept at this, I don't care what Bomber said to flatter me into it. I knew not what to do, so I simply got up and bowed what I thought was a respectful bow to Angelo and Regina and said softly—"Think about it. Will the agony of the trial be worth *any* result? I will call you later."

And I walked out the door.

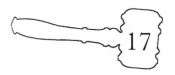

I didn't go to Angelo and Regina's diner for dinner. We'd had enough social intercourse for one day, I thought. Instead, I found a place that purported to be Mexican, but after my first bite of what I bought as an enchilada, I decided they didn't make Mexicans in New Jersey like they did in California.

I discovered it was possible to digest cardboard.

While I was eating, I tried not to think about the food. From nowhere melodies popped into my head. Then rhythms and a few harmonies. I realized a string quartet wouldn't do it for the Sciorias—I needed percussion. I didn't want to do a whole symphony because there was so little chance of it ever being played.

Phantom Virus, The title of Daimler's book, kept popping into my head as a title, and phantom conjured up all kinds of eerie sounds. Weird combinations of mystery. Oboe would be good.

The challenge was to forget *Phantom of the Opera* while writing *Phantom Virus.* A melange of off-beat instruments might do—the percussion and maybe a quartet of horns, a clarinet, oboe and bassoon, I thought.

I went back to my motel room with my head bursting with ideas. Angelo's *mea culpa* scene I had witnessed had been moving and poignant and gave me a cornucopia of musical ideas.

I opened the door to my room and reached for the light switch, eager to get to my music paper. My mind was rumbling with exotic rhythms in 7/8 time for the *mea culpa* movement— and I was just thinking that might not be a bad name for the whole piece when something came down on my head, and that's the last thing I remember.

Some indefinite time later, when I opened my eyes, I seemed to be on the bottom of the ocean looking up at an angry surf. The view was intermittently cloudy, and I was suffused with confusion. What was I doing on my back on the floor? Two hammers seemed to be at work in my head; one behind each eyeball. Bam, bam, bam! Excruciating.

I closed my eyes. Didn't help much.

I opened them again. It was daylight on the ocean surface. I tried to get up, but the pain was blinding and it felt like the pressure of all that water was keeping me down.

But I *was* breathing, that was something.

I don't know how long it was before I could perform the simplest functions, like rolling over, then sitting up, then crawling to the telephone.

Fortunately I remembered Bomber's phone number—I don't have any idea how.

Unfortunately Bonnie Doone answered in one of her I-am-God's-gift-to-men moods.

"Oh, hi, Sweet Meat," she said with that saccharine voice she put on when she was at her least sincere. "Whatcha doin'?"

I wasn't about to show and tell the latest to airhead so I said—"I'm calling for Bomber," in the coldest voice I could muster—a snap under the circumstances.

Bonnie prattled on with insufferable small talk which exacerbated the pounding in my head, so I didn't respond.

"Sorehead!" she said at last. She didn't know how right she was. Bonnie left me sitting on hold an eternity before she bothered to tell Bomber I was waiting. It was her little power play.

"Boy?" Bomber said when he finally cam on the line. "You fix it up with those Italians?"

"I was ambushed," I said.

"What?"

"Hit over the head in my motel room."

"No!"

"Yes."

"See anybody?"

"No."

"Call the police?"

"No."

"Well, do it. A full report. It's got to be on the record." Only after he got the procedures out of the way did he say, "Are you all right?"

"Been better," I said. "I've had it."

"What did you say?"

"I'm packing it in."

"Now don't be rash, boy."

"Easy for you to say," I said, my head throbbing. "You weren't hit over the head."

"Well," he reasoned aloud, "they didn't kill you. They could have, you know. Probably just trying to intimidate you."

"They succeeded."

"No, no—don't let them. You can't give in to the bozos. Life would be chaos."

"What do you think it is now with this jackhammer working over my brain?" I groaned. "I'm coming home."

"Aren't you curious who did it?"

"No."

"Obviously you've hit some sensitive areas," he gloated. "That's good work, my boy." Did he think throwing me a compliment would beat down the walls of my remaining rationality?"

"Nice try," I said and realized my head was too deadened to stutter.

"You've got 'em scared, boy," he thundered, trying, no doubt, to cheer me into action. "Now all you have to find out is who and why."

"Sorry," I said. "I want to live to finish my symphony."

"Why? Schubert didn't," he said, then added the clincher, "It was the making of him. Call the police," he said. "Then see a doctor—go to the hospital—it's all on me."

"You're too kind."

"Then decide. You want to be a quitter after you've reflected, so be it. Maybe Bonnie can fill your shoes if you aren't up to it. Trade jobs sort of."

"Not working, Bomber," I said.

"All right—the doctor first—then the cops. Do that for yourself. Then call me back. We'll work something out."

I didn't have to ask what that was. Whenever Bomber said, "We'll work something out," he meant, I would do as I was told. Nothing complex about Bomber, once you were on to his inclusive phraseology.

Seeing a doctor did seem like an idea whose time had come, so I called 9-1-1. I said it was an emergency and I needed an ambulance and nobody argued. I gave them the address, and it seemed like only minutes until I heard the sirens.

It took gargantuan will to stay conscious after I heard the sirens approaching. Who and why? I kept asking myself to keep awake. I had heard staying awake was vital if you had a concussion and wanted to stay alive. On balance, the idea of staying alive appealed to me more than the alternative.

The moment I saw the white-frocked ambulance attendants open my door, I passed out again.

I have to admit, I don't understand or appreciate hospitals. They seem to me just a depressing repository for the infirm and lame and the halt. It is sort of a way station on the way to recovery or the great beyond, as the case may be. I imagine you could make a case for hospitals, I just don't know what it would be.

I admit, I am afraid of hospitals. I've heard too many horror stories about the wrong medicine killing the bloke, inept surgery requiring re-cutting—comas, fatal blood loss—or transfusion from someone with R4.

Of course, if I were certain our star witness, Dr. Daimler, was right, I wouldn't fear R4. He says by itself it is harmless.

The ambulance attendants did yeoman service trying to keep me awake, and I remember fading in and out on the trip. I was conscious for our arrival at the sprawling building built of brick and mortar, as if to withstand the huffing and puffing of the big, bad wolf. It was what I had come to recognize as East Coast modern. That is, it would not have been out of place in the last century.

There was a lot of grass surrounding the bricks. Where I came from, too many droughts had curtailed expansive lawns. Here the grass was automatically sprinkled from above, year-round. Here, if they had a dry spell, the grass browned out—as it does in the frozen winters—and nobody went into a tizzy. There is too damn much of it to water by hand—but the light-green grass with the distant border of dark-green trees gives the place a peaceful aura.

They wheeled me inside, and I seemed to engender a fair amount of attention and concerned looks from the staff.

I was looking back. Everywhere I went from now on I would look into all the faces I saw for signs of intent to do me bodily harm.

I admit it: I had developed a sudden case of paranoia. I don't think I can be faulted for it. As Henry Kissinger said, "Not all paranoia is unfounded."

Some doctors, not more than my age, did some things to me—a shot, exams, probing, x-rays, and I was suspicious of every one of them. Wasn't this the hospital where Merilee Scioria died? Wouldn't they have a stake in a cover-up?

By the next morning, I seemed to be more aware of my surroundings. There was another gentleman in the bed next to mine. A would-be assassin? I wondered.

A cheery nurse came in to ask me how I felt. Her plastic breast plate said Lori Haberstock, R.N., and Lori was a looker. The white uniform set off her black hair just so. The body beneath suggested enough to set off a rapid recovery in any male, no matter what the malady.

In her arms was a newspaper. She laid it on the bed where I could see it.

"You're famous," she said with a Chiclets smile.

Did Lori Haberstock, R.N., have some interest in me? She wasn't wearing any nuptial rings and there was an unmistakable twinkle in her eyes.

On the other hand, *she* might have been an assassin.

I looked at the paper. I was on the front page of the local weekly.

I glanced at the headline:

BOMBER HANSON INVESTIGATOR UNCONSCIOUS IN MOTEL ROOM

"Where'd they get this?" I started to ask, but I knew the answer before I finished the question.

She shrugged. "This is a pretty small town. Not much happens. When something does," she lifted a hand, palm up…"everybody knows it."

I read the short piece beneath the headline. It said I was investigating the death of Merilee Scioria for my father, the world-famous trial attorney, Bomber Hanson, who had taken the case of Angelo and Regina Scioria of this locale. The tone turned sardonic as the reporter alluded to the fanciful notion promulgated by the plaintiff—that Merilee Scioria may not have died of Wanns disease, but of the drug JCD that was supposed to cure it.

"Oh, by the way," Ms. Haberstock said, "you have a visitor."

I froze.

She let go of a tinkling laugh—"Says his name is Buck Rogers," she said, shaking her head at the improbability of it all.

"I don't want to see him," I said, but it was too late. He was standing in the doorway with a frightening grin on his ugly face.

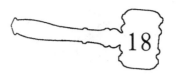

18

"Don't leave me, please," I whispered hoarsely to the nurse. Of course it carried and reverberated in the small cell of a room. She smiled and patted my shoulder. "I wish," she said. "I'd love to spend the day with you, but the boss has other plans for me. If you need anything just press the call button and I'll come running." Before I could protest, she was gone, and Buck Rogers took her place at my bedside.

"How ya doin' buddy?" he said with an exaggerated heartiness like you do when you are trying to be friendly and sincere but are neither. He seemed to be waiting for my answer.

"I've been better," I muttered, trying to contain my trembling without noticeable success.

Not what you'd call a savory looking character at eye level, Buck Rogers menaced me out of my mind as he loomed over my bed.

My heart froze in my throat, and it seemed that my breathing mechanisms were on the fritz. That didn't bother me because I thought I was cheating the assassin by taking his job from him.

"Nasty bump you got there," he said, examining my bandaged head.

"Yeah, well," I muttered as if I were telling him something he didn't already know, "it was a lot bigger."

"Yeah, well, I just dropped by to—I saw the thing in the paper and I didn't want you getting any wrong ideas or nothin'. I mean, you know I had nothing to do with, you know—what happened to you."

I'd like to say that was reassuring, but that would have been wide of the mark.

"You know," he said, and I got the startling feeling he

seemed a little nervous. "I like you, kid. I wouldn't want to hurt you."

"Thanks."

"You got any idea who done this to ya?"

I shook my head. It hurt.

"'Cause if you do, let me know—maybe I can give them a memory of their own—or a memory loss—as the case may be."

I nodded—mostly with my eyelids. And on that happy note, Buck Rogers shot out of my hospital room in a rocketlike fashion worthy of his namesake.

My paranoia was deepening. Everyone I saw fueled suspicion: doctors, nurses, orderlies; but the visit from that pseudo-savory Buck Rogers had to be the prizewinner. I had visions of him lurking in a closet on my floor, just waiting for the cover of darkness to finish me off.

Just then, Mr. Polyunsaturated walked in. I should say Dr. Bern.

"*Gosh*, you got yourself a real goose egg there," said the doc, rather gratuitously, I thought. The oil was not only oozing through his teeth, it was coming out of his ears and nostrils as well. He was a man given to the oleaginous—always affable with a billboard smile at the ready. He was my inside candidate for the culprit in this scenario—but he was so inured in grease, if you tried to stick anything on him it would be downstream in minutes.

Much as I despised the doctor, I couldn't see him hitting me over the head, much less murdering anybody.

His machinations took the form of oily subterfuge. He'd use every trick in the book to save himself, but there wouldn't be any violence involved. Not his style. Yet, I was anything but comfy in his presence. He was not a confidence-boosting visitor.

I was less sure he wouldn't contract someone to do his dirty work. In fact, why else would he be here, hovering over me with that counterfeit grin of his—that "I'm-your-big-pal" grin?

If ever there was a man born to be an ad for brill cream, Dr. Bern was it.

"A nasty business," he was clucking, but I wasn't listening. I was speculating instead on my chances of getting out of there alive.

"Well, I just dropped by to see how you were doing. I have a patient in here so it's no bother. See that they're treating you okay." He fired me with a fish eye—"*Are* they?"

"Yuh," I mumbled, hoping against hope Dr. Bern would just go away.

"You need anything you just ask for me—okay?"

"Okay."

"Well, then," he said, putting a greasy hand on my shoulder. "You take care," and, mercifully, he was gone.

My next visitor came later in the day—during the lull between lunch and dinner. His visit was more of a surprise than a shock.

Angelo Scioria came alone, and it was apparent from when I saw him walk in the door, he was not his old belligerent self. In fact, he had a hangdog expression on his face that seemed to dog his steps from the door to the bed.

When he looked down at me, he shook his head in a slow, dolorous rhythm.

"Hello, Mr. Scioria," I croaked, but he just kept shaking his head as though he had been expecting the worst and found it.

When he finally spoke, it came with a muffled sound as though he were talking through a towel.

"This is my fault," he said, the small head moving sadly from side to side. "What kind of people do these things? I ask for justice and they try to murder instead." He seemed to feel the pain more than I did.

I started to present a milder picture, but my throat was dry.

"This no good," he said. "No good. It cannot be. All I want is my baby back. I cannot get her back. God has decided he wants to keep her. I can do nothing. They want to make my baby into something horrible, then they do this to you. No, no, *NO!* Impossible to go on. I want justice when we begin. Then I see they want to smear my baby because they have done wrong. It is their only defense. They murdered my baby so they make her look like a slut! She was an angel! They killed her and they are killing me." His head swerved again—side to side. "Now they try to kill you," suddenly he broke down as he put his hand on my shoulder and the tears flowed. "Is not right! Is all my fault. What have I done? Oh God, why, why, WHY!"

"I…," I started to talk without having any idea what I would say. He pressed my shoulder to stop me.

"No!" he said. "I am giving up the case. It is too much for me. It is too much for Regina, it is too much for you. Nobody should have to go through this to get justice. *Nobody!*"

"But, Mr. Scioria," I began again.

"No! Do not argue. I will pay for what you done. If I have to work the rest of my life, I will pay for this terrible mistake. But now—is finished. I give the money back to dentist. No more do we risk life for my baby. She is gone. She won't be back," and he gave up all pretense of composure, and his body quaked with lush, uninhibited sobbing.

Angelo Scioria was feeling so sorry for me, I was feeling sorry for him. Not that I could disagree with his sentiments about dropping the case.

When he composed himself enough to leave me, he went without a sound after promising to call Bomber.

Good, I thought, maybe I'll get back home alive.

My doubts and fears increased while I reflected on Buck Rogers. Lying flat on your back in a hospital bed gave you a lot of time to reflect. He certainly was no stranger to crime and violence, but he seemed so sincere—scared even—perhaps it was a clever ruse.

After Angelo left, I tried to work it all out—in the haze of my paranoia.

Would all of these guys want to put me out of commission? Even Angelo? Not impossible. Certainly Dr. Bern and Buck Rogers. But if I was pressed for a choice, it would be Dr. Bern. Why would a guy like Buck Rogers come to see me? He'd do the job and let it go at that. Second thoughts? Doubted it. Bern, on the other hand, was the kind of guy, if you stepped on him, you'd slip to kingdom come.

It was less than an hour after Angelo left that the phone rang. He had been as good as his word. Bomber was on the line at the peak of his decibel form. If there was the slightest acknowledgement in his voice that I was infirm, I missed it.

"That little wop wants to throw in the towel," he barked at me as though I had caused the consternation.

I cringed at his insensitive characterizations. But that was Bomber. You wouldn't find a guy with less prejudice—he judged people solely on their merits, but for some reason he loved to sling words that belittled them—especially if he was not taken with them as individuals. It was a complex thing with Bomber, and I didn't pretend to understand it.

"I guess he feels pretty s-strongly about what happened to me," I said, implying it was nice *some*body cared.

"Well, Jesus Jenny, Boy, you don't want to turn into a blueberry muffin just because you got a little scratch on your head."

"Oh, no? Scratch was the size of a baseball," I said proudly. I wasn't going to let him belittle my heroics.

"Look, kid, I've been there. Korea—"

I groaned. This stale lecture was the last thing I wanted in my shape. I got it anyway.

"In Korea," Bomber said, "it was kill or be killed." He was alluding to his brief stint as a bombardier on a crew whose *first* mission was turned back midarmistice. Though he saw no real action, Bomber was perhaps the last of the great war mongers. Or so he would have you believe. I had seen too often the pussycat side of him to swallow that one whole. Like he sent me on this mission in the first place.

"Bomber," I said quietly, as Theodore Roosevelt had

suggested. But with Bomber there were no big sticks. "I want to come home."

"Stay the course, Son," Bomber said, "steady at the helm."

Whenever he called me "Son," I knew he was currying favor. "My boy" was almost neutral in its personal charge, and "Boy" was of a demeaning/hostile bent. He called me Tod so seldom I'd yet to get a firm fix on what that meant.

Circumstances were conspiring against me. My condition was weakened by the blow and by my fear that someone was bent on finishing the job.

"Your first order of business when you get out of there is to talk Angelo back into the case."

"B-b-but he doesn't *want* t-to."

"Of course he *wants* to. That was just Italian showmanship—Drama 101."

"N-n-no."

"I've been in contact with that Nazi up north." He was referring to Dr. Daimler, I'm sure, in his lump-em-all-together fashion. "It's damn fascinating what he has to say. This is a case that *must* be tried. And it's up to you to see that we try it!"

Then I did something unprecedented. I hung up on my father.

19

When the doctors released me from the hospital, they told me to take it easy for a couple of days.

I asked nurse Haberstock if I might fly home under the banner of taking it easy, and she shook her head.

"Bed, preferably," she said. "Sit up, if you'd rather—but *no* exertion."

But that didn't keep me from making my return-flight reservation once back at the motel. Or attempting to.

My charge card was rejected. I knew there had to be a mistake. I was the only one who used it, and I was nowhere near my limit.

"I'm sorry, sir," the clerk intoned as though he had switched on a recording he deployed for just such eventualities.

Hot under the collar, I called the credit card company and was told my card had been blocked. That's what she said, "Blocked."

"What does that mean?" I asked, using the timbre of kettledrums.

She went through the litany of stolen cards, lost cards, limits overspent. I protested each as devoid of truth—but each protestation became weaker than the last as the naked truth dawned: Bomber had blocked it. It was his charming way of demonstrating how dependent I was on him.

That news put me in my deepest funk since being hit over the head.

I was making some notes for my *Phantom Virus* piece when there came a knock on my door. I got up and opened it without thinking, and as soon as it was open a half inch, I knew I had made a mistake. My reflex was delayed, so by the time I tried to slam the door, there was a foot in it. My heart shot out the top of my head, and I knew I had bought it for good this time.

But when I looked down to where the floor met the door, I saw something that returned my feet to the ground—if not my heart.

A high-heeled shoe.

Quickly I fanned through my cast of suspects for the most likely to wear a high-heeled shoe. Buck Rogers was definitely out. Eldon Shaker was an unlikely maybe. Angelo—never in a million years. But Dr. Bern was *made* for high-heeled shoes.

I had all my weight against the door from the inside and was surprised that, except for the shoe, I was meeting no other resistance. Then I heard the familiar, annoying voice.

"Tod, for heaven's sakes, open the door!"

I stumbled back in shock. The door was pushed open and airhead herself, Bonnie Doone, entered pulling one of those compact, fit-under-the-airplane-seat bags on wheels.

The room was so small, when I stumbled back, I fell on the bed.

This bizarre brainchild of Bomber's was obviously calculated as a cheap psychological ploy to keep me on the job. Apparently I was supposed to tremble at the sight of Bonnie Victoria Doone, run to the nearest phone and call Bomber to plead for my job back. But under the circumstances, I didn't care two cents for my job.

Until I began to think rationally.

Angelton *was* the nicest place in the world to live. There weren't too many jobs there for a person of my inclinations and training. If there had been any hope for a composer of classical music, I wouldn't have become a lawyer in the first place. Never would I have considered working for my father.

There is no doubt this was the sneakiest trick the great Bomber had ever pulled on me. My feelings about Bonnie V. Doone have never been kept from Bomber. Yes, she had a body sculpted to kill. But upstairs, like the primeval world in *Genesis*, her brain was void and without form.

111

"How you been, Sweet Meat?" she said with the most saccharine grin as she swept her ridiculous little suitcase on wheels in an arc until it rested against the bed.

"I came right from the airport," she enthused, just like a high school girl after her first date. "Didn't want to waste a minute." And with that she dropped her Aphrodite's bod into my desk chair and glanced at the music notes I had made on the staff paper.

"This the great American symphony or something?" she asked.

The fact that she didn't know a symphony from a barbershop quartet notwithstanding, I started to explain about the *Phantom Virus* work, but it was falling on stone-deaf ears, and she cut me off with, "Yeah, well, I hope these chicken scratches will stand you in good stead after you bail the employ of Bomber Hanson."

I looked at B.V.D. in abject wonder.

"Oh Lord!" I groaned, "what are you doing here—?" The answer was obvious, but she surprised me.

"Bomber thought I could give you a hand and all," she winked the most outrageous wink. "You being in a weakened condition and all. Then if you really do party poop and go home, the great Bomber Hanson, attorney-at-law will have a loyal representative in Jersey to stand up for truth, justice and sisterhood."

"You?" I exclaimed. "You?" I repeated for emphasis. "This has to be a joke," I said.

She shook her head. "No joke," she said. "The murder of Merilee Scioria is no laughing matter."

She astounded me by remembering the victim's name.

"Well," she was saying. "bring me up to speed, and you can go back to Angelton and suck your thumb," then she added with a sly wink, "and look for work."

"Hey!" I reacted too strongly. I realized she was reveling in my discomfort, and I preferred to withhold that satisfaction from her clutches. I suddenly decided on the friendly approach.

"Come on, Bonnie, gimme a break. What's going down here?" I figured I could disarm her with the vulgate she had so easily mastered. It was one of her rare talents.

She feigned surprise. "That naive, Sweet Meat?" she said. "You want out—flaking, tossing the sponge, reneging, party pooping, you dig?" she threw out her arms—"Joan of Arc to the rescue."

My mouth hung open.

"You can't be serious—"

"Never seriouser. This is my big break. My debut as investigator. How do I look?" she twirled as though she were showing off the latest fashion.

"Ridiculous and ridiculouser."

"Sour grapes."

"Come on, Bonnie—whose idea was this charade, and what do you hope to accomplish?"

"I told you—you out, me Jane."

"Very funny."

Bomber doesn't think it's so funny," she said. "He wants to try this case."

"Even though Angelo doesn't?"

"Apparently."

"Well, how's he going to do that? You can't try a case without a client."

"I'm supposed to change his mind," she said, and I could have sworn she threw a little sexy twist into the lower section of her anatomy.

"*You?*"

"Yeah—unless you want to—"

"Why in the world would I...?"

"Look at it this way," she said, playing with her long blond hair. "Who better? Angelo Scioria wants out because of you—what happened, you know." She waved a hand at my body as though I had somehow faked the whole episode. "So you tell him in so many words, it's not necessary. You appreciate his feelings and all, but it's just part of the game, blah, blah."

"Getting hit over the head is part of the game?" I could be surprised to infinity by her naïveté. "Maybe you'll get to experience it, then we'll talk."

"Yeah, well," she shrugged, again in a deliberate effort to denigrate my experience.

Just when I was about to ask what her plans were for the night—it was almost 10:00 p.m.—B.V.D. stood and began to take off her clothes.

"Hey! What do you think you're doing?"

"Getting ready for bed," she said, as though that were the most natural thing in the world.

"Not *here!*"

"Where else?" she shrugged. "It's late—"

"Not *here!*" I repeated. Cleverness of speech was eluding me.

"Oh, don't worry," she said, stripped to her underwear. "I won't jump you. I don't molest kids."

I looked at the one bed in the room, then back at Bonnie. I shook my head. "Sorry," I said. "Not a good idea—definitely not."

She fell on the bed clad only in that skimpy underwear—took one of my pillows and hugged it. "If you don't want to stay here," she waved at the door, "you find a place—I'm bushed."

I threw my stuff in my bag and left the room. At the desk I discovered what I already knew—my credit card was blocked.

I spent the night in my car.

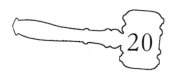

20

Next morning I awoke with the sun and a terrible back-ache, and let myself back into my room. B.V.D. was still sleeping, and I was glad I could wake her.

When she flipped open an eye, she pulled the covers up to her chin. She needn't have worried; any chemistry between us was of the demolition kind.

I picked up the phone on the bedside table and dialed my father. My approach was settled. I knew I had to get tough, but I also knew that was the most futile approach. So, I slid into my bottom line—

"Bomber, I trust all is well in Angelton."

"Tod," he said, and I knew we were on softer ground. "Well as can be expected with the entire staff doping off in New Jersey."

"Yeah, well, we're having a fine old time, all right. Want to talk to Bonnie? She's still in bed."

"How do you know that?" he seemed surprised, like this charade had been Bonnie's idea from the beginning.

"Because she came into my room last night and started undressing."

"She didn't!" Bomber was, when the chips were down, something of a prude. "What did you do?"

"Slept in my car."

"Phew," he let out a hiss of relief—it could have been bogus.

"Now the thing is," I said steadying my vocal apparatus. "Are you going to unblock my credit card, or am I going to have to go over your head to get home?"

He knew who I was talking about. Mother was the only one over him. She would give me anything I asked for.

"I'll unblock it," he said. Then he added—"You can come home and do Bonnie's job if you want. If that's what you're made of."

I was quietly seething at that one—"Okay," I said steadily. I knew a blatant bluff when I heard one. Any attempt B.V.D. made at my job would end in disaster. "She's welcome to stand in for me the next time some bozo tries to crack open my skull. God knows there's nothing inside Bonnie's head to spoil."

"You're too hard on her, Son. Tell you what," he said. "Put her on the phone. You still want to come back, after I talk to her, okay. But I am trying this case. Up to you if you want to be part of it—or the practice," he added.

I thrust the phone at Bonnie. She groped groggily for it—"Hello," she said, still narcotized by her excessive sleeping habits.

After a monotonous bout of "Yes, sirs," and a twinkle in her eye, Bonnie hung up the phone.

She looked at me and pulled the covers way up again.

"So?" I said.

"He wants us to go to Angelo. Make the case. Says you should study my tact, diplomacy and salesmanship. You might learn something."

"Yeah, right."

"Or," she said, trying (and failing) to tantalize me, "you could go alone."

I was embarrassed for B.V.D. when she came out of the bathroom and I saw what she was wearing for her visit to Angelo Scioria. A mini-mini, sheer panty hose and a sweater that accentuated the positive. The skirt was fire-engine red and put me in mind of the siren she was attempting to be. The sweater was off white—off color, get it?

"You're going to wear that!!?" I offered.

"Not *going* to—am."

"Well, if you think that sexpot outfit is going to cut any ice with Angelo Scioria, you got another thing coming."

"Think so?" she said, with that all-knowing smirk. She

looked in the mirror on the bathroom door and smoothed the wrinkles on the bikini-sized garments with her hands.

"Now, here's the deal," she said, taking charge as an inmate taking over the asylum. "You're going with me—I'm doing the talking."

"Oh, no," I protested. "You've popped your cork this time."

"Oh, yes," she said as though she were a conscientious dominatrix. "Your presence is only required to validate my claims; to wit: There is not the slightest necessity for Angelo to feel sorry for you. You are a big boy, a good soldier, who can take his knocks in the line of fire. You are not, contrariwise, the sniveling, whining cream puff you appear to be."

"No way!" I said, with finality.

It was unnerving the way Bonnie looked at me as though I were the one who was nuttier-'n-a-fruitcake. She was really starting to get on my nerves. Then she dropped the biggest clinker of all time. "Bomber said to tell you, you do this like a good boy, and he'll sport you to a ticket home."

"Why, that's *blackmail!*" I exclaimed.

"No kiddin'," she said, with her airhead wink.

What you have to understand about B.V.D. is that instead of a brain between her ears, there was a pneumatic pump which pushed the most asinine things through her mouth.

For me, the prospect of going home was so exciting, I swallowed what pride my father left me and took Bonnie to meet the Sciorias—determined to stay in the background, and give B.V.D. all the rope she needed to hang herself.

But before we left, I made one more attempt to reason with Bonnie.

"Bonnie," I said, "Angelo and Regina Scioria are old-country folk. They idolized their daughter—thought she was an angel. You walk in there with this whorehouse outfit, you're going to shock their sensibilities right off the map. You don't stand a chance with these people."

She looked at me sideways. "You don't know anything

about men *or* women," she said.

I shrugged like a good sport. "Suit yourself," I said, sublimating my self-satisfaction at her impending failure.

I kept my distance as we arrived and walked into the Scioria living room. Angelo's reaction on seeing Bonnie Doone was not exactly as I predicted. He was gallant to a fault—taking her hand, smiling into her eyes and fussing over her as though she were a long-lost girlfriend who had opted for the nunnery.

She sat and batted her eyelashes at him as though she were trying fiercely to wash some cinders from her eyes. "Mr. Scioria," she began.

"Oh, Angelo, please," he said. He had *never* asked *me* to call him Angelo.

"Angelo," more eyelash action. "My boss sent me across the country to ask you a favor."

"Oh?" he beamed at his imputed importance. "So ask away!"

"Bomber would like you to reconsider your position on the case."

Angelo frowned. His eyes darted about to let us all know he was not a man who was easily swayed from a stated position. But when his gaze settled back on mini-skirted Bonnie with the clinging sweater, I knew his game was up.

She wheedled him some more, but it was a charade to earn her keep.

"Well, if Bomber thinks he has a case, I should not stand in the way."

Mrs. Scioria said nothing. I was not called upon to say anything. There was no gnashing of teeth over my injury—no lamenting the depths to which mankind had sunk—no anguish over my pain. I wasn't needed.

But I had earned my ticket home.

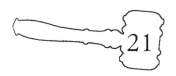

On my way home in the plane, my feelings vacillated between relief and a strange fear that I had made a terrible career blunder.

When I thought of "career," I thought of musical composition. I always had a knack for self-delusion. But on the plane I was reminded, once again, of my pestiferous need to make a living.

It triggered my old belief about how unfair the social security system was. Paying all those old fogies for doing nothing when everyone knows they are at a time of life when they can do nothing better than work. While guys (and gals) my age are bursting with self-fulfilling projects we could complete very nicely with the benefit of some government assistance.

Older people are more seasoned, more intelligent, more worldwise than we punks, and with my system we would be even more valuable when the time rolled around for us to hit the grindstone.

Unfortunately until they changed the system, I had no choice but to play by the rules of the game. Ergo, I realized perhaps I couldn't be so cavalier about my job with my father. It was always a struggle to remember to think of him as a father— since he gave me very little reason to think of him as anything but the drill sergeant he was.

So, by the time the plane landed I had worked myself up into a pretty good lather. I had convinced myself I would lose my job, either in outright firing or in a more demeaning faux swap with Bonnie Doone.

Bomber had installed a plain-looking, middle-aged temp in Bonnie's chair to answer the phone and run interference while the peons were away.

She was an improvement.

"Your father said to send you in as soon as you got here," she said.

When I knocked and I heard the booming "Come in," I opened the door to see Bomber staring at me as though he couldn't quite place me.

"Oh, well, Tod," he said, as though greeting with *noblesse oblige* some stranger. "Sit down. Tell me about your trip."

Tell him about my trip? I sat, trying to collect my thoughts and to understand why he was playing it so naïvely, as though he didn't know about my near-death experience. Then I thought he was repressing it purposely—something like he handled Sis's suicide.

"Well, the high spot was," I said, calmly as I could in the bombardier's presence, "getting hit over the head in my motel room."

He looked at me quizzically. "Oh, that," he said waving a hand as though it were of no significance.

I got flustered. "Yes, th-th-that," I stammered, perhaps hoping for a little more sympathy.

"Well, looks like you are on the mend okay," he said, belittling my trauma.

"Better," I said, then tried to spin the word sarcastically. "Thanks."

If he got my drift, he didn't let on.

"Anything more on the investigative front?"

I don't know if it was the blow to the head that did it, but I had forgotten that I had seen Evelyn Welsh, Merilee's friend, making what looked like a drug buy from Dr. Bern. I told Bomber.

He nodded as though he knew that all the time. "So, you had a couple visitors in the hospital," he said.

"Yeah—"

"Anything strike you as odd?"

"Both of them," I said. "Angelo too, coming to think of it."

"But, who was missing?"

"Missing?"

"The drug company show up?"

"No."

"Their lawyer, Carstairs?"

I shook my head.

"Say anything to you, Boy?"

I shook my head again, "Why should it?"

"If you want to use that block on top of your neck for anything more than a hat rack," he said, with his patented superiority and supercilious grin.

"Thanks."

"It's nothing," he said, waving a hand at me as though my thanks were anything but sarcasms. "I don't mind the role of pedant," he said. "You're young yet—you can absorb a few sophistries."

"Yeah? What?"

"At least one of your visitors was guilty and he was there to, one, cover up his nefarious act and, two, to see how you had survived it. Because, your superstition to the contrary, he didn't want you dead. Dead would have been incriminating," he said with a disarming understatement.

"As I remember," I grunted. He may have thought he was illuminating, but he wasn't.

"Still don't get it? The drug company, my boy, had nothing to be guilty about. They aren't in the biz of knocking people over the head. Their intimidation takes other forms. Neither is brute force Carstairs's bag." He shook his head. "No, the real culprit here is not Brogger-Wexler and certainly not white gloves Carstairs. My boy," Bomber said with the hearty voice he used to convey the thought he was convinced beyond all reason was a universal truth, "what say we settle with the drug company—get the Sciorias their dough and go after the real villain in the piece?"

"Who?"

"The doc, of course." He seemed surprised I had to ask.

"B-b-but Carstairs offered to settle and you rejected it."

"I didn't reject. I made a counteroffer."

"That they st-stop m-making JCD. Just k-kill the goose that laid the g-golden egg is all."

"So, I may withdraw that bargaining chip. You did notice he didn't flinch when I asked two mil."

I had noticed that. No skin off my you-know-what if he settled. It was not a case that lit any fires in my heart.

He read my mind. "Carstairs is an able attorney. Little too able for my taste. I say we cut him loose and let that worm with the M.D. behind his name swim for himself." He cocked an eyebrow at me. "Worms don't swim, you know."

"He'll get an insurance l-lawyer—"

"Yeah, and whoever it is won't hold a candle to Mr. Carstairs." His grin was so smug it was almost annoying.

So, Bomber made a call to Angelo Scioria to feel him out. If he got him the two million, would he be willing to stay the course against the doctor, where the depth of the pockets was much less certain? It was an easy sale.

Jude Carstairs and the Brogger-Wexler Drug Company would be a tougher nut to crack. Bomber had a rule never to initiate settlement talks. "Sign of weakness," he'd say. Yet Jude Carstairs had not mentioned settlement since he visited our office and Bomber asked that the drug company stop making JCD.

Two million was Angelo Scioria's number. It was a drop to Brogger-Wexler, perhaps a couple days' take from JCD alone. But how to bring it up without appearing weak?

Bomber had an idea.

It wasn't long after Bomber had finally come into the 20th century (at its end) that we got a fax machine. Bomber distrusted what he referred to as, "new fangled gadgets" and was always the last guy on the block to own one. "Let 'em get the bugs out," he would crow in procrastination, and in Bomber's mind that debugging process could take years.

But once we got some piece of equipment, Bomber was

intent on getting his money's worth out of it.

"The fax!" he announced after he had been fishing for the solution.

He had the temp type the following message and fax it to Jude Carstairs in New York:

> Jude:
> Sciorias considering your two mil-
> lion offer as a basis for settlement talks.
> Bomber

After the ding of the fax that signified a completed transaction, Bomber looked at his watch. "Any bets on how long until the phone rings?"

I shook my head. "Carstairs might not be there," I said. "If he is, he'll have to c-call Brogger-Wexler to get some parameters."

"Nah, he's already got those. Just a matter of him wanting to play hard-to-get for awhile. I say he gets the 'offer' and responds within five minutes. Only imponderable is, how long it takes to get the fax to him." He looked at me as though about to launch a serious question. "You don't suppose he has any other clients, do you?"

I responded with a smile and a shake of my head.

The phone rang—Bomber looked at his watch. "Three and a half minutes," he said. "Not bad."

The temp buzzed Bomber on the intercom. Bomber picked up the phone, listened, smiled broadly and winked at me. Into the phone he said, "Count to one hundred, then put him on."

After what seemed like ten minutes, I heard Bomber's false heartiness pour into the phone. A sure sign he was about to skin you alive.

"Jude, you old reprobate, how's it goin'? ...Well, I thought you said two million—I could be wrong...*I* did. Oh, well, yes, that. I know how hard it is to get a drug company to stop making its poison. Especially such a profitable one.... Yes...I think Mr. Scioria might be willing to temper that particular demand for, say another mil.... Oh, I see.... Well, no, I don't think one mil would come anywhere near cutting it, but if you force my hand I might split it with you—the three plus the one—split it at two—and I think a couple full page ads in the *New York Times*, *Los Angeles Times*, Chicago, Washington and Miami—Houston say—saying there are dangers to taking JCD blah blah blah.... You take the ads and I'll give you confidentiality."

Bomber held the phone away from his ear as a wan smile took to his lips.

"No, I don't think the ads would breach it. You won't have to mention Merilee Scioria—in any prominent way—some throw-away line should do it.... Like she was possibly one of the victims of misprescription...."

The phone came away from his ear again, but the smile didn't return. "Well, I'll certainly speak to Angelo, but I'd be very surprised if he'd take the money alone. You know those Italians—out for blood. Especially tough in his case, understand. He only wants the money to reimburse the dentist's family. ...Yeah, yeah, well, thanks for getting back to me, I'll see what I can do."

As soon as he put the phone down, he jumped up and gave his hands one whacking good clap.

"It's in the bag," he said.

I wasn't so sure.

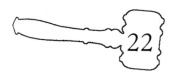

22

So far everything was falling in line. Bomber graciously dropped the demand for the full page ads in national newspapers and settled the Scioria's lawsuit against the drug company for two million smugolies, but with a creative condition.

The Sciorias would not get the two million unless we won a judgment against Dr. Bern. It could be for any amount, even a dollar, but we had to win in court—any out-of-court settlement would nullify the agreement. So, we filed against Dr. Bill Bern for medical malpractice to the tune of twenty-five million, enough to give the doc pause.

When Angelo Scioria asked how much fee Bomber would take out of the drug company settlement, he said, "No fee. My fee will come from Dr. Worm."

Angelo protested, but for naught.

Bonnie Doone had mercilessly returned to the fold with a head so swelled we had trouble fitting her though the door to the Victorian office on Albert Street. She had, she said, over and over, "saved the case"—in unsubtle attempts to belittle my efforts.

Less than a month later, I was in Bomber's office when he said, "Well, well, well," he was looking through the mail on his desk, " I underestimated Dr. Worm."

"Oh?"

"Here's a notice that, guess who will be representing him?"

"Jude Carstairs?"

"On the money, Boy, on the money."

"How d-did he get his insurance company to hire such a s-star?"

"There's the rub, my boy. He has no insurance." He

shook his head at the wonder of it all. "Bare!"

"How c-can he afford him?"

"You put your finger on it, my boy. How indeed. I intend to find out."

What that meant, of course, was he intended *me* to find out.

I summoned my courage to ask him why he was throwing himself into *Scioria v. Bern* like a demon.

"Because it's fascinating," he rumbled. "This kraut up north may be the only sane inmate in the nuthouse."

"So you b-believe his theories?"

"That's one of the great things about the human mind, Son—so damn flexible. Bend it anyway you want. The thing here is the stuff they gave her could have killed an elephant. That greasy bastard, Bern, is going to be up to his neck in lard. Can't wait to see him squirm."

I had never seen him so optimistic.

It made *me* squirm.

Bomber flew first class to Newark (I was in coach), and from there a limo took us to Birchwood.

Mercifully Bomber kept Bonnie Doone at home to man (or woman, as the case may be) the phones, bring in the newspaper and pay the bills; all of which were comfortably within her capabilities.

Though I usually did the jury investigations—to see who on the panel might be unfriendly to our cause—this time Bomber decided a New Jersey outfit might be in a position to have inside knowledge and local edge. I was not disappointed. It was easy enough for me to screen those who were pro-drugs and drug companies, those who were blinded by the good that good doctors most often do, and any secret enemies of the Sciorias. What was more difficult was ferreting out the undercurrents of local politics—the prejudices and attitudes that drive the citizenry from deep beneath the surface.

When we looked at the analyzed jury candidate list in Bomber's hotel suite just off the main drag, he said, "Not too bad."

And that attitude, sunny and positive, carried through the jury selection, right up to the start of the trial.

The drama was to unfold before Judge Elsa Packer, perhaps the only fly in Bomber's ointment. He was never too comfy in the presence of a woman judge. And though there were only a handful when Bomber began trying cases, every day there were more and more of them.

Bamboozling judges was Bomber's trademark. But he was not one to easily bully a woman. He was certainly a male chauvinist, but he also had an old-fashioned deference to women. He was wont to open doors and to stand when they came into a room or to a table where he was seated. But when it came to calling a woman "Your Honor," it stuck in his craw—and sometimes his throat. It wasn't that he couldn't display obeisance to the bench, no matter the intelligence of the sitting judge, it was rather that he had difficulty imagining any woman knowing the law. It seemed to him a man's thing—like being a bombardier.

As for my own presence in New Jersey, I know I swore I would have nothing to do with the case after I had been bopped on the head, but it became a matter of pride—of holding my head up in front of Bonnie Doone. I could have stayed and answered the phones and Bonnie Doone could have come to New Jersey with Bomber, but she would have been as useless as you-know-whats on a boar.

So, I bit the bullet, as they say. But I kept my back to the wall. Bomber had about convinced me that now that we were so high profile, it was extremely unlikely that anything would happen, but I kept my eyes open.

We only had to settle for two shaky jurors. One of them was married to a man who worked for a drug company. But Bomber thought she couldn't stand her husband, so he took a chance. The other was a doctor's receptionist. Bomber hoped she could be objective about doctors. But you never could tell what the others would do. I hate to think how many cases were lost taking the jury for granted. With the jury in place, we began our case as the plaintiff.

Bomber rose, bowed his counterfeit obeisance to the judge and said, "Plaintiff calls Dr. Walter Daimler, please."

The doc came forward, and I was sorry to see he was red in the face and appeared nervous. Oh my, I thought. If he isn't rock solid, where will we find our believers?

Dr. Daimler took the stand and held up his right hand to be sworn in. He said, "I do." resolutely enough, then turned as if to verify the chair was still there before he sat.

I noticed then that opposing counsel, Attorney Jude Carstairs, was boring his eyes into the doctor in the most intimidating fashion. Bomber took Dr. Daimler through his background and qualifications. He was careful not to let anyone glean the impression the doctor was a crackpot since on this issue he was far from the main stream of the scientific community with his view on R4 and its nonconnection to Wanns disease.

He told of his Ph.D. in molecular biology, the numerous grants, awards and prizes he had garnered; the numerous articles and books he had published, his reputation (pre Wanns/R4) as an expert on molecular biology.

Watching Dr. Daimler with his sublimated fidgeting, I was aghast at how uncomfortable he looked answering *our* simple, self-serving questions. I thought of pushing a note in front of Bomber that said, "He looks nervous."

But I was sure Bomber would scribble on the note, "An idiot could see that."

Just then Bomber shifted gears. I should have known I wouldn't sense anything that got by him.

"Now Dr. Daimler, will you tell the jury what studies you have done on the connection between R4 and Wanns disease—and give us any background you think might be helpful?"

Lawyer Carstairs was on the verge of an objection, then seemed to think better of it.

Left to his own narration, Dr. Daimler shone like the noonday sun. His color seemed to improve, his eyes got lustrous and his whole body seemed to transform to relaxation.

"Wanns is the only disease diagnosed by press conference," Dr. Daimler said. "That was when I started to get interested in it. I asked for the studies to prove the hypothesis that R4 virus caused Wanns disease. There were no studies. It was pure speculation."

Jude Carstairs was making notes furiously during Daimler's narration—in such a manner to let us know that he thought everything preposterous.

"The disease began in the gay community of Los Angeles in the early eighties. Five homosexual men contracted a degenerative condition known as Kaposi's sarcoma."

"What is the R4 virus, Doctor?"

"It is a newly discovered virus that inhabits the bodies of about a million people worldwide. The number has remained steady since it was first discovered. It was out of this first mysterious discovery that the Wanns hypothesis was born. I myself was skeptical about the causes attributed to the disease of these five men. Kaposi's sarcoma is a degenerative condition that causes structural and functional damage. The men in question had immune systems that were shot. They were all drug users. They all subsequently died of Kaposi's sarcoma. At first the cause of the disease was attributed to drugs—later, to the virus R4."

"How do you know that, Doctor? Have you made a study of Wanns?"

"Yes. I did my own studies on a group of men who had Kaposi's sarcoma. They were all drug users, they all used amyl nitrites, or popers, drugs widely used in the homosexual community. Roughly half my study group were R4 positive, the other half were not. Yet the men died in the same proportion. Those who were R4 positive were said to have died of Wanns disease. Those who were not were said to have died of Kaposi's sarcoma."

"What does that say to you, Doctor?" Bomber asked.

"That there is no relation between R4 and Wanns disease."

Jude Carstairs was scribbling furiously onto the yellow

legal pad in front of him at the defense table.

"How did those five original cases grow into the Wanns disease scourge we have today?" Bomber asked.

"The virologists who took charge—by press conference—began adding *other* diseases to the Wanns coterie. Pneumonia, dementia, and a host of others. They began with one then added three, then more until they have over thirty today. But the same criteria prevails. If you die of pneumonia and have R4 in your body, you die of Wanns disease, if you have no R4, you simply die of pneumonia."

"What in your judgment, Doctor, is the purpose of adding diseases to the Wanns coterie?"

"Public relations," the doctor said, deadpan. "The U.S. Government spends eight-billion dollars a year on this disease. Why? Because the public reaction to a sexual scourge demands it. Yet Wanns kills fewer people than TB and measles worldwide. The more they can scare people about the risk of sex, the greater the funding. More diseases, more drama. If it were drugs destroying the immune system as I claim, there would be very little sympathy for the victims and very little sentiment in the annals of government to find a cure. They are struggling to expand its victims to heterosexuals, to make it an everyman's disease, but they are having a difficult time including women in their scare. Heterosexual diseases are more dramatic than homosexual."

"Doctor, is it your opinion that there is any connection between R4 and Wanns disease?"

"There is no connection—"

There was a murmur of protest in the courtroom.

"Why do you say that?"

"Because it is not a virus that causes Wanns. Viruses do not discriminate in the population. As indeed the R4 virus is present in people of all ages and sexes. Wanns victims, however, tend to be males between the ages of twenty-five and forty-nine. And female drug users."

"Is that why they claim dirty needles pass the virus?"

"Yes—they claim that Wanns can also be spread by blood...but they completely ignore dirty drugs. For example, you would expect if this were a sexually transmitted disease, as is claimed, it would be rampant in the world of prostitution. Yet, the only prostitutes who get Wanns are the drug users. Also, if it were a sexually transmitted disease, it would spread exponentially. Some of these men have hundreds, even thousands, of contacts. Syphilis is on the rise, gonorrhea is on the rise—Wanns remains static."

"All right, Doctor, are you familiar with the case of Merilee Scioria, whose parents are sitting at the plaintiff table?"

"I am familiar with the details, yes."

"Would you tell us what you know of that case?"

"A celebrated case, very dramatic. The dentist filled a few of her teeth. He wore rubber gloves. He didn't bleed in her mouth, he didn't spit in her mouth. They claim mingling of body fluids of any type can also spread R4. These ideas are fanciful. The first thing you must understand about viruses is they attack the general population in even numbers. Wanns has notoriously passed by women of all ages and men under twenty-five and over forty-nine, for the most part.

"The dentist found he was R4 positive. He felt compelled to tell his patients. Five of them tested positive for R4. One was Merilee. Another was a woman who didn't even see the dentist. She'd had her teeth cleaned by his hygienist. Two were drug users, one got R4 from a blood transfusion. So, the Sciorias panicked, like many do thanks to the hysterical, misleading media. She thought because she was R4 positive, she would die of Wanns. The Sciorias were unaware that ninety-five percent of R4 positives don't die of Wanns. They went to their doctor. He may have known nothing of Wanns. I don't imagine he put a great amount of time into studying the syndrome. He concluded she should take JCD."

"What's that?"

"JCD was a drug developed thirty-some years ago. JCD is a DNA chain terminator—it kills cells indiscriminately. To get one harmful cell, it kills a thousand healthy ones. In time, your immune system is shot. In the case of Wanns, it actually *brings about* the symptoms it is designed to defeat. Thirty years ago it was recognized as the deadly drug it was. It killed so many animals in the experiments, they didn't dare try it on humans. It just made its reappearance when the Wanns lobby insisted the government do something to combat Wanns."

"But doesn't the government test these things before they are allowed on the market?"

"Ah, yes. Customarily blind studies are made with two groups; one given the medicine they are testing—the other given the harmless placebo. The JCD study began fairly legitimately, but when the takers began dying, the study was unblinded and blood transfusions were given to the group on JCD to prolong their lives. Superstition is strong in society. The Wanns lobby was at the boiling point. Politicians want to be loved and are generally ignorant of science. The drug was approved and rushed to the market without proper testing. It has killed everyone who has taken it steadily. The few that have not been killed are those who stopped taking it. That is, regrettably, a very small percentage."

I could hear myself breathe. "But, doctor," Bomber said, "I'm a layman. It all sounds so plausible. *Too* plausible, perhaps. I mean, why would so many scientists refuse to accept this—or at least make some studies to prove you wrong?"

"Science today is peer review. I rocked the boat," his lips formed a tight smile. "There is an interesting parallel in the United States during the Civil War. A doctor became perplexed since most of the expectant mothers wanted midwives rather than doctors to deliver their children. When asked why, the mothers responded that many more of their babies delivered by doctors died. He postulated it was because the doctors came from patients with communicable diseases deadly to infants— this was before aseptic procedures were an accepted practice. He was routed out of the medical community, accused of being a quack and died in an insane asylum."

"That won't be your fate, will it?" Bomber asked.

He smiled broadly. "It hasn't been yet."

"Thank you, Doctor. You have been most instructive. If I may turn again to the drug JCD, given to Wanns patients. Is there anything to prevent a doctor from prescribing JCD for anyone he chooses?"

"Only his knowledge, and his conscience."

"All right. Let us assume, then that a doctor gave someone JCD—prescribed it. What would typically happen to the patient?"

"The symptoms of Wanns would gradually start to appear."

"In a perfectly healthy patient?"

"Yes."

"And given enough JCD, an otherwise healthy individual would die?"

"Yes."

Bomber opened his mouth to speak, then decided to let the answer reverberate in the craniums of the jurors. After a fruitful pause during which he and I cased the faces of the jury, he said.

"No further questions."

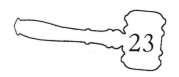

23

During the recess, Bomber talked to Dr. Daimler in the corridor.

"You going to be okay?"

"Oh, yes," Dr. Daimler said, "sure."

"This Carstairs can be a vulture. If you can, just remain confident. Remember you know much more about this subject than he does. In spite of what he will try to make it appear, don't let him bully or bamboozle you. And he will do his best to rattle you. But don't underestimate him. He's done his homework, you better believe it—with experts who disagree with you."

"They don't intimidate me."

"I'm sure not. But I must be frank, Doctor. You came across in the beginning of your testimony as a little nervous. And that was with your friend asking the questions. Jude Carstairs will try to bring you to your knees. If you seem nervous or frightened, the jury will assume you are not telling the truth. I don't mean to add to your nervousness, but you are our key witness. I have taken the case on the strength of your persuasive beliefs. I didn't miscalculate, did I?"

"I don't think so," he said confidently.

"Is there anything I should know? Any weakness in your argument that Jude Carstairs will go for? I must be prepared."

Dr. Daimler looked at Bomber with a bold confidence in his eyes. "I have held nothing from you," he said.

"Good!" Bomber said. "You answer the questions like that and we'll be in clover."

Back in the courtroom, it was Jude Carstairs's turn to cross-examine Dr. Walter Daimler.

"Now really, Doctor," he said on his feet at last. You felt

his impatience in his earliest questions. "You don't mean to suggest that a doctor who had struggled through medical school, had taken the Hippocratic oath, would prescribe a drug for a patient—a sacred charge—that he had any idea would kill that patient?"

"I'm not a mind reader," Dr. Daimler said. "I don't pretend to know another's thought. What I know is not disputed. JCD is a chain terminator. It kills cells—all of them eventually. I would expect a reputable doctor would know that."

"But you don't know that. Dr. Bern is certainly a reputable doctor..."

"I object!" Bomber was on his feet. "No foundation."

"Sustained."

"We have no idea of his reputation," Bomber went on. "Saying he is reputable prejudices the jury and doesn't make him reputable."

Judge Packer tried to wither Bomber with her glare. "I *sustained* your objection," she said.

"I stand corrected," Bomber said—my favorite of his bogus humility catch phrases—his first trotting it out of the trial.

"Now, Doctor," Jude Carstairs said, "Wanns disease destroys the immune system, does it not?"

"Yes."

"But if you die of pneumonia, as you suggest, without R4 in your blood, you say you die of pneum—"

"That's correct."

"But shouldn't your immune system defeat the disease?"

"Well, if it does, you don't die," the doctor said. "By definition, if some disease kills you, your immune system was unable to handle it."

Carstairs made a sour face to show his skepticism. "Now, Doctor, I noted in your direct examination you intimated Wanns was not a sexually transmitted disease, is that correct?"

"Correct."

Jude Carstairs got that befuddled look on his face.

"Then, Doctor, if it isn't sexually transmitted, why do you say it occurs mainly in homosexual men between the ages of seventeen and forty?"

"That is a scientific statistic," Dr. Daimler said, "not my opinion."

"But how do these homosexual men get Wanns then?"

"One—they are drug users. Two—they test positive for R4, panic, perhaps *because* they are homosexual men, then take JCD, and develop all the symptoms of Wanns as a result of taking JCD."

Jude Carstairs still looked skeptical, but he said nothing. He changed his tactic. "So, Doctor, it is your opinion R4 virus is harmless?"

"Yes."

"Could you elucidate that opinion please?"

"R4 is a newly discovered virus. That is not to say it is new. We discover new viruses that have been around perhaps from the beginning of man because we have more powerful equipment."

"You are aware the preponderance of the scientific community believes there is a causal relationship between R4 and Wanns?"

"Yes."

"How do you account for that?"

Dr. Daimler shrugged. "Herd psychology. There is big money to be made signing on to this prevailing, but erroneous, opinion."

"Surely you don't mean to suggest your fellow scientists would sell out to a theory they didn't believe in?" Mock horror took over Jude's facial features.

"I don't make those judgments. There are zero studies that prove the R4/Wanns relationship. Zero. The scientific community operates on peer review and approval."

"Now, Doctor," Jude Carstairs said with his patronizing tone—"You don't seriously contend that your fellow scientists can't brook differing opinions?"

"That is exactly what I am suggesting," he said. "I myself have had grants dry up. At the university, I have had my graduate seminars taken from me, so now I teach introductory science to freshmen."

"Could that be for another reason—other than your disagreement with the establishment?"

"No," the doctor snapped, a little too piquish for my taste. Jude Carstairs was no fool. He let the force of the over-protested answer sink into the jurors' minds. Dr. Daimler's "No" reverberated against the walls and seemed to come back at us a hundred times.

When those sinister sounds ceased at last, Jude Carstairs shifted gears again.

"Doctor, you claim prolonged drug use causes Wanns?"

"Yes."

"And its victims are all drug users?"

"Of one sort or the other," he said.

Jude Carstairs went for the jugular.

"Oh, and what does that mean?"

"As I said, JCD, the drug approved by the FDA after removing it from the market thirty years ago, is a drug. It is a DNA chain terminator—it kills cells indiscriminately, the good with the bad, and sooner or later if you take enough of it, you die."

"Without exception?"

"Unless you stop taking it in time."

Jude Carstairs's face was a tortured mask of incredulity. Then, it relaxed.

"All right, Doctor, let me ask you, how strong is your belief there is no link between R4 and Wanns?"

"Strong!" he said. There was no question there was a chemical animosity between the two men, perhaps it was professional—but it seemed personal.

"And you say the R4 virus is basically harmless to humans?"

"Yes."

"Would you, then, Doctor, to perhaps prove your point,

be willing to take an injection of R4 yourself?"

"That is a stupid question," he snapped. "There are a million people with R4. Only five percent get Wanns. Doesn't that tell you something?" Dr. Daimler was taking the initiative and Jude Carstairs didn't like it.

"I'm asking the questions, Doctor. And I'll ask it again—yes or no. Since you believe R4 harmless, would you submit to putting it in your body?"

"Objection," Bomber said. "Asked and answered."

"He didn't answer," Jude protested. "Yes or no, Doctor."

"Yes!" the doctor boomed—"under some circumstances," he qualified it.

Carstairs eyebrows shot up. "And what might they be?"

"That Dr. Valentine and the Wanns establishment agree in writing that if I am R4 positive and don't get Wanns, they agree their hypothesis has been incorrect and stop taking money from the taxpayers under false pretenses."

"Oh, really, Doctor, really? Well I guess you realize they won't do that."

"Then there would be no point in my undergoing that test."

There was further sparring between Jude Carstairs and Dr. Daimler, Jude Carstairs attempting to ridicule Daimler's beliefs. It was hard to tell the effect it had on the jury. Daimler hadn't waivered—but he did look nervous, and there was nothing Bomber could do about it. We agreed we'd look good on the transcript, but jurors didn't read transcripts, they watched and listened.

Having the opportunity for the last word, Bomber got to his feet for a short redirect—to leave his side of things on the jury's mind.

"Now, Dr. Daimler, in your professional opinion, if a perfectly healthy person takes JCD, the drug given to Wanns patients, takes it day in and day out for months, what will happen?"

"The person will get very sick and die."

"How much must be taken for how long to kill a patient?"

"Depends on many factors. The constitution of the patient, his size and weight, the size and frequency of the dosage."

"Yes," Bomber said. "Let's say a small young woman, about five-one, a hundred pounds or so—good health." Bomber was describing Merilee Scioria, but just in case it was too subtle for the jury, he added, "a person the size, shape and condition of Merilee Scioria, say. If she were given six hundred milligrams of JCD a day, roughly how long would it take to destroy her immune system, and in effect give her all the symptoms of Wanns disease?"

"Six months to a year," the doctor answered confidently.

"And if I were to tell you that Merilee Scioria, who was five-one and weighed ninety-eight pounds, took six hundred milligrams of JCD each and every day and died nine and a half months after her first dose, that would be consistent with your experience?"

"Yes."

"No further questions, Doctor, thank you."

Dr. Daimler rose from his witness chair as Jude Carstairs rose to his feet. "Just a minute, Doctor, please," he said, holding up his hand like a traffic cop.

"Doctor, did you ever diagnose Merilee Scioria?"

"No—"

"Did you ever meet her?"

"No."

"So, any comment you make on her case is pure speculation, is it not?"

"No. I have studied Wanns and R4 and JCD and its terminal effects on a cross section of the population."

"Studied, Doctor?" Jude was maximizing his incredulity. "Have you been given a grant by the government to study Wanns?"

I could see Dr. Daimler was fuming at the belittling he

was undergoing, but there was nothing we could do about it.

"My studies are independent of the establishment," he said, then added, "or I wouldn't be free to pursue pure science."

Jude's eyebrow shot up, "Oh, *really*, Doctor?" he said so broadly I was waiting for a pratfall. "Wouldn't that indicate to you the establishment's considered opinion of your work?"

"Your Honor," Bomber said, "I must object. We have covered this ground already. If the defense attorney missed it, I would recommend he read the transcript—"

"That's not funny," Jude Carstairs snapped.

"Mr. Hanson!" Judge Packer scowled at him.

"I stand corrected," said the great Bomber. "But my objection stands."

"All right," she said, "I think we have covered this," the judge said, and Bomber reveled in his small victory—bowing low to the judge.

Jude Carstairs looked mildly irked, but he also bowed to the decision. "No further questions," he said.

I could tell Bomber wanted badly to have the last word, but he decided the last victory was enough. "No more questions," he said, and Dr. Daimler stepped down, very much relieved to be off the stand.

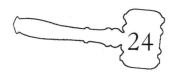

Bomber paraded several other specialists in virology, including a Nobel Prize winner, sympathetic to Daimler's theory.

Jude Carstairs cross-examined each of them with a vengeance—too much vengeance for my taste. Jurors resent vengeance. The only point he made was that none of them had ever met Merilee Scioria, let alone diagnosed her. But the cumulative weight of all those experts disputing the prevailing scientific establishment wisdom caused Jude Carstairs to stipulate that the list of Bomber's other witnesses would say the same.

You might think our next witness was a no-brainer. Angelo Scioria had to testify. And if he broke down in grief, all the better. What we were afraid of was that Angelo would get feisty under cross-examination. Our star expert witness was nervous—we couldn't afford to have our star narrative witness be abrasive.

Bomber counseled Angelo about it and he agreed to be on his best behavior. And he surprised us. He was a model witness, for us, naturally, as he relived the agony of his only child's wasting away. No actor could have performed better.

When an attorney cross-examines a sympathetic witness, he is well advised to use measured tones so as to appear sympathetic himself—all the while asking questions that hem the witness into a box of contradictions. It is always a sparring contest between advocate and witness. The danger is that the learned attorney is almost invariably more knowledgeable and astute than the novice witness, who is usually experiencing his first bout on the witness chair. The learned attorney, on the other hand, must be careful not to appear overbearingly superior lest it cause sympathy for the witness.

All these rules seem to go out the window when Bomber is doing the questioning of an unfriendly witness.

Jude Carstairs was more careful.

He warmed Angelo up with some puffball questions as though he were engaged in a courtship.

"Now, Mr. Scioria," Jude Carstairs was sliding into the nitty-gritty. "Is it fair to say you were devastated by the unfortunate, tragic death of your daughter, Merilee?" Jude was nodding his encouragement. Bomber was frowning.

"Certainly," Angelo answered stoically.

"And it must be difficult for you to relive the horror of your loss—is that correct?"

"Yes."

"Do you want to tell the jury why you felt you should bring it up again with this case?"

The tension froze the air as Angelo narrowed his eyes at Jude Carstairs. I was on the edge of my seat waiting for Angelo to blow.

Instead he answered calmly. "A wrong has been done. As unpleasant as this is for my wife and me, we felt it was necessary to remedy that wrong."

"And thanks for asking," Bomber whispered in my ear.

"But you surely realize," Jude Carstairs continued probing with his dull needle, "in the course of your remedy, it will be necessary to probe your...late daughter's...character. And we will be forced to go where that leads us."

Angelo just stared at Jude.

"You do understand that?" Jude said.

"I understand you will try anything, Mr. Carstairs," Angelo said. "I also understand if you try to make my Merilee look like the devil incarnate you will not succeed in justifying her murder. Murder is murder. The victim is not the criminal."

"Hear, hear," Bomber said, much too loudly.

"Your Honor," Jude Carstairs said, piqued, "please instruct the jury to disregard plaintiff's counsel's outburst, and remind him he is an attorney, not a cheerleader."

Judge Packer obliged Carstairs and Bomber said, with humble pie oozing from every pore, "I stand corrected."

"All right, Mr. Scioria," Carstairs said, as though conceding a point, "how did you first become acquainted with Dr. Bern?"

"He was my doctor."

"Yes, but how did you happen to go to him?"

Angelo appeared confused. "He was always our doctor."

"Did you get his name from the yellow pages?"

"I don't remember," Angelo said with a frown. "It was so long ago."

"Could he have been recommended by someone?"

"Could have, I suppose."

"Do you remember who that could have been?"

"No."

"When did you first go to Dr. Bern?"

"I don't remember. Soon after we moved to town, I guess."

"When was that?"

"Twenty-some years ago."

"Before Merilee was born?"

"Yes."

"And what did you go for?"

"I don't remember. Some illness. The flu maybe."

"And when Merilee, your daughter, came along, did she go to him too?"

"Yes."

"So, I assume you were satisfied with his service?"

"Yes. Then we were."

"Did you later become *dis*satisfied?"

"Yes. When I learned that he killed my little girl."

"Well, that is unfounded speculation, Mr. Scioria, and I will ask Judge Packer to remove it from the record."

"Yes, Mr. Scioria," the judge said kindly, "please answer only the questions. Don't add comments of your own."

Angelo threw up his hands, "I do my best."

"I appreciate that, Mr. Scioria," Carstairs said, smiling benignly.

"Did Dr. Bern ever prescribe drugs for you?"

"I suppose he did. Antibiotics, things like that."

"Did you ever get from Dr. Bern any kind of mood altering drug?"

"Mood altering—what is that?"

"Uppers, downers—any drugs for depression?"

"No."

I hoped I was wrong, but I noticed a flinching in Angelo's eyes, and I expected the jury noticed it too.

"Can you tell us in your own words what you remember of Merilee's final illness? When did you first realize she had it?"

"About a year before she died, she went to this dentist as she did every year. That time she got a letter from him soon afterwards. Said he had been tested for R4 and the test was positive, and he suggested his patients should have a test, just to be safe."

"And did she get a test?"

"She did."

"What were the results?"

He paused to let the pain pass. "Positive," he muttered.

"What did you do then?"

"We panicked."

"Why?"

"Because we thought that meant Wanns disease. We went to Dr. Bern. He prescribed JCD. And it killed her."

"Mr. Scioria—please. Do not digress and make sweeping statements. You aren't a doctor, are you?"

"No."

"You sought the advice of a doctor, didn't you?"

"Yes."

"Someone you trusted?"

"Then, yes."

"And that was Dr. Bern, is that correct?"

"Yes."

"But now you are having second thoughts about that?"

"Yes. If there is no relation between R4 and Wanns, and JCD kills all your cells, she was murdered."

"Isn't that a big if, Mr. Scioria?"

"I don't know."

"Yes, you don't know. Do you think, therefore, you should be casting these aspersions on your doctor's reputation? Dr. Bern, who cared for your family without any complaint from you?"

"Objection," Bomber said. "Calls for conclusion vague and uncertain compound."

"Well, do you want to rephrase the question, Mr. Carstairs?"

"All right. Are you a doctor, Mr. Scioria?"

"Objection," Bomber said. "Asked and answered."

"All right, you said you weren't a doctor. Do you have any special training in diseases?"

"No."

"Germ theory, virology, biology, chemistry, any of the sciences that would help you to understand illness and disease?"

"No."

"No medical training?"

"No—"

"Nurses' training?"

"No."

"Then on what basis do you come to the conclusion that JCD would kill a person?"

"I read it. Dr. Daimler said it. He studied those things."

"Have you also read and heard the opposite?"

"No."

"No?"

"Your Honor," Bomber said, "he's mimicking the witness."

"All right, move on, Mr. Carstairs."

Glancing at the response of the jurors, Bomber seemed disappointed at their seeming lack of sympathy.

"You have not read that JCD was approved for treatment of Wanns by the Federal Drug Administration?"

"I have heard the same drug was not approved for treating cancer years ago."

"Where did you hear that?"

"Dr. Daimler."

"Does he, to your knowledge, have any official capacity in scientific circles related to Wanns disease?"

"They ostracized him."

"Yes or no, please, Mr. Scioria."

"I don't know."

"All right—for twenty-plus years you trusted the judgment of Dr. Bern, is that correct?"

"Yes."

"You had no reason to distrust him, correct?"

"That's correct. That's why I let him treat my baby."

"How old was your baby at the time you refer to?"

"Nineteen."

"Years or months?"

Bomber was on his feet. "Your Honor, please," he said. "Defense counsel is ridiculing the witness, who is being cooperative though it is emotionally difficult for him. Please ask Mr. Carstairs to conduct himself as a gentleman."

"I'm just trying to be specific," Jude Carstairs said.

The judge turned to Angelo. "You say you let Dr. Bern treat your baby. I assume you were referring to your daughter, is that right?"

"That's right."

"At what age?"

"He treated her all her life. I let him."

"Thank you." Judge Packer turned to the defense counsel. "You may continue, Mr. Carstairs."

"No further questions," he said, surprising us.

So Bomber asked for a recess, and it was granted.

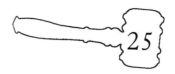

I was stumped. Bomber does the strategy for his cases and usually I marvel at his prescience. This time, all he had shown so far were the bones of the case. Angelo Scioria told how his daughter had died. Dr. Daimler said the drug she was pre-scribed killed Merilee.

But where was the malpractice? He'd prescribed a drug approved by the FDA and prescribed by perhaps thousands of other doctors. How did the great Bomber intend to turn that into malpractice?

Bomber, of course, hoped to trip up Dr. Bern. Wrap him around his little finger and "nail him to the cross," as he liked to say.

He had told Jude Carstairs that if the defense didn't call Bern as a witness, he would call him as an unfriendly witness for the plaintiff. Carstairs decided to call him as his first witness.

The doctor walked to the stand with shoulders squared and a jaunty step that gave his body a cocky sway. His smile was constant, and unlike most guys with perpetual smiles, it looked rather genuine. On the surface, he was, unfortunately, an easy guy to like.

Dr. Bern always appeared to me as a guy who was over compensating for being vertically challenged. I'd put him at about 5'5", which was a couple of inches under Bomber without Bomber's elevator shoes. All the more reason for him to wear them. If Dr. Bern could be ingratiating, Bomber could be intim-idating.

Motive? I said to myself as I watched Dr. Bern take the witness box. How much neater if we had one.

Some men want to be known by their wristwatches. With his gleaming-gold Rolex (retail about fifteen grand), Dr.

Bern was such a man. When he raised his hand to take the oath, the shiny Rolex peeked above his gold cuff-linked cuffs.

When he sat in the witness chair, he propped his elbow on the railing and put his hand to his jaw, revealing that gleaming-gold product of the Rolex people.

Under direct examination, Jude Carstairs had Dr. Bern repeat the damaging, dastardly things he had said about Merilee Scioria in his deposition.

Bern embellished a bit to drive the nails deeper. He called Angelo Scioria an hysteric where his daughter was concerned and said that influenced him in not telling the Sciorias about her pregnancies or her drug addiction.

Hearing this, Angelo leaned forward in his seat at our plaintiff's table as if he were going to throttle Dr. Bern the first chance he got.

By the time Carstairs turned the witness over to us, I felt he had made very convincing arguments that Merilee Scioria was a scumbag. Our tack, of course, was that she was murdered by a negligent doctor, but if we had a convincing motive, things might go a lot easier. Why did Bomber have so much faith in the Sciorias?

Bomber's challenge with Dr. Bern was to make a likable guy unlikable, and in the process not become unlikable himself.

"Are you board certified, Doctor?" Bomber began gently.

"No, I am not."

"Do you have any training in virology, R4, Wanns disease—?"

"No."

"Or drug abuse?"

"No."

"Since you received your license to practice medicine in the state of New Jersey, have you attended any classes, seminars, conventions where R4 and Wanns disease were mentioned?"

"No, I have not."

"And your practice is in general medicine, is that correct?"

"Yes."

"What we call a general practitioner?"

"Yes."

"Do any surgery, Doctor?"

"I can do minor things, but I rarely do."

"Mostly flu shots and stitching cuts and things like that?"

"Well, it is more varied than that," Dr. Bern said, his smile fading for the moment at hearing his life's work compared to a first-aid nurse.

"How many R4 patients have you had?"

"Just the one—Merilee Scioria."

"Did you consider sending her to a doctor with more experience in the disease?"

"Yes, I did. But she insisted on me being her doctor."

"Did she put that in writing?"

A crack appeared in the perfection of Dr. Bern's smile. "Of course not," he snapped.

"Any witnesses to her telling you that?"

"No. It was a private consultation. It *is* a sensitive matter," he emphasized.

"Can you describe how JCD, the drug you prescribed for Merilee Scioria, works?"

"It destroys the bad cells in an attempt to arrest Wanns disease."

"Does it also destroy good cells?"

"Yes. It, unfortunately, can't discriminate. The hope is, while good and bad are destroyed, the good will regenerate while the bad won't."

"Does it ever happen the other way? The bad regenerate and the good don't?"

"I don't know. Not in my experience."

"Your experience being the one patient, Merilee Scioria?"

"Yes."

"She died, didn't she?"

"Yes."

"So the bad triumphed over the good?"

"Apparently."

"Have you ever heard of JCD curing Wanns disease?"

"It's not a cure. Doesn't claim to be."

"So what is its mission?"

"To arrest the disease—prolong life."

"Did it do that for Merilee Scioria?"

"I have no way of telling how long she would have lived without it."

"Perhaps longer?"

"I doubt it."

"Your doubt is based on what, Doctor?"

"As much as I could find."

"Did you read the reports and studies of Dr. Daimler?"

"No, I did not."

"Why not?"

"Because he is considered so far out, I didn't think I could learn anything. His theories are considered, if you will pardon my saying so, somewhat crackpot."

"But you didn't read any of his work?"

"No."

"And yet you feel comfortable characterizing something you haven't read as 'crackpot'?"

"Well, no one in the scientific community agrees with him."

"No one?"

"Well, hardly anyone."

"*Hardly* anyone?" Bomber was trying to intimidate. "Does the name Dr. Werner Schwartz mean anything to you?"

"No, I'm afraid not."

"He won the Nobel Prize in medicine. Does it ring a bell now?"

"I may have heard the name."

"Are you aware *he* agrees with Dr. Daimler?"

"No, I wasn't."

"Oh, by the way Doctor, you've just told us that you never read Daimler's reports and studies. Do you own any of Dr. Daimler's books?"

Bern blinked once too often before he answered. "No."

"*Phantom Virus?* That ring a bell?"

Dr. Bern frowned, he was putting some effort into remembering, you could tell. "I don't believe so—"

"Not on your bookshelf, in your office?"

"Not to my knowledge."

"Could others have put books there without your knowledge?"

"My receptionist might. Sometimes she takes gifts people send me—promotional materials—and puts them there, and I don't see them."

It was one of Bomber's shake-up questions. Shake up the witness with uncanny inside knowledge. Of course, Bern would destroy the book as soon as he got back to his office. But it would haunt him. We couldn't do much about it—I could go on the stand and say I saw it, but there would be the suspicion I was making it up because of my connection to the case.

"Doctor, do you consider yourself a man of science?"

"Well, of course," he said proudly. "I'm a medical doctor."

"What is more important in science, Doctor…conformity or doubt?"

"Oh, I object," Jude Carstairs said. "We are getting so far afield. What possible connection could there be to the issues of this trial?"

"Your Honor," Bomber said, "this goes to the vital heart of the case. It is our contention Dr. Bern, negligently or otherwise, prescribed a lethal drug to his patient, Merilee Scioria. It is important that the jury is apprised of the extent of his negligence—of what his thoughts are on science, medicine—what his obligations are."

"Oh, Mr. Hanson, we don't need any speeches," Judge Packer said.

"I stand corrected."

"But I'll overrule the objection."

"All right, Doctor," Bomber pressed. "Answer the question, conformity or doubt?"

"Well, doubt, certainly, if it is responsible doubt."

"Are you suggesting that Dr. Daimler's doubt might not be responsible?"

"I don't think it is."

"Are you acquainted with his credentials?"

"No—"

"Or the credentials of the Nobel laureate who appeared—?"

"It hasn't been my field."

"And yet you prescribed a lethal dose of JCD to…"

"*Ob*-jection," Carstairs squealed. "Inflammatory, without foundation, speculative."

"Sustained."

"Bomber knows better."

"I stand corrected. Isn't it true, Dr. Bern, you prescribed a drug you knew nothing about?"

"No. I read the literature—talked to others."

"What others? Their names, please."

"Oh, I don't remember now."

"Could you find their names in your office?"

"I doubt it."

"Know where you got them?"

Bern furrowed his brow in thought, then shook his head. "Sorry, I asked around—medical circles—I got some names. I don't remember what they were."

"All right. Do you remember what they told you about JCD?"

"A reliable drug, not a cure, but a hope for arresting the disease."

"Tell you of any dangers?"

"Not if used as directed."

"There was no mention JCD was a DNA chain terminator? Killed all the cells until none were left?"

"Well, yes, but that is *how* it kills Wanns disease."

"No mention that JCD would give the symptoms of someone with Wanns disease to someone who didn't have it to start with?"

"Every drug has side effects."

"In hindsight, Doctor, do you have any doubt that what killed Merilee Scioria was the prescription of JCD you gave her?"

"*Ob*-jection! Calls for a wild speculative conclusion."

"Your Honor, I would submit the question is no such thing. He is the prescribing doctor. He claims to have talked to several people, though he can't remember who they were—claims to have done his homework. He must have formed an opinion. He saw Merilee Scioria when he prescribed the lethal drug—"

"Objection—"

Bomber plowed on, "And he saw her when she died. She was hardly the same person."

"Yes," the judge said, "but the question is, was that caused by the disease or the purported cure?"

"Exactly!" Bomber heartily agreed.

"All right, can you rephrase the question? No, I'll ask it. Dr. Bern, in your opinion, what was the cause of Merilee Scioria's death?"

"Wanns disease."

"In your opinion," the judge continued, "could the drug JCD have had any complicity in her death?"

"No, Your Honor."

"There," Judge Packer said. "We've got his answer without all the pyrotechnics."

Bomber was seething. Anytime a judge robbed him of his prerogative to ask loaded, intimidating questions, he was furious—and I don't blame him.

He asked more questions to show Dr. Bern was anything but an expert on the matter, but Judge Packer sustained most of Jude Carstairs's objections, and we didn't do too well with that approach.

"All right, Doctor," Bomber said, picking up a narrowly folded piece of paper from our plaintiff's table. "I show you this pamphlet titled JCD, which we will submit to be marked Plaintiff's Exhibit A."

After the court bookkeeping, the brochure was marked and returned to Bomber, who handed it to Dr. Bern.

"I hand you Plaintiff's Exhibit A, Doctor, and ask if you have seen this before?"

"Yes," he said, after a cursory glance at the paper.

"Please tell the jury what it is?"

"It is the technical explanation of the drug JCD that accompanies the dispensing of JCD."

"Have you read this before?"

The doctor looked at the paper and nodded slowly.

"Yes or no? Doctor, audibly for the reporter, please."

"Yesss."

"You seem less than sure, Doctor."

"Well, it was some time ago, and if you are going to ask me questions about it, I might have to refresh my memory."

"Certainly," Bomber agreed, awfully unctuously. "Have you any recollections at all about what this warning says?"

"Not really now, no. I did when I read it."

"And did you discuss these warnings with Mr. or Mrs. Scioria at that time?"

"I don't remember." To his credit, he was crinkling his brow in an external display of effort to recall. I imagined Dr. Bern glancing at the paper at some point, but I read it, and I can tell you it isn't what you'd call gripping reading. It probably wasn't too long before Dr. Bern began thinking of his golf game or whatever.

"Will you read the boxed portion to us, please," Bomber said, pointing to the box on page one—"the bold type here."

Dr. Bern blinked rapidly as though lubricating his contact lenses for the task. He cleared his throat as though he realized projection was in order.

"Warning," he read, "JCD may be associated with hematologic toxicity."

"What does that mean in plain English, Doctor?"

"JCD *may* be *associated* with loss of blood cells causing anemia."

"Toxic means poisonous?"

"Yes."

"And poison kills you?"

"It can."

"Did you tell the Sciorias JCD could kill their daughter?"

"I was dealing with Merilee Scioria. She was my patient."

"So, you went over this with her? The fact that what you were giving her was poison?"

"Objection!" Jude Carstairs was on his feet. "Plaintiff's counsel is distorting the warning. He's grandstanding for the jury. Obviously JCD is not poison or it wouldn't be on the market."

"Well," Bomber cut in. "It *obviously says* it *is* poison."

"Gentlemen!" Judge Packer implored.

"*He's* making argument," Carstairs insisted.

"I'm not arguing. The warning in bold, boxed type says the drug is poison."

"It does *not!*"

"Gentlemen, please calm down. I don't want to have to cite you both for contempt."

"Sorry, Your Honor," Carstairs said. "This man provokes me—"

"I stand corrected," Bomber said, with a self-satisfied smirk. "But the fact remains," he said in quieter tones, "the brochure that accompanies the drug claims it is toxic, isn't that correct, Doctor?"

"May be associated with toxicity of the blood, is what it says. *May* be."

"So, all right. It doesn't say it is *definitely* poison, is that it?"

"Yes."

"But it *could* be?"

"Associated with—"

"Now, Doctor, I'm just a simple man. Can you explain in language I might understand what that means, if it doesn't mean you risk death by taking JCD?"

"In warnings of this type, mandated by the government, the drug companies must include worst case scenarios. The warning says, in essence, this *could* be a side effect, not that it happens at all. Even if there is the slightest suspicion that is has happened once, it must be included. 'Associated with' means that JCD in conjunction with other factors—which are by no means occurring in all patients, or even many—could cause poisoning of the blood."

"You make it sound so benign, Doctor."

"Objection!"

"Sustained."

"Will you read the next sentence, please?"

"'Prolonged use of JCD has been associated with symptomatic myopathy similar to that produced by the R4 virus.' They bend over backwards to be conservative."

"Well, is that so? Let's examine that statement, Doctor. Do you consider it 'conservative' to reintroduce a drug that was taken off the market thirty-some years ago as unsafe?"

"That was for another disease."

"What was that?"

"Cancer."

"How can an antiviral drug work against cancer?"

"They thought it would kill cancer cells."

"Ah—" Bomber said, nodding, letting the statement sink in. "But now they know cancer isn't caused by a virus?"

"Correct."

"But they still think Wanns is caused by the R4 virus?"

"Yes."

"So, did you ever consider…you never tried doing nothing? I mean, letting the R4 virus exist as it does in a million people harmlessly?"

"Well, I don't agree that it's harmless."

"Is your opinion based on any study you can cite?"

"No."

"What is it based on, Doctor?"

"As I said—talking to doctors—"

"Have you thought of any of their names?"

"No."

"And reading material like this manufacturer's insert?"

"Yes."

"And you still prescribed JCD?"

"Yes, it was all that was available."

"Merilee Scioria wasn't sick when you prescribed JCD, was she?"

"Certainly—she tested positive for R4. She was devastated. She demanded a cure."

"A cure for a harmless virus?"

"Not harmless to all those Wanns victims," Dr. Bern said smugly.

"That's gratuitous, Doctor," Bomber shot back. "Read the first line of the second paragraph please."

"Rare occurrences of potentially fatal lactic acidosis…"

"All right. Fatal means death, does it not?"

"But it says 'rare occurrences.'"

"Okay. Do you know how many 'rare' refers to?"

"No—but it is very few."

"But you don't know how many?"

"No."

"Do you know how often the manufacturer of JCD updates this insert?"

"No."

"So, 'rare' could be considerably more now?"

"I haven't heard that."

"From people you don't remember, Dr. Bern?"

"Objection! Mr. Hanson is continuing to badger the witness. I ask that he restore some civility to the proceedings. That is if he is capable of it."

"Very nice indeed, Mr. Carstairs. And how civil would you be if your client's daughter had been murdered?"

"Oh, Your Honor—" Carstairs bleated.

Judge Packer turned red, and she slapped the top of her bench with her flat hand. "Mr. Hanson!" She shot him with her most venomous gaze, "I *will* not tolerate that kind of behavior in my courtroom. I want you to apologize to Dr. Bern, Mr. Carstairs and the jury, and I'll have no more of it, or I'll cite you for contempt!"

"I stand corrected," Bomber said, bowing humbly to the parties specified and to the jury. Some of them, I was happy to see, were smiling.

Judge Packer had apparently heard that humble homily once too often, for she said. "Say you're sorry—" as though Bomber were a naughty child.

"I'm *truly* sorry," he said. Words, of course, cannot do justice to Bomber's counterfeit demeanor. If he thought he convinced anyone of his sincerity, my guess was he was happily mistaken.

"All right, I'll ask only a few more questions," Bomber said, and I noticed Dr. Bern's smile broadened while his body seemed to relax.

"After Merilee Scioria tested R4 positive, did she have any symptoms of Wanns disease?"

"Well, R4 is a symptom."

"Doctor, isn't that a virus, not a symptom of disease?"

"Well, it's a cause."

"And that thesis is disputed by Dr. Daimler and others, is that accurate?"

"I suppose."

"You aren't sure they dispute it?"

"Not firsthand, no."

It took a little more sparring for Dr. Bern to concede that others might have differing opinions.

"And did you consult with anyone whose opinion differed on the connection of R4 to Wanns?"

"No."

"Did Merilee Scioria have even one symptom of any of the Wanns diseases before you put her on JCD?"

"Just R4."

"Which we have agreed is *not* a symptom of a Wanns disease, did we not?"

"It causes it."

"But, Doctor, there *were* no symptoms, were there?"

"Just that," he answered stubbornly.

"All right then. Did Merilee Scioria begin taking JCD?"

"Yes."

"And what was the result?"

"Well, when her symptoms came to the fore, her health declined. I like to think the JCD prolonged her life."

"Her life, Doctor, or her misery?"

"Objection—"

"I'll withdraw that," Bomber said magnanimously. "So, how long did Merilee Scioria take JCD under your prescription?"

"Nine and a half months," he said.

"Then what happened?"

Dr. Bern paused and seemed to glance at his attorney. "She died," he said.

"No further questions."

26

"You see that damn wristwatch on the doc?" Bomber said to me after court adjourned for the day. "Fifteen, twenty grand at least."

"Maybe it's a fake," I said.

"No fake," he said with an assurance born of I don't know what. "Ever wonder where a small town general practitioner gets fifteen grand to throw away on a watch?"

"Well, h-he's a d-doctor."

"Small potatoes. And why does he flaunt it? I mean, does he expect sympathy from the jury with a showboat watch like that?" he asked rhetorically. "I'll tell you this, Boy—if he were my client, he wouldn't be flashing any fifteen-grand watch."

"Mayb-be he wants to look successful. P-people respect success."

"Legitimate success," Bomber grumbled.

"What's next?" I got out in one piece.

"Carstairs'll put on a bunch of guys to tell what a slime Merilee Scioria was. I'll object like heck, but old Jude'll squeal how relevant it is and how he'll connect it—all B.S., of course, but that's life as a big-city lawyer."

"Is there any r-relevance?"

"Not a scintilla, Boy, not a smidgen, a skosh, a drop. Wants the jury to hate her and resent old dad for raking it up when he should have left well enough alone. It's the old why-are-you-bothering-me-with-this? ploy. Even if Wanns is caused by drugs as Dr. Daimler says it is, she used drugs and used 'em hard. So where is the sympathy in that? If they do that, of course, I'll get Angelo and Regina back on the stand to stoutly deny it, but—" he threw up his hands at the chanciness of it all.

"I'll argue until I'm blue that it doesn't matter if she was Joe Stalin and Adolf Hitler rolled into one, murder is murder and the victim is not on trial—but somehow the other side has an easier time of it."

"B-but, you seemed so c-confident."

"It's the only stance in front of Angelo. The slightest crack in my optimism and he'd go ballistic."

I thought back on his intransigent resistance to taking the case and how he had so dramatically reversed course, but I kept my mouth shut. Bomber often said the most salubrious configuration for my mouth was in the closed position.

"As of now," Bomber said, "we are losing the case. It's a shame. You know better than anyone, I don't like to lose. Especially when I have this feeling in my gut we are right as rain. The gods should be with us."

"What are you going to do?"

"Pray for a miracle," he said. "Wait, I have a better idea. You go out and find out what's with that wristwatch."

"And g-get h-hit on the h-h-head ag-gain." I was really flustered at that idea.

"Nah," he said, dismissing my trauma as though I'd imagined it. "No, no, there is something sub rosa here, I feel it in my bones."

"Yeah—I felt it in my head."

"Exactly! Wasn't that the tipoff? If Merilee Scioria were truly evil and the case were open and shut, why would anyone try to hurt you?"

"My s-sentiments exactly," I said in sort of a droll tone.

Bomber didn't respond, instead he plunged deep into thought. He was like a swami at a seance. I only hoped whatever spirit he was communing with had some good answers that didn't involve me.

When he opened his eyes, he shook his head. "No revelations," he said and I heaved a sigh of relief. "Only one thing I'm certain of—as certain as you can be about a hunch: I don't think Merilee is the rotter we are being led to believe by so many of the enemy. If I am right, they have a motive for making her look bad. What? And why? And when we find it, that motive will dovetail with old doc Bern wanting her out of the way."

"Conspiracy?" I know, only for crackpots.

Bomber said, "Get me some evidence, Boy."

"I b-been everywhere. T-talked to everyone. What's l-left?"

"That's what my ace investigator must find out. Nail it down, Boy. Get me the goods."

"Shall I w-wear a f-football helmet?"

"Not a bad idea—especially if you want to go incognito."

Bomber could afford to be so cavalier about my head injury. The closest he ever got to one was hearing about fictional characters, and those guys usually popped right up as though nothing had happened.

After the break, Dr. Bern returned to the stand. Bomber asked him for the records of the pregnancy terminations he'd done on Merilee.

"I didn't keep any," he said. "I wanted to keep it confidential."

"Oh, do you destroy records as a matter of course?"

"Of course not, and I resent the implication."

"Oh, you do? Rather serious matter in the eyes of the medical examiner, isn't it, Doctor—destroying records?"

"I didn't destroy them," he said, his face flushing. "I just didn't make them."

"Did you send a bill?"

"I don't recall."

"You don't know if you charged her?"

"I don't know if I sent a bill. Maybe I didn't charge her."

"Could she have paid you without you keeping any record of it?"

"It's not likely," he said.

"But *possible*," Bomber pressed.

"Well, in this case," he faltered, "it was so sensitive."

"You didn't want her parents to know about the abortions?"

"*She* didn't want them to know. I was only acceding to her wishes."

"So, you might not have a record of your billing?"

"I might not."

"Will you look please, Dr. Bern—and turn all records pertaining to this case over to your counsel?"

"I will look, yes. If I find anything I'll give it to Mr. Carstairs."

"I assume, Doctor, you report all your income to the IRS?"

"Yes."

"Good. Include your tax records as well, please, will you?"

Bern wasn't happy about that one, but he said he would do his best. Always a nice out, for what is one's best? Best—under the circumstances of a busy schedule that leaves so little time for record searching? Best—considering the pragmatic need to cover up illegal activity? Lot of ways you can mangle that thought.

At the break, Bomber dumped a nice project on me. We hadn't left the plaintiff table when he said, "Son, let's get the drug company records on how many feel-good pills they shipped to the doc."

"They'll just g-give them to me?"

"Use the magic word if they balk."

"What?"

"Subpoena," he said. "Would they rather give you the records or come blab about it in court?"

To give me a hand with the assignment, after the break Bomber asked Dr. Bern to list the drug companies he bought from.

"Gosh," he said, "all of them, I suppose."

"All right, who do you buy most from?"

"Most? I'd have to check my records."

"Do you have those records?"

"I can look."

"All right, to save time, if you had to use your best guess on the three companies you buy most drugs from, who would they be?"

"My nurse does the ordering. I couldn't say for sure."

"Your *nurse* does the prescribing?"

"No, I do that."

"Then answer the question."

"He's badgering, Your Honor," Carstairs said, jumping up from his seat.

"I'm not," Bomber maintained stoutly, "I'm just trying to get his cooperation in answering the question."

"He is answering," Jude Carstairs insisted.

"He is not."

"Gentlemen," Judge Packer said.

"He's evading with everything in the book. It's a simple question."

The judge banged her gavel. "Mr. Hanson! Control yourself, please."

"Yes, Your Honor. Any help you could give me to get Dr. Bern to answer these simple questions would be appreciated."

Jude Carstairs said, "Bomber wants them answered to his taste."

"I do not," Bomber said, heatedly. "I don't care what his answers are as long as he gives some."

The gavel cracked throughout the courtroom again. "All right, that's enough!" Judge Packer could get angry right along with the best of them. "Keep *quiet*, both of you."

"Your Honor, he…" Jude Carstairs tried to squeeze in his sophomoric blame on the other party (Bomber).

"Quiet!" and she rapped the gavel again.

Bomber smiled at the jury as though it were obvious

that truth and justice were ours.

I watched the jurors react, most of them sought to maintain the deadpan look.

Judge Packer's ire notwithstanding, there was more bickering between counsel, and when we finally pried Dr. Bern loose from a few names of drug companies he thought supplied him with more then the rest, Bomber leaned over to whisper in my ear, "Check the other ones first."

Bomber's whispers were, as usual, on the loud side.

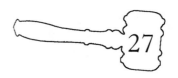

27

I telephoned the Jones, Waldron Pharmaceutical Company in Milwaukee. A woman who seemed short on human warmth told me she was terribly busy and might not get to my request for some time.

"Tomorrow?" I asked.

"Goodness, no—"

"Next week?"

"Oh, no."

"Next month?"

"Possibly."

"Next year?"

"That would be safe."

"Out of curiosity," I said, "may I ask you a question?"

"Well-l-l, I'm *very* busy, but go ahead." she hissed, impatience searing the phone lines.

"How long would it take you to pull up on your computer the purchases of Dr. William Bern of Birchwood?"

"Well, I don't know," she said. "Not long, of course. But first I have to get to it. I'm backlogged up to here. Besides, I'd have to get permission to give you this information."

"Um hum—computer time? Less than five minutes?"

"Well, more or less."

"And how long would it take you to fly round trip to Birchwood, New Jersey, with your records in answer to a subpoena?"

She got all huffy, but I suspect she grasped my drift. I said, "Here's my phone number. Shall I start preparing the subpoena or do you want to check with your boss?"

There was a chilly silence on the other end. I waited it out. "Spell your last name for me, please," I said at last.

"I'll check," she said.

She hung up first.

Two of the drug suppliers were in the Big Apple, and Bomber thought it would be nice if I paid them personal visits.

At Emory Broadbent in one of those classy glassy towers, a wacky bottle blond built like a fire engine with twice the horsepower under the hood did my bidding. Her hair, if her eyebrows and moustache were any indication, started life in a darker hue. She went by the name Francine Volga, if the plastic sign on her desk was any indication. At my request, she produced a computer printout. This was not before I satisfied her with my credentials and murmured my standard subpoena option.

I looked at the printout and what seemed to be a staggering quantity of feel-good drugs listed. Blondie explained to me that most were uppers and downers and mood alterers, and when I looked at the list I noted there was hardly anything else on it.

"Would you say this is an ordinary amount of these drugs for a doctor to order in a month, or an inordinate amount?"

"Depends," she said, "on how many doctors in his clinic."

"Clinic?" I said.

"Yes—we have him down as a clinic."

"Well, he's a solo," I said.

"Alone, he practices alone?"

I nodded as gravely as I could.

"Oh, my yes," she said, her face turning to blush. "Yes, that is quite a lot, then."

I would have been satisfied with that testimony, but I knew Bomber would want to turn all the stones.

And as the stones turned, I was glad they did.

Exeter, Miller, Dogle and Erp—sounded like an education conglomerate, a law firm or a string of cowboys, depending where you put your emphasis. But it was a drug conglomerate whose accounting office was housed in one of those cutesy colonial brick jobs that must have dated back to when the joint was called New Amsterdam.

Irma Snodgrass was my mark at Exeter, Miller *et al.*, and she went back to New Amsterdam herself.

But she was friendly and garrulous—my favorite combination in a potential witness, and I hope I won't seem immodest if I say I got the queerest feeling she was flirting with me. I don't mean to minimize my interest, but she did have some years on my grandmother.

The first thing she said in response to my query was, "Oh, my, what a lot of interest there has been in your Dr. Bern."

"Oh?"

"Yes. The drug people have gone through all our records."

"Drug people?"

"Yes—you know," she said, winking at me conspiratorially—"Cops."

"Really? The local police?"

"From Jersey, yes—but also the feds." She talked like a teenage TV addict.

"The...feds?" I asked.

"Oh, you know, they all have initials nowadays."

"DEA?"

"Sounds familiar," she said, "CIA, FBI, FDA, ATF—notice how they all have three letters, as though that were all we could remember."

I tittered along with her just to be sociable.

When she produced her computer printout, I glanced at it and asked my question about the quantity—more or less than the average, or normal for a solo general practitioner?

"Yes," she said. "Oh, my yes. There's enough to choke a horse there. He's no slacker, that's for sure. Well, you know those FRBs wouldn't be interested if he was a slacker."

"FRB?" I asked, confused—"Federal Reserve Board?"

"Oh, that what it stands for? I thought it was Feelgood

Retail Buyers or something druggie like that."

"DEA—Drug Enforcement Agency, could that be it?"

"Couldn't prove it by me. All those letters run together after while."

All in all it wasn't a bad half-day's work. To treat myself, I bought a *New York Times* and stared wistfully at all the musical events I could have attended had I been a man of leisure.

When I, instead, brought home the bacon to Bomber, he seemed pleased. Oh, the ordinary observer may not have realized that, but I was an old hand at reading eyebrows, and there was the unmistakable tic in Bomber's right one that signaled approbation.

"So," he said, "you think Doc was feeding Merilee drugs? Maybe he was the poppa of those two aborted babies."

"Think so?"

"I don't know. Speculating won't get us anywhere," he said. Then he seemed to square off against me as though we were in a prize fight and he had just put his dukes up. "So get the goods, Boy. It's up to you."

"Any idea h-how?"

"Lots of ideas. Long on ideas. Results, Boy. That's all that matters. Get me some results."

Marching orders, I called them. Bomber was skilled at giving them.

"We've got loose ends all over the place," he said. "Let's start tying them up. How does the coroner fit into this puzzle? I have a feeling the ubiquitous Dr. Bern is connected to obsequious Dr. Zukerman. Why? Maybe one too many of the doc's cash customers bought it under less than savory circumstances. How does Merilee fit in all this? We've been touting her as victim, but maybe she's not. Could be a perp—"

"N-no way," I gave him my opinion.

"I'm not arguing, kid—all I say is bring me some *evidence.*"

I'd like to say I left him with a thumbs-up sign, and on the way back to my room was struck with a lightening inspiration that paved the way to the perfect solution.

Instead I noodled ideas for my *Phantom Virus Concerto* as I now decided to title the piece I was going to get out of this case.

I decided to score it for a potload of percussion—two or three players lined up behind drums, timpani, gongs, glockenspiels, bells, whistles, ratchets, xylophones and alarm bells. Cacophony was my bag. I'd leave out the winds and brass, and use a lone viola to add some class.

The pandemonium in my head was the result of that gone-but-not-forgotten blow to my head that may have contributed to the cacophonous confusion.

Then for some unfathomable reason while I was humming the viola part—which I'd decided would represent the women in the case, Merilee and Regina Scioria for starters—I thought of that poor soul who held down the fort at the coroner's shop. It was an old saw in the investigation biz that the secretaries knew where the bones were stashed. Unfortunately they were also intensely loyal to their bosses.

Usually, I thought optimistically, but not always. At least, I thought, it's worth a call.

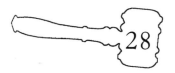

28

The next morning, Dr. Bern was back on the stand.

"Now, Doctor," Bomber began, "I asked you to search your records for certain copies of treatment records and billing records, did I not?"

"You did."

"Were you able to accomplish that?"

"Accomplish? Well, yes, I searched all right. But I couldn't find any."

"No records at all?"

"Not pertaining to Merilee Scioria or this case."

"Really? You want to tell the jury how you keep your records and how you searched them?"

"Objection," Carstairs said. "Compound."

"Well, okay, Doctor, answer either one of them, then I'll ask the other again. It will be simpler for your attorney to follow that way."

Bang went the gavel from the bench. Judge Packer's face was crimson with anger. Jude Carstairs was on his feet to protest, but she was doing it for him.

Of course, Bomber stood corrected.

"And, Doctor, if I asked what records you kept about the drugs you dispensed, what would you say?"

Jude jumped up. "I object, Your Honor. That is irrelevant—also vague and uncertain. Bomber is attempting to send smokescreens all over the place. Confusion and obfuscation is his game."

"*Au contraire*, counselor," Bomber said. "I am not the one hiding records here."

"Gentlemen! Please! Do I need to recess the court to give you a lecture on courtroom decorum? I will brook no extraneous editorializing from my attorneys, is that understood?"

"Yes, Your Honor," both men said. It was the only time there was stated agreement between them.

Bomber continued to badger Dr. Bern, dig at Jude Carstairs, and enrage Judge Packer. About all he succeeded in getting across, as far as I could see, was that Dr. Bern was a lousy record keeper.

The judge sustained Carstairs's objection to Bomber's question about how many feel-good drugs Dr. Bern dispensed, I think erroneously. But the tenor of the proceedings led me to a heart-to-heart with Bomber.

"Buh-Bomber," I said, when the court had cleared out for the day. It wasn't going to be easy.

"Yeah, kid—"

"C-can I talk to y-you?"

He looked startled. "Sure, kid, anytime."

I took a deep, deep breath. Sometimes I thought deep breathing would minimize my stutter.

"Do you think...I mean, c-c-could you be working again-against yourself? I m-mean, d-do you think the jury m-might be getting unc-comfortable...l-like it's overkill?"

"Overkill, huh? A lawyer's duty is to advocate his client's position to the fullest extent of his ability. Would you have me hold back, Boy?"

"N-no suh-certainly not. B-but when you've m-made the kill, sh-sh-shouldn't you let him d-die?"

The emotional strata I had worked myself up to was exacerbating my stutter. I certainly knew better than to try and tell my father how to try cases. I knew I'd be lucky to get through my heart-to-heart without collapsing into an epileptic fit.

"Ah, yes," he said. "How dead is dead?" Bomber mused at the ceiling. "Dr. Bern is a slimeball, Boy, do we want to sweep that under the rug? If ever a guy cried out for the overkill, it is ole doc Bern."

"B-but the jury..." I began, "and the j-judge."

Bomber turned alert— "What about her?"

"You are d-driving her n-nuts."

"Yeah," he said, with his soft tones. "She's very emotional. *Too* damn emotional for a judge."

Now I was on the spot. Bomber's Neanderthal prejudices were coming to the fore and battling *them* was as hopeless a joust as you could get.

"Women shouldn't be judges," he said, flatly. "They are bred for breeding, not for the trenches of war in the law courts. Just watch her, she about jumps out of her skin every time I get a good lick in. Going to get herself a good dose of apoplexy before this thing is over."

"Then what?"

He shrugged. "They carry her out in a stretcher, we got a good crack at getting a man. The men can usually take it. Oh, they clamp down now and then just to show who's boss, but they don't see me as a threat to their manhood as old Elsa Packer does."

"You know h-how m-many women you got on the j-jury?"

He shot a surprised look at me, "Course I know," he said. "We got nine. We wanted twelve, but life is compromise, boy."

"You g-get a chance to wuh-watch those women while you're making a f-fool out of the j-judge?"

Bomber got a sour expression his face. "Can't be done," he said, shaking his head. "You can only make a fool out of yourself. Nobody can do that for you. Either you're a fool or you're not. Judge Packer comes with the fool built right in."

"S-so wouldn't it be better politics with the j-jury to m-make the judge look better instead?"

"Not my job," he said, adamantly rejecting my suggestions. "Damn frustrating having to try a case before a woman. For millennia they've been in the background—caregivers, mothers, wives. Why, when your mother graduated from college, Adlai Stevenson gave the commencement address challenging all the women to add volunteerism to their foregone careers of motherhood and homemaking. Careers outside the home were not even mentioned. And Stevenson was a *liberal*."

I grunted, but he went on.

"So, how much can we expect of a skirt on the bench? Face it, kid. She's miscast. Women personalize everything. Everything I say is an affront to her dignity. Gets emotional. Bad for her. Can't stand the heat, she shouldn't be in the kitchen."

"But is it your job to d-drive her out of the k-kitchen?"

He shook his head. "It's my job to do everything I can for my client. If the judge lets it rankle her...not my problem."

He shook his head again. "No—you do the investigating—leave the courtroom tactics to me."

Well, I had planted the seed, I thought. It was the most I could do.

On the way out, Bomber changed the emphasis, but kept the subject. "You know what the definition of a judge is, Boy?"

"Uhuh—"

"A law student who corrects his own papers."

*   *   *

As we got deeper into the defense's case, things got bleaker. The next day Jude Carstairs put the coroner on the stand. He read his report saying Merilee Scioria's death was caused by Wanns Disease. And he mentioned her arm was a pincushion of needle marks.

Bomber set out to demolish the coroner in cross-examination, but he had no easy time of it. He asked questions about their office procedures, personnel practices, record keeping. Obfuscation questions I called them.

"Now, Dr. Zukerman, when you examine a corpse, can you tell how old needle marks are?"

"No."

"Can you tell who administered them?"

"No."

"Can you tell what was in the needles which caused the marks?"

"Not unless there are still traces in the body."

"In Merilee Scioria's case, were there traces of any controlled substance in her body?"

"I don't recall."

"Were any noted on the report?"

"No."

"So, you would not be able to tell, for instance, whether those needle marks you mentioned came from a diabetic injecting insulin or a drug user?"

"Just from looking at them, no," he said. "I don't know of a case where insulin is injected in the arms. But we do other tests. Insulin can be detected. None was."

"Is there anything else you can think of, Doctor, in your experience or education or reading, that could cause needle marks to the skin?"

"Other than insulin or drugs?" he shrugged. "No."

"What about tattoos? Aren't they done with needles?"

"Yes-s-s."

"Did Merilee Scioria have any tattoos?"

"Not that I recall." He frowned as he scanned his report. "None noted."

"Is that something you would ordinarily note on your report?"

"Only if it seems germane."

"Could it have been germane in this instance?"

"I don't think so."

"If there were needle marks that were caused by a tattooing needle rather than a drug needle?"

Dr. Zukerman shook his head. "No," he said. "Merilee Scioria didn't die of intravenous drug use, she died of Wanns disease. Needle marks were not a significant factor in her death."

"You are familiar with Wanns disease, Doctor?"

"Yes."

"You have done autopsies on Wanns victims, have you not?"

"Yes."

"How many?"

"Dozens."

"All right. Is there a unifying characteristic in the Wanns cases?"

"Their immune systems are shot. They can't fight the diseases they have."

"In your opinion, could drugs be the cause of a destroyed immune system?"

"I've read that opinion."

"What's your opinion?"

"I've also read the opposite. I'm a coroner, not a specialist in Wanns or R4. So, I don't know."

"But you would concede the possibility that drug use could destroy one's immune system?"

He shrugged. "I could," he said, without much conviction.

"And to your professional knowledge is JCD a drug?"

"Yes-s-s."

"And that could destroy a person's immune system?"

"I really couldn't say," Dr. Zukerman said. "I'm a coroner, not a virologist."

"And, as a coroner, you are charged with the responsibility of *diagnosing* the cause of death, is that correct?"

"Correct."

"So, would it behoove you to be current on diseases and their causes?"

"Objection, Your Honor," Carstairs said. "He's badgering by insinuation. Dr. Zukerman is a coroner. He testified to that. Mr. Hanson wants to make him seem deficient in some way because he isn't six other kinds of doctors at the same time."

"Nice speech," Bomber said.

"Overruled," Judge Packer said, then looked at Bomber. "And no more inappropriate outbursts from you."

"I stand corrected." Bomber turned his questions to matters of the preparation, duplication and storage of his report. "If someone wanted to change a report, how might he go about it?"

"It couldn't be done."

"Why not?"

"My signature goes on the report. I wouldn't sign an altered report."

How about altering it *after* you signed it?"

"I don't know what you mean. White out parts of it—forge my handwriting?"

"All right."

"Couldn't be done."

"Why not? Modern technology can do miraculous things."

Dr. Zukerman shook his head. "No," he said. "Access is impossible. Our reports are kept under lock and key. Original reports that I do are in my handwriting with my original signature. That can't be faked."

"Positively cannot be faked?" Bomber pressed.

"Absolutely, positively *not.*"

"Thank you for that, Doctor. Would you be good enough to write out a hypothetical report of a fictional autopsy during the lunch break and give it to me after lunch."

Dr. Zukerman stared at Bomber, giving his counsel time to hop to his feet. "Objection, Your Honor."

Bomber looked at Jude Carstairs with an exaggerated expression for the jury's benefit.

"On what grounds, Mr. Carstairs?"

"Irrelevant," he said. "If Mr. Hanson wants to make a circus out of this with magic tricks, we can always do the same. There is not a scintilla of evidence that the report was forged. He questioned the doctor at length about it. The doctor said it was genuine. We don't need to see that Bomber knows some master forgers. It is totally irrelevant to this case."

"What are you afraid of?" Bomber asked.

"It's a smokescreen, Your Honor. He's grasping at straws."

"Your witness stated unequivocally his reports could not be altered or forged. We are entitled to test his veracity."

"Gentlemen!" Judge Packer pound her gavel. "Enough! You both give me a headache. I'm going to allow it and direct the witness to produce a report during the lunch break, as close as possible to your regular reports. Is that understood, Doctor?"

"Yes, ma'm."

"It doesn't have to be an actual case, but it should pass for an actual case, all right?"

"Yes, ma'm," he said, but he wasn't happy.

"And now I'm going to recess court for the lunch break a little early. I need to break from all this bickering. I'm sure the jury does too. Be back here at one-thirty. And you two sparring partners," she said, looking at the lawyers, "take this opportunity to reconnect to your sanity."

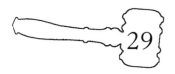

29

In spite of my realizing from years of bitter experience that my advice to Bomber would be taken *cum grano salis*, I actually thought he lightened up on Judge Packer. I hoped the jurors would recognize and appreciate it.

After court adjourned for the morning, Bomber wrote a name and New York phone number on a piece of paper. His memory for phone numbers was phenomenal.

"Who's this?" I asked, looking at the unfamiliar name, Karl Morgan.

"My East Coast master forger," he said. "Line him up for this afternoon. You can drive the thing to him in the city. If he'll meet you halfway, so much the better. When we get Zukerman's report after lunch, I'll rewrite it with some changes. You get Morgan to forge it with doc's signature. Have it back here as soon as you can."

When I looked up from the paper, I saw Regina Scioria hovering bashfully outside the railing that separated the audience from the players.

"Oh, hi, Mrs. Scioria," I said.

"Tod," she whispered, afraid she might be heard by the enemy.

I walked over to her, "Yes," I said.

"That man lied."

"Which man?"

"That witness. The coroner."

Bomber was packing up, but I wanted him to hear what Regina had to say.

"Bomber," I said. "Mrs. Scioria says the coroner lied."

Bomber got that look on his face when he suspects

someone is about to tell him how to try cases. "Oh," he said. "When?"

"When he said Merilee didn't have any tattoos."

Now we both perked up. "She had tattoos?" we said in unison.

She nodded sheepishly. "It was so embarrassing. But she covered her arms with them."

"How do you know he was lying?" Bomber asked. "He could have forgotten."

She shook her head. "Nobody would look at that beautiful girl and forget she was covered with tattoos on her arms."

"Excellent work, Regina," Bomber said. "You know the name of the tattoo artist she, ah, patronized?"

"Oh, no, I'm afraid not. We looked the other way. We couldn't even acknowledge what she'd done."

"Do you have any pictures of her tattoos?"

"Oh, no, Angelo wouldn't hear of it. If he found one of her someone else had taken, he'd burn it straight away. The only picture he took of her she had long sleeves covering everything."

"Are there any tattoo parlors in town?" I asked her.

"Oh, my, no," she said. "She would have had to have gone to the city."

"New York?"

"I guess," she said.

I knew what was coming—and it came.

"Looks like you've got your work cut out for you, Boy," Bomber said. It wasn't difficult to imagine the tedium in store for me—schlepping from tattoo parlor to tattoo dive with Merilee Scioria's picture.

If all the people who drove cars in Manhattan were certified and committed to institutions for the mentally unstable, as they should be, you wouldn't have to be nuts to drive in the city. Forty-five minutes to drive two blocks is *de rigueur* and parking is ten million dollars a day.

So, I availed myself of public transportation, armed with

a couple of pictures of Merilee Scioria, B.T. (before tattoos) provided by her mother, and the faux coroner's report from Bomber for master forger Karl Morgan.

He was my first stop. Good as he was at his trade, Karl Morgan did not live in the Golden Triangle, that enclave of zillion dollar real estate on the Upper East Side, but in an apartment on the Lower East Side where he had no less than five locks on his door.

He was a balding, affable man with a bone crunching handshake. He had a belly and a wheeze when he spoke.

I commented on the locks. "Do they do the trick?"

He threw up his hands. "You figure a con has to diddle with five of these puppies, it's got to slow him down some. That's all we can hope for here—slow 'em down some."

I gave him the stuff and he glanced at it. "Get right to it," he said. "That old man of yours, he's the best."

I had a feeling he felt that way, and I didn't question it. I got a little tired of hearing what a stud old Bomber was. I suspect he got Mr. Morgan out of a fix sometime before my time and this was the payback.

I left the blank forms, and the genuine report along with Bomber's handwritten notes on how he wanted the blanks filled in. Then I began my search for the tattoo *artiste*.

I made a list from the yellow pages and called them all first to ascertain they were in business on that fatal date some four years before when Merilee Scioria had had the job done. Then I let my feet do the walking.

Unfortunately tattoo parlors didn't inhabit the Golden Triangle either. I worked my way up from the Bowery and once I'd hit about 35th and Broadway, I noticed a drying up of the trade. Disney and Marriott had conspired to clean up the sleaze section in the heart of the theater district, and the tattooists were the second to go—right after the pornography shopkeepers. It was Disneyland on 42nd Street.

One of the guys I visited lower down said, "This art

ain't yet caught on with the swells from the Upper East, and as a consequence we can't charge enough to afford decent rents. So, we're stuck in these holes, like rats struggling to stay alive."

They say you have to kiss a lot of frogs before you meet your handsome prince. But after seeing a half-dozen of these guys, themselves covered with their "art", the frogs started to look pretty good. Tall, pudgy grizzly bears with wall-to-wall hair, with an occasional shrimp thrown into the mix. But the billboard-sized guys had more space for their art work. More's the pity. My vision became blurred with dragons spitting fire from their nostrils, reclining babes and arrow-pierced hearts.

The first seven guys looked at my pictures and shook their heads. All insisted they would have remembered working on a chick that good-looking. The only variable was the word "chick." Depending on the age of the practitioner, that changed to broad, babe, or girl, not to mention a few unmentionables.

The eighth bear was pay dirt. A chestnut beard with flecks of gray in it. Sitting behind what I'm sure he thought was a desk, his hands folded over his too-ample belly. The black eyes above the brown beard staring off into space in some unfathomable reverie. A plastic sign on his desk said Miles Konklin.

I showed him the pictures and he said, "Yuh," right away. "I done that one. Never forget it."

"Why's that?"

"Not only because she's a looker," he said, sighing his belly upward, then watching it fall back. "I tried to talk her out of it. Understand, I'm not in business to discourage business, but she was so young and pretty...." he shook his head. "Seemed such a shame."

"What did she say when you tried to talk her out of it?"

"Said it was necessary."

"Necessary? What did she mean?"

"Damned if I know."

"Was she...I mean, did she seem high on anything?"

"Nah, sober as a church mouse. That girl was class," he

said, exhaling heavily again.

"Oh? Some say she was a druggie."

He shot me a glance as though I had shot his best friend. "Who says?"

"Well," I was intimidated, "her doctor, for one."

"He's crazy."

"The coroner for another," I added. "He said her arms were covered with needle marks."

"Coroner?" he said. "What coroner?" He couldn't seem to connect his customer with a coroner.

I nodded in confirmation of the tragic news.

"Oh, no way," he said, and his face sank. "How?"

"Coroner claims Wanns disease."

"A girl?"

"We have a different theory. Think she was murdered."

"Oh, man, that's heavy."

"Yeah. She have any needlemarks on her arm when she came in here?"

"No way," he said, shaking his head vigorously.

"You sure?" I asked, cocking my dubious eyebrow.

"Course I'm sure," he said. "Wasn't a mark on her..." he dropped his voice, "before I decorated her." He sucked some air. "What a shame," he muttered. "Don't get me wrong. I ain't ashamed o' my work—just...some art goes better on some canvases than others."

"You sure... I mean, is there any way you could be mistaken about this? Wrong girl, maybe—maybe she was an addict but good at hiding it."

"No way, Jose," he said, shaking his head in one sharp motion. "You don't think I know junkies? I paint 'em all day long. I don't mind taking their money when they're outta their minds. Not just studs, I do a fair amount of broads now. It's getting big with broads." He pointed at the picture in my hands. "That's no broad," he said. "That's a lady."

"Would you—I wonder, would you testify in court?"

"Oh, court," he said, and let it hang there. "I don't do court so hot." He shook his head again. "No, I don't think so."

"But they're tearing her to shreds. Making her look like every kind of addict and hussy. You're the only one we've found who can straighten it out—save her reputation."

He drew himself up, converting his slouching persona into a formidable contender. "Give me their names," he said, with a menacing look. "I'll take care of 'em."

"Just a day in court is all it would take. We'd pick up, bring you back, pay for your time."

He shook his head again. "I don't do too good in court," he repeated. "I been. I know. Them lawyers, they twist your words around until you don't recognize nothin' you said. Sorry—wish I could help."

"Well, I hope you'll change your mind, Mr. Konklin." I gave him one of my cards with my hotel phone number and thanked him for his help.

When I turned to leave, I heard his voice as though from the bottom of a mine shaft. "Wait," he said.

My heart pounded in my throat. Was he going to change his mind and cooperate? I turned slowly.

He was staring at my hand—the one with the pictures. "Could I have one of them pictures please?" he asked awkwardly. The request did not come easily to him.

I looked deep into his black, restless eyes. "Sure," I said. "I'll make a copy of each and send them to you."

He was obviously moved by Merilee Scioria. Maybe the pictures would move him to court.

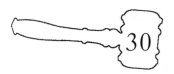

"You didn't mention the subpoena powers of the court when he told you he didn't want to testify?" Bomber grilled me after I told him the news of Miles Konklin, tattoo *artiste*. "Surely he is aware of that. And surely *you* are."

"Surely," I said. "B-b-but I t-thought you'd rather h-have a friendly witness than an angry one."

"But, Jesus Jenny, Boy, here's our breakthrough witness, and he doesn't want to testify."

I told Bomber about the pictures, ours and his, and my thoughts about broaching the testifying again when I delivered ours.

"Good thinking," he said. "Did you get the forgeries from Morgan?" he asked.

I turned over the envelope I was carrying and Bomber took the artifacts out and looked them over. A large smile broke out on his face. "Sure does nice work," he said, examining the product carefully.

Back in court, Bomber's questioning of the coroner that day was what is referred to in the trade as a fishing expedition, and Jude Carstairs objected to it, as such. Judge Packer allowed most of Bomber's questions.

It was relatively simple for Bomber to show that the coroner didn't know from straight up about forgeries. Dr. Zukerman was so cocky at the start of the questioning that it was almost fun to see him melt down as Bomber flumoxxed him with textbook ease. My only question was, what good did it do our case? Bomber was simply fishing in the hope that the demolition of the coroner would yield some residual benefit.

"He's an ally of Dr. Bern," Bomber said, in answer to my question, "and a man is known by the company he keeps.

Shakespeare said that in the Bible somewhere, didn't he?"
Bomber winked broadly at me.

Okay, so we had a small victory by confusing the coroner. Bomber thought it more significant than I did. In the hallway he said, "We're on a roll, Boy—let's tie it up with something substantial."

"Substantial?" I said.

"Yeah—what's behind him doctoring the document?"

The confusion must have shown on my face for Bomber set me straight: "You see any reason he didn't mention Merilee's arms were covered with tattoos? Not only that, but he said they were full of needle marks."

"Tattoos make needle marks."

"Hah! You think he'd have the nerve to hide behind that?"

"But didn't you just g-give him an out? Showing how easily a report could be altered without h-him realizing it?"

"Who, the doc? He's an innocent. A pawn. This thing goes deeper than some poor sap coroner."

I knew what was coming, and at times like that I tried to disappear within myself.

"So, get your buns out there, Boy. Why did Doc Bern want Merilee Scioria dead? My guess is it's sex or drugs or both. Maybe money—it always comes down to filthy lucre in the end. So, who was the guy wouldn't talk to you?"

"The Drug Enforcement Administration cops; c-close to the chest over there."

"So, break 'em down."

"Ha! I'm g-going to break d-down the drug cops? Yeah, r-r-right."

"You don't have to use a sledgehammer, boy. Wiles, use your wiles."

I couldn't wait to get away from him. When he started that kind of talk, there was no escaping. I was just about to duck out when Angelo and Regina Scioria came toward us both with hangdog expressions. I mistakenly thought good manners required me to stay.

I greeted them with a hearty relief because their presence got Bomber off his hobby horse about me being the shining-knight-on-a-white-horse hero of the piece.

"I don't like it," Angelo said.

"Don't like what?" I asked, when I saw Bomber was not going to lower himself to respond.

"This talk of tattoos," he said, with a sour face. Regina stood dutifully one step behind Angelo and let him do the talking. "I don't like..."

Bomber was seething inside. An idiot could tell that from looking at him, as he would say. The thing he liked least in the world was someone telling him how to do his job. He gritted his teeth and said, "I'm sorry about that, Mr. Scioria, but my job is to win the case. If you wanted a loser, there are thousands of lawyers in the woods who would fill the bill nicely. And if you've just decided you want to lose, I'll step aside with every gracious bone in my body, and you may retain a loser."

I could see Mrs. Scioria's face going the pain route while Angelo only seemed about to go ballistic.

"No, no," Angelo said. "We don't want you to quit. You're not a quitter, I know that much."

There was a sublimated joy in watching Bomber in a sparring match with someone who could hold his own. Angelo was such a man. That you're-not-a-quitter gem put Angelo right up there with the first team.

Bomber glowered at Angelo. "I *never* quit," he said, "when the client places his faith and trust in my judgment. If he doesn't, I become a loser and I lose interest. Your daughter is gone, Mr. Scioria," Bomber said, a little harshly, "gone, gone, gone. You knew this would be rough, and you wanted to go on with it."

"But it's so unnecessary."

"Don't you tell *me* what's unnecessary. I know my business. I know you want to preserve Merilee's memory as Miss New Jersey, but I never promised you a rose garden. Lots worse things than having a couple arms full of tattoos. We're on to something. I can feel it in my bones. You try to stop us now, I walk."

Angelo bit his lip. Was he holding back a tirade?

"Besides," Bomber said. "Your two million is contingent on us winning this case. You walk, you kiss the two mil goodbye."

"Well," Angelo said, crestfallen, "could you just...make ...go...a little easy?"

"No *damnit!*" Bomber bombed the little man with one of his bazookas. "*I* will try the case—you may want to consider trying it in *persona propria*. That's your option at this point. If you want me to continue, leave me alone," and Bomber walked away from us, with me staying behind to repair the damage, salve the wounds, which was so often my task.

Angelo was on the verge of tears. I had the feeling if he hadn't thought it contrary to the macho image he wished to project, we would have been knee-deep in tears. He moaned and groaned, whined and whimpered about his angel's memory and the needless besmirching of same, and I did the only thing called for under the circumstances: I agreed with him. And furthermore, I pledged to do all I could to keep the memory of her pure—the implication was I would bring this off with my expert investigative practices. I left him with the impression I would work nothing less than miracles, and she would come out of this thing as Joan of Arc and Mother Teresa all rolled into one.

When the Sciorias left me, I thought there was a slight bounce back in their step, but I couldn't be sure.

That was when I finally realized what this case was about for the Sciorias. It wasn't about money, it wasn't even about winning: it was about restoring their daughter's good reputation.

That was their perspective. To Bomber, the case was always about winning.

It was my job to see that their perspectives didn't become mutually exclusive.

I decided it was time to put in my call to the coroner's secretary. So, when I got to my room I called the coroner's shop and she answered the phone—on the fourth ring. Why so long? I wondered. I had visions of her sitting there staring at it trying to think of reasons for not picking it up.

"Coroner's office," she said, as though she didn't want to.

"Hi," I said, with a cheerfulness I hoped didn't sound too forced. "This is Tod Hanson. I was in there the other day to look at the records on Merilee Scioria. We're trying this case—Bomber Hanson is my father." I paused several times for a response of recognition from her—but it was not to be. I couldn't even hear her breathing. "Are you still there?"

"Um hum," she said.

"Well—good—I was wondering if you would allow me to take you to lunch?"

Dead silence.

"Hello?"

"Why would you want to do that?" she said, and I detected a hopeful, not a discouraging tone in her voice.

"Because I'd like to," I said. "I only spoke to you briefly the other day, but I have a feeling you are an interesting person."

"Interesting," she said flatly. Not a question—not a mimicking, just a flat mater-of-fact word.

"Yesss—" I let the sibilant sibilate, if that's possible. I think it was my grandmother who told me liars went to hell, and I did not reject that notion out of hand. Rather, I reasoned:

(1) All well and good if you are a grandmother.

(2) But in this business sometimes situation ethics are called for to save your skin.

(3) Where is hell anyway? Is it possible that is where all the interesting people are?

(4) If there is really a hell calling, perhaps I can redeem myself in the meantime. Like saving the case and vindicating Merilee.

She seemed all choked up when she said, "Since you put it that way…. When did you want to go?"

"How's tomorrow look?"

"Looks okay," she said, without having time to look anywhere.

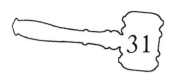

31

My luncheon with Elsie: I picked her up at her office. I
didn't see the coroner, but I couldn't miss Elsie. She was made
up to a fare-thee-well, and her hair was pushed to the top of her
head and held in place with the assist of a cold blast of aerosol
hair spray. She had chosen a sedate restaurant on the edge of
town. It was festooned with lacy Victorian frills, old dolls and
knickknacks from that era of excess. It was a small house con-
verted to this tea-shop kind of place, the clientele of which
seemed to be largely women—some of them quite large.

I always think hefty-sized patrons bespeak good food—
if you equate rich with good, and I am not above that equation
myself.

It turned out to be true. Little biscuits with strawberry
butter, créme fraîche, dainty sandwiches chock-full of cream
cheese and butter. Desserts dripping with whipped cream. Elsie
liked to eat, I could tell by watching her.

"I just love this place," she said when we were handed
menus. We sat on curvy wrought iron chairs with a table
between the size of a napkin.

I asked her for suggestions for ordering and she had
plenty. I settled for a pile of biscuits and the chicken swimming
in butter. The tablecloth was crocheted, as were the curtains.
There was a faint covering of dust on the place, which was
understandable. There were so many dust-catchers, it would
have taken a full-time crew to keep it clean. And then there
would be no room for patrons.

"Thank you for bringing me here."

"My pleasure."

"Ah," she said, "pleasure. Yes. Eating is one of the few
left to me."

"Oh?"

"Oh, yes. Expectations," she sighed. "I used to have them."

"You mean, you don't anymore?"

She twisted her lips. "Not so much," she said. "When we're young, we have hopes. I wanted a family and children. I thought that was after all, what women did, was it not? But that sort of activity requires the cooperation of a man and there were simply no men to be found."

I frowned. "It's tough," I said. "Sometimes I can't comprehend how so many people get together. Where did you try to meet men?"

"*Every*where." she said. "Bars, classes, churches, friends. I had a few close calls, but somehow the years slipped by and the men slipped with them."

Her crooked smile carried with it the years of coping with frustration.

She had been fairly attractive, I could see that in her expectant eyes and nubile nose. But the weight of disappointment had dragged her down while it puffed her up.

"All I have," she said, "is my job. I go home at night to an empty apartment—now even empty of expectations. You're young yet. You can't imagine what it's like not to dream—not to hope. I hope you never have to."

"Well," I said, after we ordered, "it must be interesting working for a coroner. How long have you been at it?"

"Going on twenty-eight years," she said.

"Wow."

"Yeah, I'm on my third coroner."

Is that right?"

She nodded.

"Have a favorite?"

"Oh, they're all so different."

How so?"

"Oh, personalities." She didn't seem to want to say more.

"It seems such a, well, an unusual way to make a living."

She shrugged. "We do what we have to," she said.

"Do you ever—I mean, go in there while he's cutting them up?"

"Oh, I've been, sure. You can't help it. But I don't look. I'm a clerk mostly. I don't get into the operation part of it."

"Files and stuff?"

"Yeah."

"Challenge you at all?"

"Not much."

"Can you keep your interest up after twenty-eight years?"

She shrugged. "It's a job. My life is outside the office."

"Oh—what's that?"

She stared at me blankly, as though she didn't understand the question. Then all of a sudden she burst out crying. I tried to placate her, but I didn't know how. Heads were turning, and I just knew they all thought I was some kind of heartless villain who had caused this outburst.

Her mascara was running, and the beehive on top of her head seemed to wilt. This was not turning out to be what I'd hoped.

"I'm sorry," she sniffled at length, trying to control her blubbering.

"That's all right," I said, and if my grandmother could have heard me she'd have known I was on a slippery slope to hell. But I could see getting herself under control was taking a lot out of her and anybody would have said the same under the circumstances.

"Oh, I'm sorry," she said again. The labor she expended controlling herself took a lot out of her.

"Was it something I said?" I ventured when she quieted down. "If it was, I'm sorry."

"Oh, no," she said. "On the contrary. You asked me a simple question about myself, and while I thought about it I realized no one had ever asked me anything about myself and suddenly that seemed tragic, and I just lost it."

"That's okay," I said again, not being too creative with my responses.

"I mean, why would you be interested?" she said, "a perfect stranger. Why would you care about me? Does it have something to do with the case you are working on?"

"Oh, no," I answered quickly. Forgive me, Grandma. "I told you, you seemed an interesting person to me. I'm across the country from home, I get lonely, too," I said.

She looked me over as if to test my veracity. I kept a straight face—and the funny thing was, I *was* getting interested in her. A woman whom no one ever asked about. In her late forties—that *is* intriguing, honestly, Grandma.

But during the ensuing silence, I realized I had backed myself into a corner. I sank back in the chair, strangely relaxed with the release of tension. I was not comfortable deceiving her to get information, and decided Elsie's worth as a person superseded our narrow needs. It was not a stance that was calculated to further my career or the goals of our case, but sometimes we have to give in to the human element. That is not, by the way, a hypothesis that my father would understand. Not, I suspect, because he couldn't but because he wouldn't.

We ate and talked mostly about her disappointments and the many puncturings of her balloons. My heart went out to her and I could tell she was pleased to have someone to talk to, and I was pleased to be able to do my bit in that regard.

The dessert she chose for me was strawberry shortcake—the same buttery biscuits covered with bright red strawberries topped with gobs of whipped cream.

She hummed in ecstasy as she took the first bite of hers. We ate in silent enjoyment for a spell, then she looked at me expectantly. I looked back and smiled a smile devoid of expectation.

She cocked her head. "But you haven't asked me anything about the coroner for your trial."

"I only came to talk about you."

"Sure," she said, "and butterflies give milk."

"No, no," I protested, "really. I've just enjoyed meeting you and hearing about you."

"But what did you get out of it?" she wanted to know.

"A great lunch," I said.

She looked at me in what I considered admiration at first, then I detected some small measure of disappointment. But I was committed. I had set my course in concrete and I saw no way of wiggling free.

Then without warning or fanfare Elsie opened the floodgates, and I floated with the tide.

"When the coroner came back from court he was fit to be tied. I expect your father got him really riled up."

"Oh, well, that's Bomber," I said modestly.

"Yes," she said, slowly. "So I've heard."

"You don't think the coroner thought it was personal?"

"Why I certainly do."

"But it's a lawsuit," I said, perhaps more naively than was reasonable in the circumstances. "He's just a witness."

"*Just*," she harumphed. "Well, he thought it went hard on him, I can tell you."

"I'm sorry to hear that," I said. "Bomber gets a little carried away at times."

She rolled her eyes. "I guess," she said. "The only other time I've seen the coroner so mad was when that drug officer came and looked at the same report."

"Merilee Scioria's, you mean?"

She pursed her lips and nodded. "That poor girl," she said. "I have a bad feeling about that whole thing."

"So do I," I said.

"That girl...she wasn't what they say she was."

I nodded with sage encouragement. "Do you remember his name—the drug officer?"

"Why, yes, I do. It was Adams," she said, then dropped her eyelids sheepishly. "I remember because I thought I'd like to be his Eve. He was a handsome devil, that one."

I don't know why I blushed. In this day that was pretty tame fare, but I blushed anyway—perhaps because she had shared this intimacy with me—perhaps because she was *volunteering* the information and my grandma could rest easy.

On our way back to her office amidst the cadavers, she gave me a lot of fascinating details that Bomber would find useful. Perhaps the tide was turning to our side.

We shook hands, she smiled a broad, contented smile. "Let's do this again," she said, and I agreed. (and you would too, Grandma!)

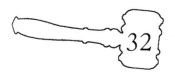

32

Bomber's subpoena of Dink Adams of the DEA met with the predictable hysteria. From the reaction you'd think Bomber was a Communist advocating the overthrow of the United States Government.

The feds hardly had time to read the subpoena before they shot back their:

MOTION TO QUASH.

Judge Packer said she would hear arguments in her chambers because of the "sensitive nature of the matter."

So, we lined up there on Monday morning like toy soldiers: Bomber and I, Jude Carstairs, Dink Adams and the DEA attorney Fred Imhoff, and of course, Judge Packer, who eschewed her robes and sat before us in a fetching burgundy creation, tailored as befitting one of her calling.

"All right, gentlemen," Judge Packer said. "Find a chair and sit in it." There was something about her manner that put me in mind of my sixth-grade teacher.

From the look of her chambers, studded with framed pictures on her desk, there was a man in the mix somewhere. I'd like to say he was ruggedly handsome, but that would be a little strong. He was nerdy, and I could see Judge Elsa Packer wielding the gavel at home, too.

Then I thought of Bomber's description of a judge being a law student who corrects her own papers.

Being reasonably capable adults, we found chairs and pulled them around her desk. I left mine floating behind Bomber, who sat facing the judge straight on.

"It seems we have a motion to quash a subpoena here," she began, giving a cursory glance at the documents. "Mr.

Imhoff, do you want to speak to your motion?"

"Yes, Your Honor, thank you, Your Honor," he said. He was a round-faced blond gentleman somewhere between Bomber and me in age, who carried with him the pomp and glory of the United States Government. He seemed to know his business, but he did ramble a bit. Hence we were treated to an engaging history of drug enforcement, as well as a heartrending account of how vital the work was for the insurance of a safe and sane society.

Bomber just looked on dumbfounded, wondering, I suppose, how much of this the judge could take.

After Attorney Imhoff waved the flag until we were all seasick, Judge Packer said, "Bomber?"

"Thank you, Your Honor. To reduce this to its prime elements, we have at hand the means of winning our case. The defense naturally doesn't want to hear it. There's a lot of smoke released into the atmosphere about sensitive government investigations—well, my clients are sensitive too. They've suffered the loss of their only child, as well as wanton destruction of her reputation. Now, we have the means of correcting that heinous slur on her good character and the defense wants to hide behind the *sensitivity* of the government. But in this country the *individual* is supposed to matter. She is supposed to count for something. We don't cavalierly trample the rights of the individual. This is not some totalitarian banana republic, this is *America!*"

Bomber was showing he could wave the flag with the best of them.

Judge Packer turned to Fred Imhoff. "How exactly would bringing Dink Adams as a witness in this case effect your investigation—and vice versa?"

"It would destroy our investigation," he said. "Years of work would be lost."

"And not calling him would destroy our case," Bomber added. "It would be unconscionable to leave the jury with the impression that Merilee Scioria was a no-good drug addict and Dr. Bern was an upstanding member of his profession when

Agent Adams has it in his power to set the record straight."

"You are surmising, counselor," Jude Carstairs said smugly.

"Surmising? Oh, really," Bomber said with his incredulous eyebrow hike. "If it is only surmise, what does Mr. Imhoff have to hide?"

"Sensitive matters—" Imhoff said.

"There we go again," Bomber said. "Maybe we should all take sensitivity training."

"You could use it," Jude Carstairs said.

"Very funny," Bomber said. "I'm sensitive to this entire case," he said. "I'm sensitive to the agony the Sciorias have suffered seeing their daughter falsely painted as a drug-addicted slattern. Merilee Scioria was a heroine—an undercover agent, working to nail Dr. Bern, a.k.a. Dr. Feelgood, the mass marketer of happy drugs. Merilee went so far as to get tattoos up and down her arms so she would fit in to the drug culture. The defense has gone to great lengths to hide that fact."

"We have not," Jude Carstairs objected.

"Will you stipulate to it?" Bomber asked.

Jude Carstairs waved him off.

"So, let me ask Attorney Imhoff what he is willing to have Dink Adams testify to in this trial."

"Mr. Imhoff?" the judge said, looking at the round face.

Imhoff shifted. "The department feels any testimony would irreparably compromise our investigation."

"Oh, come on," Bomber said, impatiently. "Surely you can find it in your heart to admit that Merilee Scioria was one of your undercover agents."

Fred Imhoff's lips tightened. "Open a can of worms," he muttered.

"Oh, for God's sakes—she's dead!"

Fred Imhoff shook his head. "Doesn't matter."

Bomber threw up his hands and looked at the judge.

She looked in turn at Jude Carstairs. "Mr. Carstairs?"

"I certainly understand where Bomber is coming from.

I just don't see how we can justify compromising an important—make that vital—federal investigation for the narrow interests of an insignificant law suit."

"It is nothing short of astonishing to hear Mr. Carstairs characterize this case as insignificant," Bomber said. "If it is so insignificant, let him stipulate that Merilee Scioria was an undercover agent, not an addict, and Dr. Bern was one of her targets—and he knew it—so he killed her."

"Oh, Bomber, that's preposterous."

"Preposterous is it? I suppose you have a more rational explanation? I mean, what are you hiding from?"

"We're not hiding at all."

"All right, gentlemen," Judge Packer said. "It seems to me you might reconsider some settlement in this case. I will, of course, seriously consider the motion to quash. The government's case on its face is persuasive. If Dr. Bern's comeuppance is one of your goals, it might be in the offing through the government's case. On the other hand, if you can't reach a settlement, I might let the jury hear the bare bones of the government's investigation."

"It would ruin our investigation," Fred Imhoff lamented.

"I think it might be worded in a guarded enough manner—but I will take that under advisement. I will welcome your suggestions in writing, Mr. Carstairs and Mr. Hanson. Now, counselors, do you think there is any possibility of a settlement?"

Jude Carstairs nodded noncommittally.

"So?" Judge Packer looked from one attorney to the other.

"I am willing to enter into further discussions," Carstairs said. "Subject to my client's approval, of course."

"Mr. Hanson?"

"Of course, once you give him the lay of the land he should be only too eager to settle. But if I know my clients, their main goal will not be dollars, but clearing their daughter's name. How we can do that without hearing from Dink Adams, I couldn't imagine."

"We shall see," Judge Packer said.

"May I humbly submit for your consideration, Your Honor, the minimal acceptable course for the plaintiff would be a signed and stipulated statement that there is a secret, ongoing drug investigation in which Dr. Bern is involved, and Merilee Scioria was an undercover agent," Bomber said. "The investigation is incomplete, Dr. Bern has not been and may not be charged with anything, and no inference of his guilt or innocence is to be drawn. Further information could compromise the case."

"Your Honor," Fred Imhoff fairly exploded. "That would be totally unacceptable. Any mention of Dr. Bern would not only compromise our investigation, it would *ruin* it."

"Very well," Judge Packer said, and it had that unwanted finality to it, so Bomber interrupted.

"Just a minute," Bomber said. "Who are we saving by hiding this? I submit only the defendant. He knew about this investigation long ago. Long enough ago to put Merilee Scioria on JCD knowing he would remove the person who was fingering him. In the extremely unlikely event he didn't know of this specific investigation, I've no doubt his attorney will tell him, hiding behind the shield of attorney/client privilege. Bern isn't going to be surprised by any of this."

"Your Honor," Jude Carstairs spoke. "This information will only inflame the jurors against my client. It is nothing but supposition at this stage—an investigation. My client's rights will be trampled if this innuendo is allowed to pass to the jury."

"Then avoid innuendo. Have Dink Adams testify and we'll get straight facts."

"All right, gentlemen," Judge Packer said, "you will have my ruling by morning."

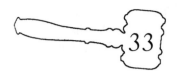

33

We gathered in Judge Packer's courtroom at nine sharp the next morning with the jury out of the room and the court reporter in place to take down the pearls of wisdom from the bench.

"In the matter of the motion to quash the testimony of the witness from the DEA, I have weighed the benefits to both sides, as well as the consequences to the government. I am ruling that a worthwhile and important investigation—one in which the government has invested considerable sums of money—might be destroyed by the testimony of Mr. Adams. While I do not in any way agree with Jude Carstairs that ours is an insignificant case, I do think it is relatively modest in the larger picture. Motion to quash is granted."

Bomber groaned. I must have too. At least I uttered a most unhappy sound. "She wants us to swim with concrete shoes," he said, as Judge Packer asked for the jury to be brought in.

Bomber quickly stood up. "Your Honor, may I make a request before the jury is brought in?"

"Yes, Mr. Hanson."

"Your decision is a stunning blow to the plaintiff. If he doesn't prevail in this case I'm sure he will appeal that decision."

Judge Packer allowed herself a curt nod of acceptance. No judge likes to be appealed; they all hate to be reversed. It's impossible to escape the former, difficult to avoid the latter, no matter how hard they try. Man is, after all, fallible.

"Under these trying circumstances, plaintiff would respectfully make two requests. One, that we may recess for the rest of the day; and two, that we may reopen our case."

Judge Packer's eyebrows lifted a couple of floors. If her eyes had been elevators, we might have been in the penthouse.

"Reopen?" she said. "Isn't that a little extreme, counselor?"

Bomber shook his head. "I don't think so, Your Honor. Under the circumstances I don't see an alternative if we are to give any consideration to the rights of the plaintiff. The defense has given us a hefty load to refute, and I feel the testimony of Dink Adams from the DEA would have put the case in the bag for us. That is not to be—so as an attorney with a sacred duty to my client, I must now look for a way to make my case without the witness who would have made it for me."

"Well," Judge Packer said, "that is far from certain."

"I beg to differ, Your Honor, though certainly nothing is certain, in my experience it would have been what the police call a slamdunk. Whereas now, I am obligated to find a way to prove my case peripherally."

"Highly irregular," Judge Packer said. "You can't do it on rebuttal?"

"I'd be happy to do it on rebuttal if the rules are relaxed to permit me to tread new ground."

"Mr. Carstairs, would you have any objection?"

Jude Carstairs arose with magisterial seriousness. "Your Honor," he said, buttoning his jacket, a nice houndstooth piece of goods that struck me as pretty racy for the New York lawyer. "I represent a client whose rights are every bit as important as those of Mr. Hanson's clients. I understand his disappointment at your learned, and, I think, eminently correct ruling. But if we are to turn court procedures on their head every time we are ruled against, there will most assuredly be no tomorrow."

Interesting phraseology, I thought, if a little florid.

"I would respectfully submit Mr. Hanson has had ample opportunity to prepare his case. I would have at any time been amenable to postponement, but he seemed eager to rush headlong ahead. Now, in the midst of the trial, he asks more time to prepare his case. I find this serves neither the cause of justice nor the concept of fairness."

Bomber seemed to have a secure feeling because he merely lifted his eyes as if to say, what a vacuous argument.

Judge Packer said, "Well, Mr. Carstairs, I am inclined

to assent to Mr. Hanson's request. I leave it up to you, what form you prefer it to take. Would you prefer to hold him to rebuttal, in which case you may complete your case now; or would you rather we reopen the People's Case, giving you the opportunity to retry your portion in a manner that suits you?"

Carstairs hung his head. "May I have time to consider the options?"

"Certainly," she said. "How much time?"

"Well, perhaps if Your Honor is amenable to granting plaintiff's request to recess today—though I would be opposed to it as prejudicial to the flow of the defense as well as an inconvenience for the jurors—I would request the same time to make our decision."

Bomber smiled. "Well, Your Honor, since you were kind enough to offer Mr. Carstairs the option when we all know you were not compelled to do so, I think it would behoove him to make up his mind in ten minutes or so. He is obviously attempting to disadvantage the plaintiff by equating this simple decision with our repreparing our case."

"But his case will be essentially the same," Jude Carstairs protested. "Why is it Bomber always gets out of joint when we ask the same accommodation he does?"

"Gentlemen," Judge Packer said, "are we getting petty again? Why do you feel you need so much time, Mr. Carstairs?"

"Well, I have to consult my client—"

"He is sitting right there," she said.

"And I'd like to do some case research in an effort to get you to reconsider—"

"Very well," she said. "Court will be adjourned until tomorrow at 9 a.m., at which time I expect to grant plaintiff's motion to reopen his case—unless you convince me otherwise, Mr. Carstairs."

When we adjourned for the day, Bomber turned to me, shook his head and said, "You've got a lot of work to do and so little time to do it."

He wasn't telling me anything I didn't already know. The object, he told me, was to make the DEA case without the

DEA witness.

"Not easy," I said.

"Not easy," he agreed. "It'll be like getting blood from a turnip, but it's all we got. Sink or swim."

"With those c-concrete shoes," I said.

Then he told me what he wanted me to do.

Blood from a turnip was putting it mildly.

I had forgotten my promise to make prints of Merilee's picture for Miles Konklin, the tattoo artist. So, my first project was to take the negatives to a one-hour place in the mall on the edge of town, where I was instructed in no uncertain terms that the one-hour motto referred to developing and printing, not to enlargements or special prints. "Two to three days, best I can do," said the gent with the stunning earring.

I smoothed a twenty dollar bill on the counter. "Would this help?"

He wrinkled his nose, and I could swear I saw the earring twitch when he said, "Nah."

Luckily I had a fifty and he sucked in some air. I could see the bulldozer grinding to clear the roadblock when he said, "Those two go together?"

"Could," I said. The hands with the dirty fingernails engulfed the greenbacks.

I called Miles Konklin from the wall phone in the mall. He answered with his downer voice—*sotto voce*—and I feared the worst. "Hi," I said *allegro con brio*, "how's it goin'? Tod Hanson here—"

"Who?"

"Tod... I was in there with a picture of Merilee Scioria."

"Oh, yeah," he said, brightening at the sound of her name. "What now?"

"Well, I wanted to tell you her pictures will be ready today."

"Pictures?" he asked, and my heart sank.

"Yeah," I said. "Remember—when I left, you asked to keep a picture? I said I'd have some prints made?"

"Oh."

"Yeah. I made 'em big—eight-by-ten."

"Oh, well, thanks. You have my address?"

"I...that's why I'm calling," I said. "I'm coming to you with the pictures. Did you find your pictures of Merilee?"

"Yeah—I took my art on her arms. No face though."

"Great!" I said. "Listen, Miles, I'm going to have to ask you a really big favor."

"Uh, oh," he said. "I don't like the sound of that."

"You'll be paid for your time—travel, everything."

"No."

"Afraid it's vital, pal," I said, then told him our dilemma of having to prove our case without the indispensable witness. "We *need* you, *and* your pictures. I wouldn't bother you if we didn't."

"Look, I'll write you a letter."

"Uh uh," I said, shaking my head, even though he couldn't see it. "Won't fly. Name of the game is cross-examination—"

"Yeah, I don't do so hot."

"Hey, you aren't on trial..."

"That's what those mouthy shysters make it seem."

"We'll see you aren't abused."

"No, thanks."

The impasse gave way to my petrified silence.

"Look, Miles, you want me to bring you the pictures?"

"Mail's okay."

"I want to talk to you. Look you in the eye."

"What for?"

"To convince you this girl you were so crazy about will drown in the slime of those 'mouthy shysters' as you call them. You want her to come off as the secret heroine she was or the slut they're making her out to be?"

"Who'd do that?"

"Dr. Bill Bern—to save his skin."

"What am I gonna do about that? I mean, all I can say is I tattooed her."

"She never told you why she was doing it?"

"No."

"Well, that's all you have to say. No sweat."

Silence.

"For Merilee," I pleaded.

"Yeah," he sighed. "Well, when would it be?"

"How does tomorrow morning sound?"

"Too soon. I got a couple appointments."

"Can you change them? Good cause."

"Gee-zus," he said, "you drive some bargain."

I gave him directions. "I'll have the pictures," I said. "You bring yours."

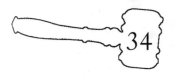

34

At six o'clock I went to The Three Bears bar. The barkeep was gearing up for the nightly rush and he greeted me with
an inquisitive, make that dumbfounded, glance—as if to say
back, "Are you nuts?" There was one old guy at the end of the
bar. He was staring into his glass. It was half full.

"Just felt like playing a little piano," I said. "You were
closest. Mind?"

He stared at me, and I hoped in that stare were visions
of his daughter. Everything was predicated on his vision of his
daughter. I could have just gone over to the keyboard and
pounded away, but I had an inkling it would be better to wait for
a sign from him.

I finally found it in an almost imperceptible bob of his
head. I went to the piano and saw that it had been moved at an
oblique angle to the bar. I sat and quickly began playing *Für
Elise*, the Beethoven piece that got the curious reaction from
Bartender Sam the last time I played it for him. Without turning
my head, I caught the bartender out of the corner of my eye.
Tears were forming in his eyes.

He didn't look at me when I returned to sit at the bar.
"She played it better," he said, and for some reason I knew he
would cooperate.

"The Sciorias lost a daughter too," I began gently. "And
her reputation is being unfairly destroyed. To what cause? The
cause of crime. I think you can help." I didn't press him, I didn't
ask for a commitment of even an answer.

He stared at the playerless piano and didn't speak for an
eternity. Of course I exaggerate, but at the time it seemed like
seven or eight weeks.

"You know," he said, after I thought I had earned a

week's vacation time, "what they had in common was their eyes." He moved his head slowly, one side to the other at the wonder of it. "Blue as the sky on a sunny day."

Wow, I thought. *He* should be writing the books.

"They were friends?" I asked, astonished.

"Oh, no," he said. "We were from different sides of town."

"So, how do you know Merilee had blue eyes?"

He stared at me as though I were tilling unwelcome ground.

Then it dawned on me. "She came in here, didn't she?" I said.

His stare didn't waver.

"To meet Buck Rogers?"

He didn't deny it.

"What happened?"

He looked at the piano then turned his head slowly in my direction. "My girl, she sure could play," he said wistfully. "You're bringing back memories," he added, in a way that let me know he wasn't happy about it.

"You have a lot in common, you and the Sciorias," I reminded him gently. "I expect you understand what they are going through."

He looked away again. "Merilee didn't play piano, did she?"

"Not that I know of. Even if she did, she couldn't hold a candle to your daughter."

"No."

"Hurts," I said.

"Yeah."

It was one of those times I wished I had a magic key to unlock the secret recesses of his subconscious or whatever I had to unlock to get him to give me what we needed.

I saw his chest heave before I heard the large vacuuming of breath that seemed for an instant to clear the entire barroom of its oxygen content. "I saw something," he said, softly.

"What?"

"It was back there," he threw his head toward a table in back. "Merilee came in here to meet Buck. She was dealing. It never made any sense to me. She wasn't the kind of girl got mixed up with those bastards. It just didn't fit. "Experiment a little," he threw out his hands palms up, "sure, but that was it, far as I was concerned. So, she shows up here with tattoos to hell and gone doin' business with Buck Rogers." He shook his head. "No way—

"They seemed to be getting into it pretty heavy, back there—I couldn't hear the words, but Buck Rogers was gesturing like a wild man. She was subdued. Suddenly he starts feeling her up and I'm ready to shoot over there and give him what for when he lifts her blouse and sweater and yanks this wire from her." He shook his head solemnly.

"Anything after that?"

"Nah—not so I...I didn't want any part of it. Oh, I heard her beg him not to tell Dr. Bern."

"What did he say?"

"He didn't commit. I expect he wanted *her* to commit to something."

"Will you tell your story in court?"

"No way. I like my shoes the way they are."

"Shoes?"

"I don't want 'em made of cement."

I'd hoped to find a ready rejoinder to that, but it was not forthcoming, perhaps due to my experience with that tap on my head.

"Okay," I said, "fair enough. But, just let me throw out some ideas." I was fiddling absently with the small, square paper napkin I found on the bar. I didn't even remember how it got there. "Stop me if I get out of line," I said, magnanimously. "Your daughter was a heroine to you. You loved her, she loved you, and you both knew it."

I watched him out of the corner of my eye. He was rigid, but he was taking it. It wasn't easy to talk to Sam about his late daughter, that much I'd learned.

"Now just imagine if you didn't know it and she didn't know it. Imagine how painful that would be—after she was gone. But maybe you had some people who could have cleared her name...but they wouldn't. Too dangerous—"

"Not my problem," he said, with a grunt.

"I understand," I said. I told him about the DEA refusing to testify at the trial and what a blow it was to our case and how we were trying to resurrect it without the use of the key government witness.

"I'm sorry, kid," he said, and *looked* sorry.

"Yeah, I hear you," I said. "But sometimes, don't you wonder what life is all about? Is it only playing it safe? Shouldn't there be factored in there somewhere taking a risk or two in a worthy cause? Sometimes stretch a little to give our lives some meaning?"

"You stretch if you want to," he said, wiping the bar which was already shining so brightly I could see our reflections in it. "Me, I'll take the few years I have coming to me."

I stretched my lips into a configuration of doubt. "I hear where you're coming from," I said, "but let's think about it a moment. If we nail the doc and Buck Rogers, haven't we pretty much disarmed the top echelon? I mean, who would be left to get worked up?"

"Oh, man, are you naïve. This is no mom and pop. This is big."

I was skeptical. "All the drugs are funneled through the doc. Any of his flunkies have licenses to practice medicine?" I didn't wait for an answer. He didn't have to give it to me anyway. "You put smiley doc in that all-expense-paid government hotel up the river, I expect the organization locally will pretty much grind to a halt."

"You kidding? Supply and demand. Demand is never ending. Take out the doc, there'll be someone else in here like that," he snapped his finger.

"But who?"

"Doesn't matter," Sam said.

"It doesn't? You get someone new in the territory, is he going to be angry at you for opening it up for him?"

"Bern will finger me from the slammer."

"In the slammer, Bern will be a flea," I said. "He's not Mafia—he's mom and pop. I expect he started small doing a legit service and it just sort of grew. Merilee Scioria was probably one of his charter members. Got out of hand. Then *she* got out of hand when she turned informer. It's an old story, the cops nailed her a gave her the choice: jail or tattletale. But I expect she took to the latter like a duck to you-know-what. Buck Rogers discovered she was an informant, told Bern and the doc panicked and gave her lethal doses of JCD. He managed to panic her until she thought that was her only hope."

"Why go to him?"

"Her doctor? Since she was a kid? Habits die hard. I know a woman who moved four hours from a town and still goes back—four hours each way—once a month to have her hair cut! Call it getting in a rut, call it comfort in the familiar— she certainly had no idea JCD would kill her. It's in all the media as the only inhibitor of R4. She got the letter from the dentist—had herself checked." I threw up my shoulders, "You know the rest. Maybe he phonied the results."

"Why don't you find out?"

"Yeah, good idea. Only the smiling doc seems to keep no records of anything."

"There can't be too many labs in this town who do R4."

"Good idea," I said. "I'll make you a deal. If I find out he never had the test made—phonied it—you'll testify?"

"Nah," he said. "Find that out, you won't need me."

"We'll need you."

He shook his head. "Too risky."

* * *

I was back at the bar at quarter to nine, laying in wait, as they say, for the nightly appearance of Buck Rogers.

When he came through the front door with his patented swagger, I saw Sam, the barkeep give him the eye and shift his line of sight in my direction.

There was less spring in his step as he strode over to the table.

"Busy," he said. "Another time."

I shook my head, "This time," I said, waving to the bench facing me in the booth. "Buy you a drink?"

"No, thanks," he said, but he sank his lanky body into the bench. "Make it quick."

I sucked up the bravado. "We know everything, Buck," I said.

He raised a noncommittal eyebrow. "What's everything?"

I told him. He listened impassively. "I also know," I said, "it was you who hit me on the head. The concerned visit to the hospital was a nice touch. I thought you were sincere. Still do. Underneath it all, I think you're a good guy."

"Heavy into the compliments..."

"I really believe you're in this deeper then you want."

"What makes you think so?"

I shrugged. "Call it intuition—a feeling for people. Gut feeling. Whatever. Something about that hospital visit. I saw real remorse there—not just some hard case trying to cover his rear."

Buck Rogers smirked at me. Could he have been saying he was playing me for one big fool? I listened to him breathe until I thought I'd explode. My thoughts turned bleak. What was keeping him from bopping me on the head again?

A wild-eyed runt came haltingly to the table. He looked like he had a major problem keeping food down.

"Buck," he pleaded.

"Outside," Buck Rogers snapped.

"Yeah, I know," he said with a pathetic turn of his mouth, spittle forming in the corners, "but, man, I gotta have some stuff."

"Outside—"

He turned and pointed himself more or less in the direction of the front door and somehow managed to navigate in that direction.

Reading about junkies can cause contempt in the heart of man. Seeing them is a different matter. How easy it is to say something glib like, we are captains of our fate—pull yourself up, fella—rise above your petty problems. But when you look into those blurry eyes, you get a different take. There are people who cannot rise above it, who wouldn't have any idea how to handle their own fate, who just can't get a handle to pull themselves up. A little dope will do it for them. Nothing else works.

It's okay for those of us who can more or less cope to pontificate about the evils of these controlled substances, as long as we don't have to see the suffering, the misery, the hopelessness.

I looked at Buck Rogers. "Ever get the feeling you are performing a service?" I said.

"All the time," he said.

"Let me tell you something else," I said, trying to keep the jitters out of my voice.

He raised an eyebrow.

"I think you liked Merilee Scioria. I mean, *really* liked her, and you were sorry to see what they were doing to her. But you couldn't stop it. You were in the middle of it—and when push came to shove, she *was* working against you. You and that smiley Dr. Bern. But even so—she was a beautiful girl—even with those tattoos up and down her arms. Turning on her must have been a lot harder than turning on some macho guy."

His blink gave me his answer.

"Let me let you in on a little secret I'm sure you already know. The feds are on to you. You and smiley Bern and the rest of the crew. I were you, I'd be looking for ways to earn some brownie points."

"Yeah?" He tried to look disinterested.

"Yeah. Like testifying for us at the trial."

"You crazy?"

"May seem that way at first, but think about it. Might signal the feds to offer you immunity. Way the wind is blowing, that might not be a bad idea for your side."

He seemed poised for the clincher. I gave it to him. "Scuttlebutt is you busted Merilee. She had on a wire and you felt it in the process of feeling her up, I believe—"

"Wasn't like that."

"Okay," I said. "Whatever. She's dead now. You ever doubt that R4...Wanns disease was a phony?"

"I'm no doctor."

"Me neither. Don't have to be. They killed her with JCD. You fingered her. Having any trouble living with that?"

He shrugged. "It's a rough business."

"Yeah, for the boys."

"She got in it by choice."

"You trying to convince yourself? I don't think it's working."

He didn't disagree.

"Think it over," I said. "I don't see any downside. Dr. Bern testified under oath he didn't know you." I shrugged my shoulders nonchalantly. I was looking like a cool cat. "Immunity," I said simply. "Way to go."

I got up and dropped a card with Bomber's local phone number written on it.

"How you gonna get me immunity?"

"Bomber'll arrange it," I said. "He's good at that stuff. Give him a call."

I winked at Sam on the way out. He was polishing glasses and didn't wink back.

Outside, I broke into a cold sweat. The bravado and bluff were coming up like a bad dinner. I sounded more like Bomber in there than like myself.

Maybe there is something to the genetic theory after all.

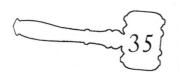

35

The next morning, Judge Packer ruled for Bomber all the way. Jude Carstairs had made only cursory motions of protest so we were reopening our case.

Bomber began with three drug company reps who read from their sales records the copious amount of feel-good drugs delivered to Dr. Bern.

Of course, Jude Carstairs objected strenuously, insisting (perhaps rightly so) that the matter was irrelevant to the matter at hand—the wrongful, negligent and perhaps preplanned death of Merilee Scioria.

"Most relevant," Bomber countered. "Dr. Bern had an enormous drug operation and this was the downfall of Merilee Scioria."

"Indirectly at best," Jude Carstairs said. "Let him show that Merilee Scioria was using these drugs, that the doctor prescribed them for her, that she sold them to others—*any*thing that connects them to her. His showing that Dr. Bern bought all the drugs ever made won't show that. He's fishing, he's slandering, he's speculating in such a fashion to prejudice the jury."

"Your Honor," Bomber chimed in, "in trial work, we lay foundations, one step at a time. I would think Mr. Carstairs was cognizant of that fact. He does, apparently, have a law degree from some accredited institution."

"All right," Judge Packer said, frowning. "I'm going to let it in."

Bomber told me later she was leaning to him because she had ruled against him on the big issue, that of the DEA agent testifying that Merilee Scioria was an undercover agent working on Dr. Bern.

Bomber told the court he was prepared to call five more

drug company representatives, but would offer their testimony for stipulation.

Jude Carstairs was glad to oblige, and the enormous purchases were read into the record.

Through it all, Dr. Bern sat at the defense table quietly, his expression showing only abject indifference. His confidence was uncanny.

News of the morning show was provided to me through the auspices of the great Bomber, and, accounting for his usual embellishment, it was more or less accurate.

I had been dispatched to visit the district attorney for the county of Essex to see what I could arrange on behalf of Buck Rogers and the immunity I foolishly promised him. It was Bomber's idea of punishment for the audacious and unfounded inducement I'd offered to get Buck to open up.

I don't want to say District Attorney Walt Esterhauzy laughed me out of his office, because he was not a guy noted for a sense of humor.

We sat in his office, which was Spartan next to Bomber's rococo melange of photographs and testimonials.

He listened impassively to my pitch, which was a naked plea for immunity for Buck Rogers to spill the beans at our trial. His hands and forearms rested neatly on his orderly desk.

When I ran out of steam on notes of duty, God and country, how mankind in general would benefit with Dr. Bern behind bars, a thin, meager smile played on Esterhauzy's stingy lips.

He shook his head once, "Bomber should have come to me in the first place. If he wants to go after a citizen of this county for murder one, this is the office to handle it. Now, mid-stream—under a precipitous waterfall, I'd say, whitewater from hell to breakfast—now, *now* he wants our help."

I suppose I could have said a lot of other things like making a stirring defense of the heroine's reputation, wrongfully sullied by the bad guys, but I had enough sense to know the D.A. was not interested.

He was the kind of guy who gave you an insatiable appetite to get back at him. I had only one recourse. That was my *Phantom Virus Concerto* for percussion and viola. I'd score the D.A. with kettledrums and low brass cords of frightening dissonance in the rhythm of a brisk jackboot march. Viola tacet.

When I fessed up my failure to Bomber, he smiled, not unlike the D.A., and said, "Politics, my boy, it's all politics. And ego, of course, but the two come down to the same thing."

* * *

That afternoon, Bomber got the preliminaries with Miles Konklin out of the way: name, address, occupation—to which he answered, "tattoo artist." He had wanted to say "epidermal design artist," but Bomber talked him out of it.

"Don't want to get too highfalutin'," he said. "Cuts into your believability quotient."

Miles Konklin was good on the stand. His worry seemed misplaced. He came across as a guy who'd rather be somewhere else, but while he was here, he'd tell it like it was.

Bomber asked if Miles ever turned away business.

"Well, I'm not in business to turn it away," he said, eliciting a laugh.

"Ever have people come in for tattoos you don't think are suitable candidates?"

"Yes, though I'm selling tattoos, understand. It's how I make my living. I got nothing against 'em, see. But ever' once in awhile someone comes in don't hit me right."

"How did Merilee Scioria hit you?"

He twisted his nose, then shook his head sharply, "Not too good."

"Would you explain that please?"

"She's a very pretty girl," he said. "Oh, I don't mean I get only lowlifers. Used to be more that way I suppose, but these days you're just as liable to get a society matron as a drunk sailor."

"Merilee Scioria tell you what she wanted done?"

"Yeah. That was the strange thing. See, the society matrons and them want something small, simple—an' usually it's out of sight—or maybe a butterfly on the shoulder so you can cover it up or show it just as pleases your fancy at any given time."

"Is that what Merilee wanted?"

He shook his head in disdain. "Said she wanted stuff up both her arms. I tried to steer her to something more, well, becoming, but she wouldn't hear of it."

"What did she want on her arms—what drawings?"

"Marijuana plants, coca, poppies—"

"What do they have in common?"

"They're the plants drugs come from."

"Did you notice anything about her demeanor?"

"De what?"

"How she looked or acted."

"She looked good," he said, as though he were trying to relive the time. "She was a looker, all right."

"Did she seem strung out on drugs?"

"Oh, no, she was perfectly sober."

"Not drunk or anything?"

"No."

"I suppose you get drunks from time to time in your business?"

"Lots of 'em."

"Dopeheads?"

"Sure."

"So you know them when you see them?"

"Oh, yeah."

"And Merilee...?"

"Definitely not."

"All right. How would you characterize her mental attitude?" Bomber asked.

"Troubled," Miles answered without a beat.

"What makes you say that?"

"She was gruff, uptight, frowning. I said to her, 'Hey you're an attractive young woman, but you don't look too happy. The thing about tattoos is they're permanent. Can't wash 'em off in the morning. Not the kind of thing you should have done in anger.' 'I'm not angry,' she snapped at me. 'Coulda fooled me,' I said. 'Who you think you gonna get back at running all these drug plants up and down your arms?'"

"What did she say to that?"

"Just tightened her lips. I tried again to have her go for just a leaf on her shoulder or belly to try it out—see how she liked it. She was definite. She wanted the whole ball of wax—"

"So, what did you do?"

Miles shrugged. "I'm in business to make money," he said. "She'd a gone down the street. So, I did it."

"Did she say anything else to you while you were tattooing her?"

"She was pretty close-mouthed. When it was all over, she looked at her arms—up and down one then the other and she said, 'That ought to convince them.'"

"Thank you, Mr. Konklin. No further questions."

Jude Carstairs looked startled, like he wondered, since Bomber didn't follow that up, if he was being set up for a trap. That was just as Bomber had planned it. He knew Miles Konklin would not testify that Merilee had said anymore, or explained what she meant by 'that ought to convince them'.

You could see the gears grinding in Jude's head, weighing the relative risks of leaving that statement to the jurors' imaginations without identifying who the "them" was. Bomber would have them believe the "them" referred to Dr. Bern and Buck Rogers. But no one said it did. So, Jude Carstairs must have wondered if he asked that question what response he'd get. Bomber could always come back on redirect and ask. But Jude Carstairs knew, and he knew that Bomber knew, the impact would be much greater if the answer came to a question of the defense attorney on cross-examination. Bomber knew there was no answer, but rather than clarify that with a question of his own, he enjoyed seeing Carstairs squirm.

Then Attorney Jude Carstairs made an elaborate shrug of his shoulders as if to say to the jury that testimony amounted to nothing and with a studied, insouciant tone said, "No further questions." This also forestalled Bomber from asking any more questions of Miles Konklin, the epidermal decorator, and leaving the jury to wonder if Bomber might have had anything more to ask.

He hadn't.

*　　*　　*

I went back to the The Three Bears bar at slack time—around dinner. Sam was behind the bar polishing glasses again. It seemed to me that was all he did when he wasn't serving drinks. And now that I think of it, I believe he had to keep his hands moving so he wouldn't go nuts.

He seemed to stiffen when he saw me. I could tell what was going through his mind—I told you no, kid, and I mean no.

I didn't say anything, but nodded in the direction of the piano.

He fixed me with his meanest stare. (He was really a pussycat. How could he have been anything else, still selling booze after his daughter was run down by a drunken driver?) He held that stare for a long time while polishing the life out of the glass at hand. I could tell he wanted to make me sweat, but I don't think he realized how easily that was accomplished.

He finally let his head bob, but not without telegraphing his feelings of disgust.

I went to the piano and started with some gentle Chopin preludes. I didn't look up. The corner of my eye caught Sam at the bar polishing away, making a Herculean effort to look insouciant.

I swung into Mozart's twelve variations on *Twinkle, Twinkle Little Star*, then his popular C Major Sonata. On to

Mendelssohn's E Minor *Rondo Capriccioso*. A few snippets from Bach's Well Tempered Clavichord, Book One—all the while trying to divine what moved Sam. I decided I had to get more romantic. I switched to Schumann: The *Träumerei*, the *Aufschwung*, opus 12.

The place was filling up when I hit him with Debussy's *Clair de Lune* again and *Arabesque.*

I thought I heard him draw a breath, or perhaps sniffle during the schmaltz. So, I continued it with some Brahms, Liszt and Rachmaninoff. The schmaltzier I got, the more affected Sam seemed to be.

By this time I was at the keyboard about three hours, and I vowed to stay there until (1) they closed, (2) he threw me out or (3) he agreed to testify. I felt that was about the order of likelihood.

For a change, I did a few Bartok and Prokofiev simple pieces. I'm not a great pianist—I couldn't make my living on the concert stage, but that night something came over me, and I don't believe I ever played better. It was as though I had a cause and that cause was Merilee Scioria, and I felt things coming out of me I didn't know were there.

I made a point of not looking at Sam. But I was just as careful to steal the sidelong glances that told me whether or not my music was striking a chord.

I had been holding back on *Für Elise*, but I wanted to play it as well as Sam thought his daughter played it, and who knew how that might have been. It was a piece so many played—often mechanically—often pitifully, but I wanted to pack it full of all the pathos, delicacy and gusto Beethoven must have thought he was putting in it.

When I began the single notes that started the piece, I felt an adrenaline rush that almost knocked me off the bench. I had neither the energy nor the opportunity to check Sam at the bar. The place had thinned out and Sam was not extra busy, but I had been transported, and the notes flowed out my fingers as though drawn by the goddess of music.

Those main theme notes just floated on air as Beethoven (and I) returned to them again and again. The arpeggios of 16th notes swept along with a soulful sweetness I had never imagined.

As I arrived at the end, I closed my eyes for the theme and closing. I was so emotionally spent, I didn't think I ever wanted to open them.

When I finally did open my eyes, I saw Sam standing over my right shoulder. His gaze was straight ahead and steady—as though he were visualizing an apparition.

It seemed like I could have replayed the whole program before he spoke.

"You win," was all he said.

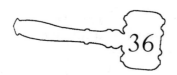

36

Sam the bartender did us proud, as they say. On the stand, he recited what he told me about Buck Rogers discovering the wire on Merilee Scioria and the ensuing argument.

Jude Carstairs cross-examined.

"Are you an expert on concealed listening devices?"

"No, sir."

"Any training in them whatsoever?"

"No, sir."

"And just how much of the alleged conversation did you hear?"

"I heard Merilee say 'Don't tell him—please don't tell Bern.'"

"Did you hear any response from Buck Rogers?"

"Not actual words, no."

"Well, any gestures, movements, sounds that you could quantify in words?"

"He seemed angry, is all I can tell you."

"All right, but you don't know angry about what?"

"Well, the subject was her wire. She was obviously trying to entrap him."

"I move that be stricken from the record, Your Honor, it is nonresponsive and speculative. I would also appreciate if you would admonish the witness to only answer the questions asked."

The judge obliged.

"All right," Jude Carstairs proceeded. "Isn't it true that all your conclusions about the scene you witnessed are pure speculation on your part?"

"No—"

"No? What is not speculation?"

"I know Buck Rogers. He came in the place every night. I know he's mixed up in drugs."

"How mixed up?"

"He sells them." Sam wet his lips. I hoped he knew how proud of him I was. It didn't look easy.

"Ever sell any to you?"

"No—"

"So, you have no firsthand knowledge...."

"I've seen it."

"What did you see?"

"Money exchanged for drugs."

"What kind of drugs?"

He shrugged. "All kinds."

"Did you ever intercept any of these so-called drugs and test them?"

"No—"

"So, you don't know—it could have been powdered sugar?"

"Expensive powdered sugar," he smirked. I was, as I said, proud of him, but I was beginning to wonder if I had done the right thing begging Sam to jeopardize his safety with this evidence which Jude Carstairs seemed to be easily demolishing.

Carstairs kept hammering away at Sam who seemed to sag a bit, as who would not? We always hope the enemy will overkill a witness and lose the sympathy of the jury doing so, but Jude Carstairs was no piker. He made his points, then sat down.

"Damage control," Bomber whispered to me as he rose to take another turn at bat.

"Sam, how long has Buck Rogers been coming into your place now?"

"I expect it's going on seven, eight years."

"And you said he came in about the same time every night?"

"Nine o'clock," he nodded. "You could almost set your watch."

"When he came in at nine, what did he have to drink?"

225

Sam turned his head the once. "Didn't drink."

"Oh? So, he just came in to schmooze with you?"

"Didn't schmooze neither."

Bomber raised an eyebrow. "Oh? So, why did he come to your bar at nine every night?"

"Objection—calls for speculation."

"I'll withdraw," Bomber said, magnanimous was his bag. Rephrase. "What did you observe, if anything, Buck Rogers doing at your bar?"

"He met people. Transactions were made. Money given to him in exchange for packets—"

"You see how much money Buck Rogers sold these packets for?"

"Twenty to fifty—varied."

"Did you form an opinion what was in those packets?"

"Objection," Carstairs bleated. "Indefinite. He claims there were many packets."

"A great many," Bomber agreed heartily. "Seven or eight years of nightly rounds. I asked for his opinion."

"He may answer," Judge Packer said.

"Drugs," Sam said simply.

"In your opinion?"

"Yes."

"Can you tell us how you formed that opinion?"

"I know what drugs look like. I've seen 'em around for years. And I know no one pays twenty bucks for powdered sugar. And I know what druggies look like."

"Thank you, Sam—one more question if I may. Did you want to come here to give this testimony?"

"No."

"Why did you come?"

"Your boy there," he pointed at me, "talked me into it. For the good of mankind," he smirked.

"Why didn't you want to testify?"

"Because," he shrugged. "I'm afraid of being murdered."

"Thank you, Sam, and thank you for coming. You may step down."

"Just a minute," Jude Carstairs bounced to his feet. "Not so fast. You don't walk away from an insinuation like that so easily. Did someone threaten to murder you?"

"Don't have to," he swiveled his head. "You don't mess with drug traffic and live to tell about it."

"Is that so? What is your authority for that?"

"Read the papers," he said, as though that were self-explanatory. "Look around you."

Jude Carstairs looked around the room as if to mock the witness. "Well, did anyone specifically threaten to kill you?"

"Objection," Bomber said, feigning fatigue and not getting up. "Asked and answered."

"Sustained."

"Who do you think might kill you?"

"Any of them."

"Who is them? Buck Rogers?"

"Sure."

"Surely you don't think Dr. Bern would kill you?"

"Why not?" Sam shot back, giving the doc an opportunity to work his plastic face in the service of outrage. That dissolved into a shaking of his head at the ridiculousness of it all. I didn't know much about Dr. Bill Bern personally, but I knew no one could expect to beat him at trial by underestimating him. He had a winning way about him, even if he was a moral pygmy whose word was as good as three-week-old hamburger.

The questioning petered out, and we were given a much needed recess.

At the plaintiff table, Angelo and Regina Scioria looked glum. Strange, I thought, how these amateurs had a sense of the way the wind was blowing.

Bomber stood, patted Angelo on the shoulders with both hands, as if that would buck him up, and left the courtroom without a word.

*   *   *

It was Fifth-Amendment time with Buck Rogers. And the two fit each other like a kid glove. The fun thing about the Fifth is if you take it at all, you must take it in response to every question. So, if you are asked, among other things, what you had for breakfast, you have to say, "I refuse to answer that on the grounds that it might tend to incriminate me."

But Bomber had a field day bombarding Buck Rogers with questions that tended to incriminate him by his evasive answers.

"Mr. Rogers," Bomber began. "You're a drug dealer, aren't you?"

"I refuse to answer that on the grounds that it might tend to incriminate me."

"Why would it incriminate you?"

"I refuse to answer that on the grounds that it might tend to incriminate me."

"Did you know Merilee Scioria?"

"I refuse to answer that on the grounds that it might tend to incriminate me."

"She worked for you pushing drugs, didn't she?"

"I refuse to answer that on the grounds that it might tend to incriminate me."

"But she was really an undercover agent for the Drug Enforcement Agency of the federal government?"

"I refuse to answer that on the grounds that it might tend to incriminate me."

Bomber kept up the questions as though establishing his case with the questions themselves. Buck Rogers used the same Fifth-Amendment shield to answer each of them.

"Are you familiar with The Three Bears bar?"

"Don't you stop there at nine every night to make drug deals?"

"And didn't you meet Merilee Scioria there in the course of this commerce and discover she was wearing a wire to record conversations with you to entrap you?"

"You worked for Dr. Bern, didn't you? He supplied the drugs for you to peddle?"

"You hit my son Tod—seated here at the plaintiff's table—over the head in his motel room, didn't you?"

Jude Carstairs rose to his feet with a posture of reluctance. "Your Honor, Bomber is trying to badger this witness with unfounded, unsupported innuendoes to establish some evidentiary base with no foundation other than his own recitations. I must object to this as being without foundation and inflammatory."

"Your Honor," Bomber said. "I am trying my best to establish foundation, but the witness refuses to answer anything. All he has to do to defeat my questions is say no."

The judge looked down at the witness. "Mr. Rogers, are there any questions you would answer?"

"On advice of counsel, Your Honor, I must refuse to answer all questions on the grounds that they might tend to incriminate me."

"Very well, that is your constitutional right and I can't do anything about it, except suggest to the district attorney some investigation of your activities might be in order. You may step down."

Bomber thought, and I agreed, Buck Rogers did us more good than if he had just said no to all the questions.

*   *   *

The local paper played into our hands, as I had hoped it would.

BARTENDER FEARS FOR LIFE

ran the headline. The story told it pretty much as it was. Later that day Sam called to tell me he had had all kinds of calls and visits from patrons who had banded together to protect him. They were taking shifts watching the bar and his house, and the thought of this simple goodness brought out the old tears in me.

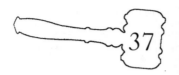

37

Jude Carstairs put on an effective rebuttal case. Not only did Dr. Bern find the two lab reports that classified Merilee's blood sample as R4 positive, he produced the lab technician who did one of the tests. She was a tough-looking broad on the witness stand. If women played football, she would have been a linebacker. Her name, fittingly, was Olga Tartoff. She wore clear-rimmed glasses and a severe business suit, medium blue, cut for her by Oram the tent maker.

Bomber's cross-examination was predictable. He had been reduced to the chore of creating doubt. He did it the simplest, most obvious, way. "Miss Tart-off," he said, emphasizing the Tart (as though any juror would be able to imagine her in that role). "You testified you tested Merilee Scioria's blood for R4, correct?"

"Yes."

"How did you know it was her blood?"

"It was on the form. Her name was on the request for analysis form from Dr. Bern."

"You didn't take the sample yourself?"

"No. Dr. Bern did that."

"Were you there with him at the time?"

"No, I was not."

"So, what besides his scrawling her name on this sheet do you have to support the contention that the blood was hers?"

Olga Tartoff looked baffled. Bomber had asked the question with enough convolution to give her pause. "Well," she said, "whose blood would it be?"

"An excellent question," Bomber said. "I'm supposed to be asking the questions here, but I like yours better."

"Objection," Carstairs said, "he's ridiculing the witness."

"Ridicule? I told her she asks better questions than I and you call it *ridicule?*"

"All right, Mr. Hanson," Judge Packer said. "You know better."

"I stand corrected." The low bow followed. Judge Packer had no talent for hiding her annoyance.

"Let me ask you this, Miss Tartoff: other than the name on the request form, do you have any way of knowing whose blood you are testing?"

"No."

"Ever mix up the forms?"

"No."

"Could it happen?"

"I suppose anything is possible. Hasn't happened to me."

"How do you know?"

"I make only one test at a time. The form is attached to the vial. There are no other forms on my testing table."

"Could someone switch forms before or after you tested?"

"Why would anyone do that?"

"You're asking the questions again Miss *Tart*-off. Please just answer. Is it possible?"

She shrugged her massive shoulders. "If you had criminals working in the lab, I suppose."

"It would take a criminal to mix up some forms?"

"Well, no one else would do it on purpose."

"You can't imagine any scenario where someone would want to change blood samples?"

"No."

"Well, let me give you a hypothetical example and you tell me if it's possible, all right?"

She nodded with taut, dry lips.

"Someone wants another person to think that other person is R4 positive. Scare him, whatever. So that someone puts the form on another vial—already positive—"

"Why do that?" she said. "He could just fill out the form positive. If you are going to lie about it, why bother with the test?"

"Another excellent question, *Tart*-off. Or how about the doctor sending you a sample from someone known to be R4 positive—putting a different name on the form. Possible?"

"I guess—but why would he?"

"Thank you, Miss Tart. You've asked enough questions for today." If Bomber added the off to her name, I didn't hear it.

Jude Carstairs offered to produce the technician from the second lab, but Bomber was willing to stipulate the technician would say essentially what Olga Tartoff said. "And," he whispered to me, "not half so wonderfully for us."

A modest parade of doctors followed, who proclaimed virtually in unison that Dr. Bern did exactly the right thing and handled the Merilee Scioria case in the highest traditions of the medical profession.

On cross-examination, Bomber asked them all the same question. "Doctor, did you ever examine Merilee Scioria?" ("No.") "Ever even meet her?" ("No.") "Ever do any tests on her blood or anything else?" ("No.") "Do you have any personal knowledge of how the blood test was conducted or if in fact the sample that went to the lab was Merilee Scioria's blood or someone else's?"

This last question met with various evasions and forms of protest, but they all came down to the negative.

Smiley Bern made another trip to the stand in his inimitable, affable manner to answer the question, "Now, Doctor, did you personally take the blood samples in question from Merilee Scioria?"

"I did."

"And were they in your possession at all times from the time you extracted them from Merilee Scioria's person, until they were sent to the labs?"

"They were."

"Why did you take *two* samples?"

"To be sure there was no mistake in the analysis of her blood. Sometimes blood changes. It's just safer to get a second opinion."

"Thank you, Doctor. Now, did you at any time exchange Merilee Scioria's blood samples for anyone else's?"

The broad smile of incredulity bathed the doctor's face. "That's *ridiculous!*" he exclaimed, with admirable outrage.

Jude Carstairs smiled, too. They were a happy bunch—and no wonder.

Bomber rose to his feet. "Doctor," he said, "that was an admirable display of outrage—I wonder if you are familiar with the Shakespeare line that goes, 'The lady doth protest too much, methinks'?"

"Objection!"

"Oh, let him answer," Judge Packer said.

"I've heard it."

"What does it mean to you?"

"Objection, Your Honor," Jude Carstairs said. "I must object. Completely irrelevant and highly prejudicial—just the question, even unanswered."

"Overruled."

Dr. Bern shrugged. "I think Shakespeare was trying to say that if you protest too much that something is true, maybe it isn't."

"Very good, Doctor. Could that apply to you?"

"Objection—vague and uncertain."

"Well, Mr. Hanson, clarify the question. Rephrase."

"All right. Doctor, you just answered your attorney's question about whether or not you exchanged blood samples with Merilee Scioria's sample by saying 'That's ridiculous.' Am I correct?"

"Yes. It is a ridiculous notion."

"Just so," Bomber said. "But in that histrionic reply—"

"Objection!"

"Yes, leave out histrionic, Mr. Hanson."

"All right. In your *reply*, Doctor, were you aware you did *not* answer the question?"

Dr. Bern looked surprised. "I answered it."

"No, you said it was ridiculous. The question called for a yes or no answer. Granted your attorney let it go—he apparently didn't think you were passing judgment on the quality of his questions."

"Objection."

"Yes, Mr. Hanson, no speechifying, please."

"I stand corrected," Bomber said, with the bow. "Now, Doctor, if you please, will you answer finally the question your attorney put to you before he turned you over to me? Did you switch Merilee Scioria's blood samples with someone you knew to be R4 positive?"

"That's...rid..."

Bomber held up his hand. "Don't comment on the question, just answer yes or no—"

"No!"

Bomber stared at him for a few seconds, then said. "Thank you for your answer, Doctor. It was a long time in coming."

Jude Carstairs was on his feet, pleading. "Your Honor, please—"

"Yes, Mr. Hanson, if you don't want to be cited for contempt, let's have no more of that."

Bomber faced her and bowed his head. "I stand corrected," he said, and she rolled her eyes.

On our way to the lunch break, Bomber whispered to me, "We're going to need a miracle, Boy."

Then I saw Elsie Lichtenwalner sitting in the audience, still and white, as though she had seen a ghost. Everyone around her had left, but she sat there as if she were some waxen mummy.

I would be less than honest if I said in that moment I saw her as our miracle.

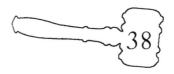

38

After I spotted the coroner's secretary in the audience seats, looking so strange, I naturally went over to her and gave her my hail-fellow-well-met greeting, "Elsie! Nice to see you. What brings you out to this circus?"

"Guilt," she answered with surprising strength.

The weight of her pronouncement dropped me into the seat in the row in front of her, I turned to face her as Bomber continued on into the corridor, oblivious of my absence.

"Guilt?" I asked.

She nodded solemnly. If I didn't think it impossible, I would have said Elsie looked exactly as she had when I took her to lunch. Same beehive hair, same makeup, same outfit—maybe she had only one.

"Guilty secret," she said, without adding a great deal to the available fund of knowledge.

"Yours?" I asked, "...or someone else's?"

She looked straight at the judge's bench and pursed her lips.

"Can you tell us about it?" I asked. "Have lunch with Bomber and me and tell us all about it."

"Oh, that's not necessary," she said. "You already took me to lunch—and that was one of the nicest times of my life."

I'm sure I blushed. I could tell she wanted to go, but didn't want to impose. She didn't seem to grasp how important her information might be to our case. Innate modesty, I suppose. "Please," I said. "You'd be doing us a tremendous favor."

"Me?" She couldn't believe it.

"You—" I held out my hand as I stood. "Please."

She took my hand and I led her to the hallway where we found Bomber looking like a lost puppy.

"Where the Sam Hill you been?" he said to me as though I were alone. "I've been looking all over for you."

"Bomber, this is Elsie Lichtenwalner. She's the coroner's secretary I *told you* about." I emphasized told you in hopes he would either remember or make believe he did.

"Oh, yes, Elsie," he said, putting out his hand in a very uncharacteristic gesture. "Good to meet you at last."

It did the trick. I could feel the warmth of Elsie's gratitude in her smile.

"Elsie may have some very helpful things to tell us," I said.

"Oh?" Bomber's eyebrows showed his interest, though by this time I think any crumb would have escalated his brows.

"She has allowed me to persuade her to go to lunch with us—though she expresses some reluctance about being a bother."

Bomber took the bait. "Nonsense," he said. "I'd be honored. How about the Sciorias' place?" he suggested, to my surprise. He'd never darkened the door. Considered them too maudlin—spoil his meal, all that. But now it seemed appropriate—not only because of the subtle effect it might have on Elsie (some subliminal spur to aid the Sciorias), but also because it was the least likely place in town to run into the enemy.

After we were inside, Bomber ran his eyes over the place in silent appraisal. "Class," he said.

"Class?" I questioned him. The Sciorias ran a nice enough diner, a clean, well lit family kind of place, but I thought 'class' was a generous appellation.

"Any place that has dishes that break if you toss them on the floor is class in my book."

Angelo Scioria came rushing over to the table. He hovered, fawned. "I'm deeply honored," he said, looking at Bomber, who tried to pass it off. "Please have anything you like, there will be no bill."

"Nonsense," said Bomber. "I'm still solvent...pending the verdict." But Angelo was gone and he quickly returned with three clean menus. Bomber commented on that too. "How many places you go nowadays where they give you menus without catsup all over them?"

I was glad Bomber was satisfied here. But his comments did betray his taste in eating places.

I don't think he could have made Elsie any happier than if we had driven into New York and eaten at the Four Seasons or one of those elegant, overpriced gourmet palaces.

"My, everything looks *so* good," Elsie said, and I could almost see her smack her lips. She settled on the Wiener schnitzel, and I had an inkling that was a daring choice for her. Bomber had the T-bone steak and fries, and I, priding myself on sensible eating habits, opted for the minestrone soup and the linguine with clams. The Sciorias were, after all, Italian.

Elsie sang us another chorus of gratitude for including her, and we waited patiently for her to sing the main aria on the program. I prodded her gently. "Can you tell Bomber what's on your mind, Elsie?"

"Oh, well, that, yes," she said, as though she had given it no thought. "I don't know what made me come to court today," she began, as though in a fog. "I took the day off—I have only seventeen weeks of unused vacation due me," she tittered. "I don't know, Mr. Hanson, I—"

"Oh, call me Bomber, please," he waved a hand at her. I was, I must admit, knocked over at Bomber's display of chivalry.

"Oh," she purred, "really? I'd be honored, but I don't know if I can," then she shaped her lips as if to try out the sounds. "Bomber," she said at last, with it coming out quite musically, I thought.

We were getting the red-carpet treatment, no doubt about that. Waiters jumping to every imagined need—a sip of water, wham, the glass was full. Our order went right to the top in the kitchen. Boss's orders. And no one appreciated it more than Elsie.

"Well," Elsie began, "What I'm about to share with you is going to cost me my job—if you decide to use it in the trial."

I made a mild, uneducated protest.

"No, I've come to terms with it," she said, looking at me, then turning to Bomber. "The only reason I'm even considering this is your son..."

Bomber registered predictable astonishment. "Tod?" he said, as though he had two sons.

Elsie nodded. "No one has ever been nicer to me in my whole life," she said, and that statement alone was enough to fill the Red Sea with tears. But she meant it—there was no denying that. I will fess up to an unwarranted feeling of elation at the accolade and at the strange, admiring look I got from Bomber.

When Elsie finished telling us her tale, we sat with our mouths open. The food had arrived and though Elsie had managed a few bites, Bomber and I were more or less frozen with forks in midair. It wasn't every day this kind of information dropped into our laps.

But we both knew, and at the same instant in her recital, that it *would* mean the end of her career, and I felt it sort of incumbent on me to reintroduce that hateful subject, though I could see Bomber frowning in my direction. His philosophy was always, don't rock the boat with musings that might tend to upend the applecart.

I forged ahead anyway. "But, what would you do, Elsie? How would you live?"

"I worked it out," she said. "The county owes me a pension—I'll get Social Security after awhile."

"We could get you assigned to another county office," Bomber suggested. "I'll see to it."

She shook her head. "I don't think so. I think I'll be pretty much finished with the county."

"Another job—private sector?" I asked.

She sighed. "I've been going to work every day for almost thirty years. I'm ready for a rest. Don't worry about me," she said. "I'll be all right. It's the right thing to do."

I was dying to tell her what I knew, but couldn't be told because it would sound like a bribe, which, if discovered, could queer the case. Bomber would, without fanfare and discreetly, send her handsome checks a couple of times a year. For while he may have been stingy with my salary, he could be startlingly generous to virtual strangers. And to someone who had done him a favor, a virtual cornucopia.

Then I sat back to bask in the glory of Elsie's praise while she and Bomber discussed her testimony.

*   *   *

Lawyer Jude Carstairs fought tooth and nail to keep Elsie Lichtenwalner from testifying. He tried every tactic in the book, each seeming more spurious than the last.

Settlement talks intensified, but Angelo Scioria was adamant he wanted a verdict—open and public vindication of his daughter's honor and integrity.

"No secret deals," he insisted. "Maybe we get less money—so what? Money is not the thing here—honor—my little girl's honor—that's what's important!"

After Elsie was sworn in, Bomber stood up and smiled the smile of the magnanimous victor. It was as though he had borrowed that smile from the defendant, Dr. Bern. The jurors could not fail to see and feel the shift in fortunes.

The smile on Dr. Bern's face had lost its perpetualism. And no sooner was that sappy smile gone than I had forgotten what it looked like.

Bomber's argument won the day, and Elsie made her way to the witness chair, head high, but with an undisguisable undercurrent of nervousness.

Jude Carstairs, and/or Dr. Bern, bless them, had found it in their hearts to induce Dr. Zukerman, Elsie's boss, to come to the courtroom where he could do his darndest to intimidate his employee. It wasn't lost on the jury, thank goodness.

"How long have you worked for the coroner?"

"For Dr. Zukerman since he came to the office seven or eight years ago—and for two other coroners before that—twenty-eight years in all."

"Are you familiar with the defendant in this case, Dr. Bill Bern, seated at defendant's table there?"

"Yes."

"How do you know him?"

"He visited the coroner's office."

"How often?"

"Several times. Four or five, that I've been aware of."

"Could he have come more often—times you didn't know about?"

"Yes. I could have been out, he could have gone to Dr. Zukerman's office without me seeing him. Or gone to the lab."

"Was he introduced to you?"

"No."

"But you recognize him?"

"Yes."

"Did he ever speak to you?"

"No. He smiled once or twice."

"Is he smiling now?"

Elsie looked at Dr. Bern. "No," she said.

"If the Court please, could they direct the defendant to smile for the witness?"

"All right—Dr. Bern, would you smile please?"

Bern flashed a forced smile and the scene had me in internal stitches, while I was struggling to limit myself to my own smile. It was vignettes like this that kept working for my sometimes-insufferable father interesting.

"Is that the smile?"

Elsie pondered, studying the now fading smile. "Well," she said, "it seemed more real before." The smile instantly disappeared from the doctor's face, but it was replaced by a larger one on the face of Bomber.

There is something in the atmosphere that transmits signals invisible to the naked eye that something important is afoot. I got one of those signals and turned around to see the D.A. of Essex County, Mr. Walt Esterhauzy, enter the courtroom and stride to the front where he took a seat on our side of the railing that separates the pros from the just-folks. I looked at Bomber. He winked at me.

"Now, Elsie, did you know Merilee Scioria?"

"I saw her once in the office. She came to see Dr. Zukerman."

"Do you have any knowledge of the nature of her visit?"

"I think she was trying to make a drug buy."

"Objection," Carstairs said. "Calls for speculation."

"I'll withdraw," Bomber said. Then to Elsie, "Did you hear any conversation between your boss, Dr. Zukerman and Merilee Scioria on her visit to him that you referred to?"

"She said she was feeling low and someone told her Dr. Zukerman could provide her with something to make her feel better."

"What did he say?"

"He got quite angry. He was shouting at her that she had no business coming here. He wasn't a drug dealer and he was going to call the police if she didn't get out of there."

"What happened then?" Bomber asked.

"She asked if he knew if Dr. Bern could help her."

"What did Dr. Zukerman say?"

"He yelled, 'I don't know any Dr. Bern, now get out.'"

"Can you describe her? Any outstanding features?"

"She had tattoos on both arms."

"Do you know what these tattoos depicted?"

"They looked like plants."

Bomber consulted his notes on the desk. He gave her the date of the tattooing and asked if the visit was before or after that time.

"After."

"And did you see Dr. Bern in the coroner's office after that time?"

"Yes. It was a matter of days that he came back."

"Do you know the nature of that visit?"

"I overheard Dr. Bern talking with Dr. Zukerman."

"What did they say?"

"Dr. Bern asked Dr. Zukerman for a sample of R4 blood—"

"What did Dr. Zukerman say?"

"He had a cadaver who was R4 positive, and he took Dr. Bern into his lab."

"Did Dr. Zukerman ask Dr. Bern why he wanted the blood?"

"Not that I heard."

"What did you think of the request at the time?"

"That it was odd. There was a terrific scare about being contaminated with R4, so I couldn't understand why Dr. Bern would take that chance—I didn't understand what he could want with it."

"Do you understand now?"

"He wanted it to send to the lab in place of Merilee Scioria's blood—to make it look like she had R4."

"*Objection!*" Jude Carstairs jumped to his feet, red in his face. "Completely speculative, outrageously inflammatory. I move it be stricken from the record."

"Sustained," the judge said, but the damage was done.

"Your Honor, I would urgently request that the jury be instructed to completely disregard all this witness's speculation. She's not a doctor. She's not an expert on disease, viruses, anything. She's only a *secretary!*"

Oh, I thought, and Bomber winked again. Jude Carstairs has overdone it. Bomber got him to lose his cool. Jude Carstairs was right, of course, but there is a little rhyme that occurred to me at that moment.

> *Here lies the body of John Jay.*
> *He died maintaining his right of way.*
> *He was right, dead right, as he sped along.*
> *But he's just as dead as if he were wrong.*

"Your Honor," Bomber said, standing tall in his elevator

shoes. "Being a secretary is a noble profession. It is honest work," he said eyeing the jury which was peopled by those in similar walks of life. "A secretary has ears to hear, a secretary has eyes to see. We must credit her with instincts worthy of a doctor, a judge, or even a defense attorney—and we could hardly get loftier than that."

Carstairs waved his hand as if shooing a fly. "I stand corrected," he said, and I was sorry for the laughter he evoked. Funny how the balance could shift so quickly.

The judge (she could do no less) admonished the jurors to listen only to answers to questions not to opinions of witnesses.

"Okay, Elsie," Bomber picked up the threads, "did Dr. Zukerman give Dr. Bern a blood sample?"

"He did."

"Did you hear either of them say anything else after the blood sample was given to Dr. Bern?"

"Dr. Bern looked at it and smiled. He said, 'That ought to fix her.'"

Dr. Zukerman, the coroner, was trying to stare down Elsie, but wasn't weakening. At the same time, the district attorney was dividing his gaze between Bomber, Elsie and Dr. Bern. I saw the doc look over at the D.A. furtively, and I think I saw him wince and quickly look away.

"Now, Elsie," Bomber asked. "Do you remember by any chance what date Dr. Bern visited the coroner?"

"Yes, I do."

"What date was it?"

"August eighteenth."

"How do you remember that?"

"It was my birthday," she said.

"Did anyone wish you a happy birthday?"

She hung her head and I saw the tears welling. She shook her head.

"I'm sorry, Elsie, the court reporter requires a verbal response."

"No."

"No one in your office wished you a happy birthday?"

"No."

Bomber turned to glare at the coroner in the audience. I was happy to see Elsie's boss squirm.

In cross-examination, Carstairs, of course, tried to make Elsie look like a blubbering idiot—a mere secretary who was hallucinating. At one point, he seemed to take innuendo to an all-time low. "You're just getting back at Dr. Zukerman because he spurned your sexual advances."

"Objection," Bomber boomed as Elsie turned red at the mere thought of that suggestion. "Utterly without foundation, desperation tactics, an ugly, unfounded smear."

"Sustained."

"Well, Miss Lichtenwalner, how do you account for these two doctors, respected members of their community, talking about these sensitive—illegal, secret and clandestine—operations in your hearing?"

"They never thought of me as a person. I was like a piece of furniture—" and then she delivered the *pièce de résistance*, for which Bomber and I will forever love her. "I was only a secretary."

There was a groan of recognition in the courtroom and if I'm not mistaken I heard more than a few from the jury itself.

Carstairs went on to characterize the words Elsie claimed to have heard—even if true—as having so many possible meanings as to be meaningless.

Elsie, bless her, held her ground.

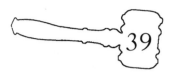

39

Dr. Bill Bern was such a world-class liar, Jude Carstairs put him back on the stand to deny everything. And deny he did. Who could deny better? If I hadn't known better, *I* would have believed him.

It was preposterous to think Merilee Scioria was an undercover agent going after him. If she had been, she would soon have realized there was nothing to find. He was, according to himself, as clean as a hound's tooth. Yes, he dispensed a lot of drugs. He was an active doctor, not a lazy one. Everything was legitimate. Most doctors didn't want to be bothered—they sent their patients to pharmacies. He, the knight in the white coat, saved his patients all kinds of money selling to them directly.

The blood vial he got from the coroner, Dr. Zukerman, was for some experimental work Bern was doing on hepatitis. He claimed Elsie misunderstood what he said from the distance. He didn't say, "That ought to fix her," he said, "That is the trickster," referring to the blood contaminated with hepatitis.

He was, when all was said and done, a conscientious doctor who prescribed the prevalent, medically accepted medicine to a patient with a terminal and hopeless disease.

When Jude Carstairs finished, Bomber got another chance at Dr. Bern.

"Doctor, you use the word trickster often?"

" Once in awhile, I guess."

"Can you remember the last time you used it?"

"Not specifically, no—except," he added hastily, "when I picked up the vial of blood from the coroner."

"Oh, yes. And what was that for, an R4 experiment?"

"No, hepatitis."

"Oh, yes. And how did you come to do that experiment?"

"I had done some reading and I got interested."

"Any other areas of medicine interest you enough to do blood tests on your own?"

"Well, a lot of areas interest me. I've done experiments, yes—"

"With blood?"

"This time—hepatitis is a blood disease. If I took an interest in bone fractures, for instance, I wouldn't need blood."

"What kind of equipment do you need to do this hepatitis experiment?"

"Well, I have test tubes and agents used to test blood."

"Satisfy you, did it? Your equipment, I mean. Were you able to get the results you were after?"

"As I said, I got interested in hepatitis and I wanted to learn more—that's all."

"What did you learn?"

"Well, that's rather technical."

"Over our heads, is it?"

"Well…unless you are a trained doctor."

"I see. Did you report your findings to anyone?"

"No, it was only for my own interest."

"Write anything down?"

"No."

"Let's say I asked you to put the results of your experiment in the simplest terms, Doctor. Something that even I could understand. Could you do that?"

"Not really," he said. "The number of pathogens in a contaminated sample, that's about as simple as I can put it."

"Was this a result that was not readily available in medical literature?"

Dr. Bern was no dummy, he saw the trap coming. "I'd have to say I didn't discover anything new—but you don't know that when you start an experiment."

"Have you ever treated a patient for hepatitis?"

"Well, ah, not that I recall."

"Did some tests on hepatitis blood, but you can't recall even having a patient with hepatitis?"

"That's correct."

"All right, Doctor, can you use the word trickster in a sentence—other than the one you say you said to the coroner?"

"Oh, 'He's a trickster', 'She's a trickster,'" Bern said. "'I thought he was on the level, but now I think he's a bit of a trickster.'"

"Ever use any of those phrases, Doctor?"

"I don't recall."

"Have you ever heard anyone refer to you as a trickster?"

"I don't believe I have."

"Like, 'That Dr. Bern is a trickster'?"

"No."

Jude Carstairs stood. "You Honor, I think we've exhausted this line of questioning. I'd have to object on the grounds of needless repetition."

"Yes," Judge Packer said, "I think you made as much of that line as you can. Sustained."

"Doctor, what is the date on the first blood test?"

Dr. Bern looked at the test report the bailiff handed him. I could see he didn't want to give the date, but he had no choice.

"August eighteenth, two years ago."

"And that was the day you got the blood from Dr. Zukerman, the coroner?"

"I don't remember that."

"Can you estimate?"

"No, I can't."

"All right, Doctor, if I may summarize your testimony..."

"Objection," Jude Carstairs said wearily. "We've heard his testimony. Let plaintiff's attorney summarize in his jury speech."

"Yes, sustained."

"Thank you, Your Honor," Bomber said, as though he had been granted a rare privilege.

Both sides rested, mercifully, and Judge Packer gave the attorneys the rest of the day off to prepare their summations for the jury.

That night Bomber holed up. That time in a trial was always solo flying time for the great Bomber, and I steered clear of the flight path.

I took some time with my musical composition celebrating the trial. I had a thought to depict Merilee's needle marks with pizzicato scales up and down the strings of the viola while all the other instruments were tacet. So, we have this booming percussion rattling along and suddenly they stop and, before the reverberation dies down, the viola takes off pluck, pluck, pluck, pluck, pluck, pluck, pluck—in the Aeolian mode known in the vernacular as the temptation mode for the old pop song *Temptation.*

You came, I was alone,
You were temptation.

Then I got going—couldn't stop—I was on a roll and rhythms and melodies flocked to my brain like the swallows returning to Capistrano. I pressed on, I was helpless against it. Boom, boom ta dum. Graght. Bah, bah boom. Hearing the percussive sounds of those banging instruments exhilarated me. I knew that sleep was impossible with all that banging going on in my head. I had no choice but to press on.

It was after two in the morning when I completed the section before the end. The ending would have to wait for the verdict.

Then I tried to sleep, an unsuccessful effort for another hour or so, as the pulsing rhythms and the contrasting viola's pizzicato and plaintive melodies crowded my consciousness.

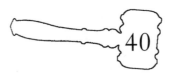

40

It was a sunny day in Birchwood for the jury arguments, but precious little of that liquid gold spilled into the courtroom.

Summarizing the case to the jury is an art. The surprising thing is how few true artists there are. Argument and persuasion are less natural to the species than warring and storing.

It is one thing to rehash the testimony, highlighting the incidents that help your case and hurt your opponent's. It is another to win the hearts and minds of the solemn twelve sitting by the side of the arena as spectators at a gladiator/lion match.

Perhaps the big difference between Bomber and his fellow advocates was Bomber felt his cases in his bones. And he communicated that feeling to the jurors.

They say there are no secrets to success in any of life's endeavors, there is only enthusiasm, and in front of a jury, Bomber walks away with the enthusiasm prize every time.

Bomber, as the plaintiff's lawyer, went first.

He was always a commanding presence before a jury. His clothes were not always a perfect match, and he usually suffered by comparison to the Wall-Street, Brooks-Brothers look of guys like Jude Carstairs, but he made up for it in bravado and with his elevator shoes and his high-school-football-coach-macho-bearing.

While he spoke, he looked the jurors square in the eyes and watched them intently—they could do no less than watch him back. Now and then, he'd drop his eyes in his humble-pie mode, when he felt that effect was called for.

"There is a saying at law, ladies and gentlemen, they put it in Latin so as not to make it too easy to understand. It goes *Falsus in uno, falsus in omnibus*—False in one thing, false in all things. That dictum enables you as a jury after catching a witness in a lie, it allows you to regard everything he says as false.

"Ladies and gentlemen, never in my long years of practice have I heard more falsehoods from anyone than I heard from Bill Bern. And he lies with such panache. He is the man for whom that phrase was written. We can call him Dr. *Falsus in Uno, Falsus in Omnibus*, or let's shorten it—Dr. *Falsus*. It will save time when I use it again… and again.

Bomber then launched into the testimony of the case, lauding Elsie Lichtenwalner for her courageous testimony of what she heard Dr. Bern say about Merilee Scioria, "That ought to fix her," when he took the blood sample from her boss, the coroner, and how Dr. Bern changed it to the unlikely, "That's the trickster."

"Now that hepatitis experiment, that takes the cake," Bomber smirked. He wasn't one for subtle facial expressions. "By his own admission, Dr. *Falsus* is a general practitioner. He's not a hematologist, he doesn't work with blood; yet he decided one day, what the heck, hepatitis fascinates me, I'll just run over to my pal the coroner and get a little hepatitis blood to fool around with.

"And isn't that interesting timing? That same day he sent the blood sample to the lab and called it Merilee Scioria's blood. The *same day*, ladies and gentlemen. He never had a hepatitis patient in his life, remember. He was just *curious*. Isn't that *curious*? The kids have a wonderful expression for this kind of tomfoolery—'meh bee so!'

"The coroner was not called back to corroborate what the doctor had to say about the blood. Could he be afraid of the perjury laws?" Bomber shrugged. "Of course, this is the man who swore categorically under oath his reports could not be altered—until we showed him how embarrassingly easy it was to alter them.

"What do you make of a man like that? A man who has breached his oath of office passing out blood from one of his stiffs—even if they convince you it was only for a vampire's breakfast? Perhaps the district attorney will take some interest in him too.

"The coroner's report did not mention Merilee Scioria's tattoos. They were up and down her arms, ladies and gentlemen, not an obscure butterfly hidden in an armpit somewhere. Yet, the coroner's report said she had *needle marks* on her arms.

"This is a suit for malpractice. In the course of investigating our case, certain evidence has surfaced that may make it seem like a murder case. Murder is a criminal offense the district attorney must look into." Bomber turned to the D.A. and nodded slightly. "But, ladies and gentlemen, murder is malpractice.

"Why would this nice, smiling doctor murder this innocent young woman? Because she was threatening his lifestyle and his freedom if she collected evidence of his drug operation as she was in the midst of doing.

"Now I expect it was the doc who hooked Merilee in the first place, though she isn't alive to corroborate that. And I don't expect Dr. *Falsus* to tell us the truth on that one. Merilee was one of the lucky ones. She got clean. How much credit goes to the drug boys who turned her from a drug experimenter to an informant, I don't know.

"Now I expect, Dr. *Falsus* had become fond of his fifteen-thousand dollar Rolex watch—I'm sure you saw him flash it on the witness stand awhile back. And his $300,000 Rolls-Royce he parks in the lot with his personalized license, 'Dr. B.B.' Maybe you've seen it out there as you go to your Fords and Chevys on your way home at night. It would be hard to miss. I look at it as I get in my rental car and marvel how he manages it all. If I had only one suggestion, it would be to change that personal license plate to 'Dr. Drugs'. Dealers should be labeled. We have to label our food now, why not label drug dealers? If Merilee Scioria had lived, she'd have labeled him; labeled him good.

"You know the government is moving into medicine. Lot of folks think that it might be good to move into law," (he got his laugh, even from Bern and Carstairs), "but doctors are on harder times now. Malpractice insurance is through the roof and Uncle Sam has cut doctors' incomes drastically."

Notice how cleverly Bomber inserted the idea of insurance in the minds of the jury. It was forbidden to mention insurance coverage or the lack of it. Dr. Bern didn't have insurance. That might have worked against us, had it been known. Jurors might sympathize with a person with no insurance coverage. It could lower the awards from the jury. So Bomber mentions malpractice insurance, implying Bern had it. Carstairs could have made a fuss, but he would have only emphasized the insurance without being able to tell the jury Bern had no insurance.

"But Dr. *Falsus* has found a way around that cut in income," Bomber went on. "I suppose in some circles that would be considered admirable. I would think it admirable if he had found some *legal* avenue to the great wealth he enjoys. And I don't care what you hear, you can't take it with you—to jail."

Then Bomber talked money—the locus of every lawsuit, and I've never heard anyone do it more creatively.

"In my time I have seen a lot of bizarre behavior at the altar of the almighty dollar. Money does strange things to people, ladies and gentlemen, perhaps it goes back to the days when our ancestors were hunters and gathers and had to store up food for the winter. I don't know what it is, but I do know that while money may not be the root of *all* evil, it *is* the root of a *lot* of evil.

"Ladies and gentlemen, my clients, the Sciorias, are frank to say they aren't interested in money. If they could have ten million dollars without vindicating their dear daughter's name, they would reject it out of hand.

"They are hardworking people who struggled all their lives to provide the best for their daughter—but she was taken from them. The Sciorias will be embarrassed to hear me talk money. Now, that may strike you as a stupid thing for a lawyer to say, especially one you suspect is in for a piece of the pie, and it should be music to Dr. *Falsus's* ears.

"What do you think Old *Falsus* would say if we offered him a deal? He is a man accustomed to making deals. Oh, Mr.

Carstairs likes to call him a healer, but he's more of a wheeler-dealer in my book. That's the best face I can put on him.

"Our deal is this—confess the murder of Merilee Scioria and we will drop our case for monetary award. Tell the jury and the world you found out through your associate—that sterling character Buck Rogers—that Merilee Scioria was an undercover agent out to entrap you. She wasn't the hopeless druggie you painted her as. Tell the truth Dr. *Falsus*, and we'll fold our hand. The pot is yours.

"Anytime, Dr. *Falsus*, anytime right up to the verdict."

Bomber hung his head as though he were embarrassed to go on. Then lifted it as though he were martyring himself to some cause larger than himself.

"Ah, but, ladies and gentlemen, if we are left with this civil case, this suit for medical malpractice, we must have an anchor to weigh responsibility. There is in this venue, alas, no other harbinger of right or wrong than cold, hard, old-fashioned American cash.

"How much cash?" Bomber made a face that said how distasteful this all was to him. "This is not a criminal case. We can't put Dr. *Falsus* in jail, though that may be where he belongs. No, all we have is the punitive damages award. Of course, we are asking two million dollars to reimburse the estate of that unfortunate dentist who was caught in the middle of this cesspool. That poor, unfortunate man, perhaps better off dead than to see the lies spread about him. Why? That two million, to reimburse his estate—which was bankrupted by a misunder-standing—is simply an expense. Two million dollars is peanuts in a case like this. If you want to send a message—and I frankly can't think of a case where a message was more urgent—send a big message. Two million is no message at all—no wake-up call against shoddy doctors who use their inside knowledge to take advantage of the unsophisticated of this world.

"This is not a case, ladies and gentlemen, where the scalpel slipped in some young intern's hand—where a tragic substitution of medicine or a mistake in the dose caused damage or death. No, this is a case where a deliberate attempt was made to murder the patient—an attempt which unfortunately succeeded all too well.

"I may be wrong, I often am, but I can't think of a more despicable act than to have a licensed physician abuse the trust placed in him by a patient. And who knows what he told that young, idealistic, yes, unfortunately naive girl? Dr. *Falsus* is a sweettalker. You heard him on the stand. Why, that man could charm the honey from the bees.

"I can just see him sweettalking that innocent Merilee. 'Look, I'm a doctor. I've taken an oath. What you have is life-threatening. I dispense prescription drugs—approved by the United States Government. My whole focus is on relieving pain and suffering. I expect Mr. Carstairs will play that tune for you. Just remember, Dr. *Falsus* sold enough drugs to sink a battle-ship.

"He'll call them medicines, mark my words." Bomber looked over at Jude Carstairs, who was scribbling furiously on his yellow legal pad. That was the defense attorney's *schtick* for most of Bomber's speech. I don't know if he didn't want to forget anything the great Bomber said, or he was trying to distract the jury with this show that said, he's speaking heresies and I must vigilantly keep track of them to vigorously refute them.

"I'm just about to wrap it up, ladies and gentlemen. You've sat still for a lot of stuff and I thank you for it.

"Let's just quickly look at the plaintiffs and the defendant in this case.

"Angelo and Regina are people like you and me. They don't wear fifteen thousand dollar wristwatches, they don't drive Rolls-Royces. They are just hardworking, plain folk who struggle day in and day out to make ends meet.

"I leave you to wonder how Old *Falsus*, this simple, small-town family doctor, got so rich.

"We have offered our theory on that, ladies and gentlemen, by simply producing the records of feel-good drug purchases Old *Falsus* made.

"Perhaps the defense has an explanation other than illicit drug dealing. I haven't heard it if they do." Bomber shook his head again to convey the sadness of it all.

"We've all read a lot about R4 and Wanns. It is a terrible affliction and it is unthinkable that anyone would administer lethal drugs to a young woman who has trusted him with her care. What kind of evil does it take to give a young, innocent girl enough JCD so she develops Wanns disease and dies?

"Well, Dr. *Falsus* did it," Bomber said, pointing at the defendant. "In order to smear Merilee Scioria, *Falsus in Omnibus* faked not one pregnancy, but two! Said he performed the abortions without witnesses, without telling her parents or anyone. 'It was just between us' he said. And, of course, he kept no records. How convenient! *Falsus in Omnibus!*

"Merilee Scioria was a young girl. Full of life—doing the right thing—the brave, courageous thing. Circumstances conspired to place this young innocent in the path of some big-time drug pushers. She turned informant, got tattoos on both arms to make her more believable. She believed in her cause to the extent of virtual self-mutilation.

"She wore a wire, as they say in the law-enforcement trade—to entrap Buck Rogers, and her goal was information on his supplier. None other than Dr. Bill Bern—defendant in this case—the man at the defense table with the incredible smile."

Jude Carstairs rose slowly and held his hand up like a school street-crossing guard. "Your Honor, I must object to personal derision—"

"Fair comment," Bomber grumbled.

"Personal attacks have no place—"

"Hey, this is argument," Bomber cut in, "I was merely identifying your client. I'll be glad to drop the bit about the swell smile or whatever I said."

"You said incredible smile—suggesting there was no credibility in it."

Bomber looked on dumbfounded at Carstairs who was emphasizing something he wanted stricken.

Judge Packer banged her gavel. "Enough! You will address your matters to me, not to each other. Now sit down, Mr. Carstairs, Mr. Hanson has the floor. You will have your chance to argue your case after he is finished. You are aware of the wide leeway allowed in argument, I'm sure. You will have an opportunity to rebut. Continue, Mr. Hanson."

Bomber turned back to the jury. "Sorry for the interruption, ladies and gentlemen. At my age it's hard to get back on the track—where was I?"

This was a ploy I'd heard Bomber use before. Then he'd watch the jurors for signs of moving lips—of wanting to help him. He seemed to suddenly take a cue from a juror. "Oh, yes," he said. "She wore the wire—Merilee did—a dangerous business for a man who can defend himself—for a young defenseless girl?" He closed his lips and shrugged.

"That nice Buck Rogers caught her with the wire. You saw him take the Fifth Amendment here time and again. Didn't want to incriminate himself. I wonder why. Do you wonder? If you'd be willing to take him home to dinner, you're braver than I am. Sam the bartender testified Merilee pleaded with Mr. Rogers not to tell Dr. Bern. Of course that brute told Dr. Bern—his boss—and the rest is tragic history. Merilee Scioria is in her grave, and the smear machine is in high gear.

"Ladies and gentlemen, if I impart nothing further to you in my ramblings, let me impress on you how honored and privileged I am to be in your beautiful state on behalf of Merilee Scioria.

"She is my Joan of Arc. She gave her life to leave your corner of New Jersey a little better place.

"For what kind of difference can any of us mere mortals make in the world? Many of us don't bother—but Merilee was young and idealistic. She gave her life..." Bomber stopped abruptly, overcome with emotion. His voice cracked, his eyes teared. "Merilee was, I venture to propose, a saint."

He paused, took a step back, as if to compose himself. I knew he would be surreptitiously reading the jurors' faces. I was reading them from the plaintiff's table—that was one of my tasks—though by that time it was probably too late. But once in a while, I could mention that something may have not seemed to have the desired effect, and when Bomber returned to the table in his peregrinations, I could put my hand next to the yellow legal tablet with my message there—and virtually without missing a beat, Bomber could throw out some memorable thought that might address the grievance.

Was calling her a saint too strong? Would it offend someone's religious sensibilities? The faces of the jurors remained impassive. Bomber came to the same conclusion and plowed on.

"Well, ladies and gentlemen," he said, clearing his voice of his emotional burden—his face and demeanor remained sad but resolute, "the choice is yours now. Dr. *Falsus* or...the late young and vital Merilee Scioria. Oh, how I wish she could be here in person so you would have a better take on her than my woefully inadequate reminiscences. Because I know to a moral certainty that if you saw our Saint Merilee, and heard *her* testify, it would erase whatever doubt you might harbor in your thoughts.

"But it was not to be, was it, ladies and gentlemen? It was not to be—" he paused, tears welling again in his eyes. "Take her with you to the jury room for your deliberations...please. Hold her in your hearts and minds. Think of the sacrifice she made of her young life. How it didn't have to be—

"Merilee Scioria or Dr. *Falsus*? Good and evil—right and wrong. You have the goods. Mr. and Mrs. Scioria implore you for their final peace of mind—vindicate their loving daughter's honor by finding—whatever is in your hearts for the plaintiff.

"And may God bless you for your sacrifice to this holy cause."

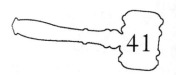

When Bomber finally sat down, I looked over at the Sciorias—they were smiling from ear to ear. They thought, as I did, we had it in the bag.

I often wish our side could make the *only* speech to the jury. So much simpler for them to decide the case our way if their minds aren't cluttered with another perspective.

Unhappily, it doesn't happen that way.

Jude Carstairs rose and buttoned his jacket. He smiled at the jury in a way that made them feel kindly toward him.

"I must say I salute the imagination of my colleague, Mr. Bomber Hanson," Jude Carstairs began. "The story he made up about my client is worthy of afternoon television. And he shamelessly cut it from the whole cloth, ladies and gentlemen. Shamelessly.

"Let's not let this master obfuscator cloud the issue here. Let's not let our emotions be toyed with. Dr. William Bern is a respected member of the local medical community with twenty-five years of blemishless practice on his record. The action brought against him is medical malpractice. Of course, Bomber would like to make it a murder case on the thinnest supposition I have ever heard in my entire career. Don't you swallow it!

"Let's look at the evidence and how Bomber stretched it and hammered it to fit his own agenda.

"Medical malpractice, remember, that's all we have before us. This is not a criminal case. It's not about robbery, assault, embezzlement, rape or murder. No, the question here is simply, did Dr. Bern make a *mistake*, a *mistake*, ladies and gentlemen, in prescribing JCD to Merilee Scioria? You heard the testimony of the experts that JCD is an FDA approved medicine, that it was, at the time Dr. Bern prescribed it, the only medicine available with a hope of arresting the dreaded Wanns Disease. Dr. Bern prescribed it for his long-time patient, Merilee Scioria, in the recommended dosage. It was printed on the instruction sheet Bomber made so much of. Merilee Scioria understood that, she took it willingly. There is no testimony she was fed the medicine by Dr. Bern, or that he was anywhere near her when she took it. That's really it, ladies and gentlemen. That's the simple issue in this case. I don't care if Dr. Bern had a monopoly on depression medicine. Even if he were the only doctor in the world able to prescribe pharmaceuticals, that is not the issue here. Don't let Bomber confuse you. Stick with the proven facts. And remember, please, *none* of plaintiffs' attorney's speculations are proven facts.

"Bomber made a lot of Dr. Bern's smile. Well, he does smile a lot. I'm frank to say I've never seen a defendant smile nearly so much. It's not a crime, ladies and gentlemen—not a crime. To me it connotes innocence. I don't see defendants smiling because they are scared to death—most know they are guilty—and in civil cases, such as this one, they are scared of what might happen.

"I'm glad Bomber made such a thing out of Dr. Bern's smile. I think we should consider what it means. To me it means he's not afraid. He has nothing to be ashamed of or be guilty about. He's not worried, ladies and gentlemen; not worried at all. He truly has nothing to worry about. He did nothing illegal or unethical. And for the life of me, I can't understand what the beef is here.

"The most telling point in our favor is that Merilee Scioria trusted this man to the end. There are lots of other doctors around, yet she chose to let Dr. Bern, her family physician, treat her for Wanns disease. Would she, *could* she have done that had she the least suspicion he was engaged in illegal activity, if she were some cloak-and-dagger agent spying to expose him? There's no evidence here that Merilee Scioria was stupid. That she would submit her life to someone who suspected she was out to destroy him.

"A word here about Buck Rogers. Bomber will have you

believe the moon is made of green cheese because Buck Rogers elected to employ his constitutional right to remain silent. That Fifth Amendment is in our constitution for a very good reason, and it is not our place to second-guess its legitimacy, or to ascribe sinister motives to anyone who takes it. It was not my idea Mr. Rogers take the Fifth. I would much rather he told the truth here. Because I too have a theory—much simpler, much more believable.

"Buck Rogers is a drug pusher. He didn't want to incriminate himself and risk arrest. He had no ties to Dr. Bern. Dr. Bern said he didn't know him. Dr. Bern testified without once invoking his constitutional right not to. He has nothing to hide. And Buck Rogers said nothing about Dr. Bern. The plaintiffs' lawyer is reaching for straws to tie those two together. And I can see how that would make a neat little package to bolster his sagging case. But it just didn't happen, ladies and gentlemen—it just did not happen.

"Bomber is a clever man. A wily man, yes, a cunning man—and he spins a marvelous tale—and if I didn't know better *I* would be tempted to believe him.

"Bomber Hanson has made a reputation for being a persuasive speaker. It is well deserved.

"Be strong, ladies and gentlemen, because as sure as I stand here, Bomber is making it all up to serve his client. Remember please, that a reputation as a persuasive speaker does not mean your case is just, as the plaintiffs' is not.

"No, ladies and gentlemen, the plaintiffs don't have right on their side. Let me bring you back to earth with the facts.

"Perhaps the most boldly audacious thing Bomber said was that his clients were not interested in money. Well, I'm sure it comes as no surprise to you that lawsuits are about the money. The plaintiff sues for a certain sum of money, then the defendant tries to protect himself from having to pay for something he deems unjust.

"Bomber talks about saving Merilee's reputation. Well, as far as I can see, there was nothing wrong with her reputation before we began this trial. We were forced by the instinct of self-preservation to bring certain facts to light in the matter of the young woman's background, so you might judge for yourselves if she was really Joan of Arc or just a confused young girl who went through the fires of youth as most do, coping with the temptations that life has to offer. Perhaps her life was no better and no worse than her peers—I don't know. But we are only publicly examining that life because the Sciorias brought this case for medical malpractice where they asked for *money*, ladies and gentlemen—money." He let the second 'money' deflate as though the thought were silly.

"Now he talks reputation. Suddenly money doesn't matter. It's her *reputation*—posthumously—that is important. No matter they seem to be bent on destroying Dr. Bern's reputation in the process.

"Well, I have news for you. Dr. Bern's reputation is more important to him than money also. In fact, he is not asking the Sciorias for money. He didn't even send them any bills for Merilee Sciorias's treatment.

"No, ladies and gentlemen, if the Sciorias were not interested in money you would not be here. You could have, over these many days, done many more pleasurable things, I'm sure. If it's not about money, we will happily shake hands and say Merilee Sciorias was a fine girl, let's drop the case. But no, see how cleverly the old master brings his noble crusade around to cash. 'Cold, hard American cash' I believe he called it. And cold and hard it is, for in the process of the pursuit of this cash they have launched a war on Dr. Bern's character. They have sunk so low, with such desperation that they have assaulted his smile. His *smile!*

"No, ladies and gentlemen, it's money they are after. Perhaps they are jealous of Bill Bern's financial success, I don't know. But the prayer, as we say at law, is for money—cold, hard American cash.

"*Falsus in uno, falsus in omnibus?* I'll let you judge whether one shouldn't stick that cute appellation on Bomber instead. Because when he says the Sciorias don't want money—

they only want to teach Dr. Bern a lesson—I smell the odor of falsity. *Falsus in omnibus*—Bomber himself said if we catch him in a lie we are entitled to consider everything he says is false. And it is, ladies and gentlemen. His entire case is built on a false premise, and it is such a far-fetched one on its face that I feel uncomfortable dignifying it with argument. Dr. Bern *is* a healer. His reputation in this community has been impeccable for twenty-five years. To postulate that he would murder a patient whose family he had served for over twenty-years is preposterous. To do so to get a lot of money would be pathological.

"I won't go into the gory details of Bomber's fabrications because I frankly don't want to remind you of the fantasies lest you give them the slightest credence. But they are just that, ladies and gentlemen—fantasies. Concoctions spun to gain a large sum of money for the Sciorias.

"Let me renew our offer. We will sign any statement they make up about the shining goodness of poor Merilee Scioria in exchange for dropping this case."

Jude Carstairs looked over at Bomber who seemed momentarily on the spot expressionwise. Then Bomber managed a grim smile and a gentle shake of his head as if to say, you don't get it, pal.

"To hear the great Bomber Hanson talk to you, you'd think he was a pauper." Jude Carstairs gave the jury a display of his impression of a dolorous shake of his head. "I don't know what it is about these lawyers that seems to begrudge success to anyone else, doctors especially.

"I must confess I have no idea who he is talking about when he refers to the doctor as he has. It is not the committed healer I know. No resemblance to the man of medicine whom I've had the honor of sitting by throughout this trial.

"Bomber comes in here from California and casts aspersions at our own. Oh, we Jerseyites—and I consider myself one—my residence is New Jersey, my heart is New Jersey—sometimes resent carpetbaggers from the West casting aspersions at our own. That's just my feeling as a Jerseyite.

"You know we are all sorry for what happened to

Merilee Scioria. It was a tragedy. Wanns disease is a blight on mankind which must be defeated—at all costs. It was most unfortunate she contracted the symptoms. Dr. Bern treated her like any other doctor would have. Experts testified to that. Dr. Bern's treatment was the accepted medical treatment. He even took a second sample of Merilee's blood and sent it to a second laboratory for a second, independent test.

"And what is his reward for a lifetime devoted to healing the Sciorias and others like them? The Sciorias turn on him because their daughter died a tragic, unavoidable death. Turn on him after twenty-some years of serving them flawlessly.

"Well, there it is, ladies and gentlemen. Perhaps the greatest testimony for our side is the silent testimony of the Sciorias themselves. Mother, father, *and* daughter. They *all* chose Dr. Bern as their doctor. Stuck with him right to the end of Merilee's too-short life. Yes, they trusted him. Why? Because he is a trustworthy family doctor who had treated them all well all their lives.

"Naturally, the Sciorias were distraught when Merilee died. Who wouldn't be? I am just saddened they felt called upon to take out their grief on Dr. Bern. One life has been tragically lost. Don't ruin another. It won't bring Merilee back.

"And here—finally—let me give the plaintiffs the victory they claim they want. We stipulate Merilee Scioria was a fine young woman. And remember what Bomber said on behalf of his clients—her reputation is what they care about, not money.

"Well, we will concede her reputation, so there is no need to give them any money.

"Thank you for your attention, ladies and gentlemen. If you will put aside the considerable drama in this case and search your consciences in your deliberations, you will find for the defendant and award nothing to the plaintiffs."

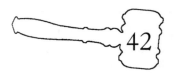

After lunch, Bomber made his rebuttal.

"Ladies and gentlemen, in my years of representing the diverse interests of this great land of ours, I occasionally have cases I can feel in my bones. This is such a case. There are slam-dunk cases, good cases, fair cases, poor cases where the prospect of winning is marginal.

"But every case has its Achilles heel—we can choose to bury those weaknesses under the rug as the defendant does when he says he doesn't want to talk about our case because it would dignify fantasy.

"Well, so be it. That is his philosophy of trying cases. Mine is to admit to weakness and hit it head on. And sometimes we may risk being crushed in the process. But to ignore important aspects of the case insults your intelligence. It says 'Oh, I can't possibly take a chance on the jury hearing this or that because they won't understand it—my way. I'm better off leaving them to wonder about it.'"

Bomber pursed his lips, shook his head and looked at Jude Carstairs. "No, ladies and gentlemen, you are more intelligent than that.

"So, I am frank to tell you the weakness of our case is just what Mr. Carstairs said it was. Poor Merilee Scioria, a young girl just beginning to taste the nectar of life, is told by her dentist he has Wanns Disease, and he recommends all his patients get blood tests. Now put yourself in her shoes, if you can. You are young, not worldwise, panicked at the prospect of contracting this dread disease and you need a simple blood test. You have seen one doctor all your life. Your mother and father chose this doctor. You have never had any indication he was incompetent medically speaking. A simple blood test, ladies and gentlemen, where's the harm in that? Would you dream—at nineteen—that your lifelong doctor would substitute a dead person's blood for yours? Would you imagine your doctor *could* do such a thing? You are nineteen, remember.

"On the heels of that admission, I am bound to say, I am very much afraid our learned defense council has completely missed the point. Merilee Scioria did *not* have R4 positive blood. The person from the morgue whose blood Dr. *Falsus* sent to the lab had R4 positive blood. It was the treatment Dr. *Falsus* prescribed that killed Merilee Scioria. He knew she didn't have it. He knew the blood he sent to the lab to test was not hers.

"And consider just how clever Dr. Bern was in his treatment of young, naive Merilee. He *claims* to have taken a second sample of her blood and sent it to a second laboratory. The results were identical. Both labs concurred in their findings. Why? Because Dr. Bern sent the same blood his pal the coroner stole for him to *both* labs. Taking the second sample from Merilee was a charade. A second opinion? Give me a break. We can all say that now, but if we were young and impressionable taking a second blood sample for a stated 'second opinion' might be reassuring. If he really had her interests at heart, wouldn't he have sent her to another *doctor* for the second opinion? Obviously, he didn't dare. He would have taken *Merilee's* blood and sent it to a lab. I venture to say it would have come back *negative!*

"After he sent the phony blood to the lab, it didn't much matter if she had gone to another doctor who prescribed the same thing. Sure it's approved by the FDA and if she took that blood test result to any other doctor he might have prescribed JCD. But, ladies and gentlemen, that prescription was for people with R4—she didn't have it. Some dead person did. JCD is *not*, may I repeat, *not* for healthy people. It makes healthy people sick and gives them the symptoms of Wanns disease. And, eventually, it kills them. Dr. *Falsus* knew Merilee Scioria was healthy, and he killed her with JCD. If that isn't malpractice, I don't know what is.

"Merilee's generation has a saying for situations like that, 'It blows my mind.'

"Well, it blows *my* mind, ladies and gentlemen, yes it does.

"My Lord, taking a blood sample from a coroner for *any* reason is enough to convict Dr. Bern of malpractice. He's not a laboratory. You heard him say he sent the sample he put Merilee's name on to a lab.

"Oh, I wish we could exhume Merilee's body and do a DNA test. I've never been so sorry a person was cremated—you know and I know and Dr. Bern knows that her blood was not R4 positive.

"I suppose I was naïve to think the doctor would understand how there are other things more important than money. Rolexes don't come cheap. It takes a heap of money to buy a Rolls-Royce—more than most people make in ten years.

"Now, Mr. Carstairs calls me a *carpetbagger*. Hopes, I suppose, to make you dislike me because he has found a convenient label to stick on me. I come from California, so I'm an outsider—an intruder—whereas he comes from New York and a fancy practice down on *Wall Street*. Well, I've been to Wall Street. I suspect you have too, and I'm darned if I don't think California is preferable—and my home town sure as heck is more like this fair town of yours than that Wall Street jungle.

"But I'm not unfamiliar with the—carpetbagger curse." Bomber made a face of distaste. "I try cases all over this country. I don't advertise in the local papers, people find me. People in trouble find me and invite me into their homes. I could refuse, of course—tell them I'll be labeled a carpetbagger. Tell them the enemy will try to tamper with the minds of the jurors and prejudice them against me because I don't live down the street.

"But then I tell 'em most jurors are too smart for those cheap shots anymore. We're all neighbors under the skin. You insult people's intelligence if you try to obfuscate a strong case with these peripheral diversions."

Bomber shook his head. "I don't know," he said, "does

Billy Graham apologize for leaving home to deliver his message? Does the pope? Our presidential candidates?

"Well, I'll tell you this, ladies and gentlemen, in my time, people have disapproved of me because they misunderstood me. But that's not nearly as bad as what they'd have thought of me had they understood me." Bomber smiled grimly at his self-deprication. Then he looked at the jury to see if any of them caught the humor. A few of them seemed to.

"Now, as you retire to the jury room to deliberate, take with you please the indomitable spirit of Merilee Scioria. Examine it all you will, cherish it, hold it high. If you can convince yourselves Merilee Scioria had this coming to her, find for the defense.

"But don't let the flame of her indomitable spirit—so pure in heart—die out.

"You are guardians of the spirit of Merilee Scioria. In spite of Mr. Carstairs's grandstand play conceding Merilee's reputation, you alone can vindicate her—only you.

"Mr. Carstairs may pooh-pooh the evidence, but it is solid. You know, he knows it, and Dr. Bern knows it."

Bomber paused, his eyes gliding over the faces of the jurors, then he turned to face Dr. Bern, *Falsus in Omnibus*.

"Well, ladies and gentlemen, I could talk for a hundred years about this case. I feel it so in my bones. I feel it so deep it tears at my guts when I think about the wanton waste of this young life." The tears welled up in his eyes again.

"Defense counsel asks you to believe that this is *only* a malpractice case. And yes, technically it is. But certainly we all agree on this: murder...is malpractice."

With that, Bomber looked each juror in the eye and bowed silently, humbly toward them, closing his eyes for a moment of silent prayer, then sat down.

I glanced at the jury. They stared into space, jaws set in determination—I just couldn't tell for which side.

In the audience, the district attorney sat looking grim.

43

Perhaps the most boring point of the trial is the judge's charge to the jury—telling them what they may consider and what they should not consider. Before the judge's charge, each side gives her points it wants her to include. She decides which are appropriate. If a judge isn't careful to deliver this in a dry, deadpan way, she is liable to tip the jury off to her view of the case, and it could be influential in their decision.

Judge Packer bored with the best of them. She did tell the jury they weren't allowed to conjecture what Buck Rogers might have said had he not taken the Fifth Amendment and refused to testify. She also told them they were not allowed to draw any inferences from the district attorney's attendance at the trial. Court trials are open to the public and anyone may or may not attend. The presence or absence of anyone in the audience is immaterial to this case. These points had been requested by the defense.

She did take from our suggestions the *Falsus in uno, falsus in omnibus*.

All in all, she did a credible, monotone job of it, and we returned to the hotel to await the verdict.

I don't care how much you prepare or how well you think you did, there is always a carload of tension while you wait for a verdict.

So much is always riding on it from the principals' perspective. In our case, it seemed Merilee Scioria's whole life was on the line.

So, it is pins-and-needles time for everyone. Some hang around the courthouse for hours hoping for a quick verdict. More seasoned players like Bomber and Jude Carstairs return to their homes or offices awaiting a call from the court clerk that the jury has returned with a verdict.

Bomber returned to his hotel suite where he caught up on the status of his other cases via telephone with Bonnie Doone, his so-called secretary, who, if it turned out well, would surely take credit for the outcome of this case.

I retired to nudge my *Phantom Virus Concerto* for percussion and viola toward completion. I used a combination snare drum roll pianissimo and intermittent timpani strokes while the viola was sustaining a low C to depict the suspense of this phase of the case, building, of course, to a rousing finish on a positive note, or a dolorous letdown befitting a disappointing verdict.

The jury gave me time to consider both endings in my head—the one with all the percussion going wild, glissandi on the xylophone and marimba, bells clanging, gongs gonging; ratchets, tambourines, wood blocks, cymbals, triangles, and drums (snare, bongo, bass and timpani) banging and bonging away.

Or the converse, an ending with slow knocks on the wood block with a downward slide on the viola, diminuendo.

The jury went for lunch without reporting a verdict. Either they were stymied or they wanted a free meal on the county. Pity they couldn't eat at the Sciorias'. We'd have our side's victory before the dessert.

I wasn't too hungry, so I sketched out the verdict for the plaintiff in all its glory. I thought it might be good luck to think positive. Besides it was a lot more fun writing all that celebratory noise than it would be to write that doleful diminuendo.

An hour after their return from lunch, the jury sent word to Judge Packer they had reached a verdict. You might glean several meanings from this—one might have been the jurors wanted a free meal all right, but they didn't want to over-do it.

Bomber and I walked over to the courthouse from our hotel. The air was damp and cool. Some rain had fallen. Though the town was becoming more familiar, it still felt strange to be walking down the street in the gray rain. Like someone was still lurking in the bushes to jump out and hit me over the head. I don't know how long it will take me to get over that. I knew better, but I asked him anyway, "What d-do you think?"

He shot me a look that said, "That's a damn stupid question," but he answered it anyway. "We gave it our all, Boy. More cannot be asked. There are a couple mysteries—a couple imponderables," then he paused. It looked like he was going to leave it at that.

"So?" I asked.

"So—? Yeah, well, of course—so. The carpetbagger thing. You never know when that will hit home. Everybody in this case is local—except me."

And me, I thought—I hoped he'd include me in that, but that was not Bomber's way. "And...?" I said, hoping he would answer either question.

"And our Achilles heel," he said. "Merilee was a drug user, a rebel, and then let the very doctor who got her hooked treat her. How could she not have feared him? He knew she was trying to bag him for the cops. She was just so innocent—so naïve." He shrugged his strong shoulders as if to say, what can you do? "But who would think her doctor would kill her with a prescription medicine? Who knew it could have been possible?" he sighed. "Carstairs is right, Merilee took the JCD willingly. Bern didn't have to force her."

The principals were all in place when we got into the courtroom. The Sciorias looked scared but expectant. Dr. Bern was frowning, but still managed a crooked smile. Hearts were anxiously pumping all over the courtroom. I could feel it in my bones.

Judge Packer entered and nodded to the attorneys. She instructed the bailiff to bring us the jury.

We always hope to read on their faces the verdict, but we never can. This bunch looked forebodingly serious—but that could have been foreboding for either side—but not both.

"Ladies and gentlemen of the jury," Judge Packer said. "Have you reached a verdict?"

The foreman stood up—a grumpy looking plumber who had not been selected for his looks. "We have, Your Honor."

"Hand it to the bailiff, please."

All the passing back and forth—bailiff to judge, judge to court clerk—before the reading was, I swear, only to draw the thing out to build the suspense.

The clerk—a woman who seemed to be in her mid years and all glasses—opened the envelope which had already been opened and closed by Judge Packer, whose expression gave no hint of the contents.

The clerk read the verdict as though she couldn't have cared less. "We the jurors, in the case of *Scioria v. Bern* find for the plaintiff in the amount of two million dollars damages and five million in punitive damages. The vote was unanimous," he said.

A small cry went up from the Sciorias who hugged each other and wept freely. "Thank God!" Angelo said. "Thank you, God," Regina murmured.

I wasn't sure if they were talking about Bomber or not.

Things were grim at the defense table. The smile was completely gone from Dr. Bern's face. Jude Carstairs stood up gravely and announced he would appeal the decision.

Judge Packer eyed him skeptically. "You're going to appeal a unanimous verdict?"

"Yes, Your Honor."

There was a hubbub at the defense table. When I looked over I noticed two uniformed marshals arresting Dr. Bern. I heard only the words "For the murder of Merilee Scioria."

I thought of my grandmother and what a stickler for the truth she had been. Liars go to hell and all that. She would not have been pleased at the rewards I got from bending the truth with Elsie. Conversely, she would have been pleased at Dr. Bern's comeuppance.

All life is rationalization, of course, so I rationalized that

I only bent (okay, mangled) the truth for a limited time, then backed off and *that* was when I got my results.

Elsie did it for us. I don't think there can be any disputing that. We owed her everything. The Sciorias were aware of that, and their gratitude was almost embarrassing—especially when they turned it on me after Elsie told them she never would have done it if it weren't for me.

I could see Bomber standing by us getting bent out of shape that no one was mentioning him and his part in the drama. I thought briefly of ignoring him—watching him squirm, but I realized he expected something of me that I was duty-bound to deliver. So I gave in—

"Let's not forget the real hero here," I said. "The nation's greatest trial attorney," and I bowed to Bomber, who had the smile of satisfaction on his face.

"*World's* greatest," he corrected me.

I asked Elsie what we could do to repay her.

"The feeling I have of having once in my life done the right thing is payment enough."

"Well, that's big of you, Elsie," I said. "At least I can take you to dinner one more time before we leave."

Her eyes lit up. "I'd like that," she said.

Before I picked Elsie up for dinner, I put the finishing touches on my concerto for percussion and viola with a flourish of scales for piano and xylophone in the Aeolian mode to paint the sound picture to match the pizzicato viola, denoting that Elsie won the case.

Elsie wanted to go to the Sciorias' for dinner, and I couldn't have been happier. It was like old home week—except Bomber begged off. He was exhausted, he said. He is not always knocked out after a trial. Sometimes he is exhilarated. I suspect he thought Elsie would have preferred to be with me alone, so I didn't push it.

As soon as we walked in the door of Sciorias' restaurant, we felt like royalty. Angelo and Regina fell all over themselves to treat Elsie like a queen.

For some reason I felt I could call Mrs. Scioria Regina now. It must have been the victory.

"Elsie, my darling," Angelo said, holding her hand in a gallant manner which tickled her no end, "to you we owe the rest of our lives. You will eat in my place every meal if you like, and you will never see a bill. That is my promise to you, my queen," and he bent over and planted a noisy kiss on her hand.

The chef outdid himself with a rosemary encrusted rack of lamb with scalloped potatoes and a red-beet soufflé.

"This is the happiest night of my life," Elsie said.

"Mine too," I said.

Grandma was with us in spirit.

The following are excerpts from other
David Champion books:
Bomber Hanson Mysteries
Celebrity Trouble
Nobody Roots for Goliath
The Mountain Massacres

The Snatch

Excerpts from *Celebrity Trouble*
A Bomber Hanson Mystery
by David Champion

James stared straight ahead. I looked at his profile. What a lousy spot for a kid to be in, I thought. Pleasing his father (which must not have been a lead-pipe cinch) and telling the truth to a stranger. His mother would have encouraged him to tell the truth, of course, but it had always been so hard to please his father.

"Did he offer to give you some money—or buy you something if Steven gave you money?"

"Said I could have a bike."

"You don't have a bike?

He shook his head. "Stolen," he said.

I had a sudden despicable thought (and I *am* ashamed of it) that dad stole the bike and hocked it. "Would you like me to get you a new bike?"

There was a sudden movement beside me, and there was no more profile, it was face front. "Would you?" he said, in a sense of hope but disbelief.

"Yes, James, I would, and I will. But first you must first do something for me."

He sank back, deflated. I got the profile again. "What?"

he said with the dullest inflection.

"Easy," I said. "Just tell me the truth about what happened at Steven's house, when you were in bed with him."

I could feel him cringe. From the look on his suddenly pale face, I wasn't sure I wanted the truth.

His eleven-year-old mind was working, but I couldn't tell if it was working for us or against us. I had complicated the mix by throwing in the bicycle offer. How did he know which truth I would find acceptable?

"Can you just tell me this: Did anything happen before you went to sleep?"

"We just talked, like I told you."

"Was he touching you at all?"

"I told you, he was holding my hand."

"Nothing else?"

"No."

"So then you went to sleep?

"Yes."

I paused, hoping he would volunteer the rest. He didn't.

"After you went to sleep, what was your first next memory?"

James paused a long time. We were at the crux and he knew it. He probably also thought his father would kill him if he told me—but I had nullified one of the big convincers, I had offered him a bike, too. As if to verify my sincerity, he looked over at me again, before he gave me the profile again.

"It was morning when I got up," he said so softly I almost didn't hear him.

"Where was Steven?"

"Already up—"

"Then what happened?"

"He came back in the room and said he was sorry he left me alone, was I okay?"

"Were you?"

He nodded.

"Then?"

"I got dressed and we had breakfast and went outside and I drove the cars and the planes and rode on the merry-go-round."

"And nothing bad happened?"

He shook his head.

"Did you tell this to your father?"

He nodded.

"What did he say?"

"He said you never knew what could happen when you were asleep. He said Steven was a fag and those fags were all alike. He wouldn't trust a naked fag in bed with a little boy further than he could throw him, including the bed and the little boy."

James was still in profile, but he was crying—I reached out and put my arm around him.

"You don't like him calling you a little boy do you?"

He shook his head.

His mother came in. She'd heard the sobbing. "Oh, James, what's wrong?" she asked him, then looked to me for the answer.

"James just told me the truth. It wasn't easy. There are a lot of conflicts. He doesn't want to displease his father."

She looked me in the eye. "Then everything's fine?" she asked.

I nodded.

She seemed flooded with relief. She had been so sure, and yet—

"Well, young man," I said, "you've earned your bike. What kind do you want?" It wasn't until I said that that I realized he could ask for an Italian racing model in the thousands. I hoped and prayed Bomber would be good for it, but couldn't be sure. Making decisions based on economic considerations were not his thing. He could have easily overlooked the triumph for the client and say, "You made the promise; you deliver the goods."

But, no, it was a modest bike as new bikes go. We'd get

out of the shop for under two hundred. There was this model in the window and it was a metallic-silver paint, and he had been looking at it every day going to and from school, hoping it wouldn't be sold until his father got the money from Steven as he assured James he would.

"Was it still there today?"

He stopped crying to say, "Yes!"

I took his mom aside and told her what to expect. I thanked her profusely for her help and offered to do anything to help them if the going got rough.

"Just to be safe," I said, "I wouldn't tell his dad about this talk—or the bicycle."

On my way out, I shook James's hand. "You were a soldier," I said, not realizing that that line probably works better on a five-year old. Then I added a gratuitous platitude: "The truth never hurts as much as a lie, does it?"

He looked at me as though he didn't understand the question or I wouldn't understand the answer.

On my way back to the office, I stopped at the bike shop, and there was the coveted bike in the window as advertised.

I was pleasantly surprised at the reasonable price and the small gratuity it took to have it delivered right at closing time.

"Little kid been coming here ever'day," the store owner said, "drooling over this bike." He shook his head. "He's gonna be mighty sad it's gone."

I smiled so much it hurt. "No he won't," I said.

Excerpts from *Nobody Roots for Goliath*
A Bomber Hanson Mystery
by David Champion

She was driving so damn fast I didn't know what was going to give first, the engine mounts of the old pick-up or my liver.

It was probably nerves that gave her the lead foot on the gas. Her nerves. My nerves were already shot.

Carrie Zepf was her name, short for "Carol" she had told me. She was strongly built with dishwater blond hair that was sheered off above her shoulders, by one of her sisters from the look of it. She was old enough to vote, but way too young to drive. She had written the letter that got me into this death trap in the first place. It was a beguiling letter—poignant and engaging—about her blind father on his last legs from lung cancer and her institutionalized mother with twelve girls at home. I had pictured the sender as younger, less worldly—not someone who would pilot a hundred-year-old Ford pickup on these rutted-country dirt roads at a million miles an hour.

"Carrie!" I yelped, my hands braced on what was left of the dashboard. "If I don't get there alive, I guarantee we won't take the case."

"Sissy," she said, taking a corner so fast I was thrown against her. She giggled, "Not my fault your plane was late. Dinner be gettin' cold by now."

"I'm not hungry," I said.

"I am," she said.

My father had flipped out this time—sending me across the United States to look into the feasibility of taking a smoking case on a contingency. It was a loser for sure, and I was against it from the beginning.

It was a harebrained idea. Of course, that is not a sentiment I would have the nerve to express in Bomber's presence. I didn't say "Boo" to my father, Bomber Hanson, who claims to be the leading trial lawyer in the country—and he doesn't get much argument. Not many people have the nerve to say "Boo!" to Bomber Hanson, except a few judges who are appointed for life.

I am unable to explain how we arrived at the Zepf farm without any structural damage. My nervous system, I was sure, was irreparable. And when I saw the flock of hens in their Sunday-go-to-meeting dresses fly at me from every angle, I got a lump in my throat as big as that battered pick-up I was just stepping out of. And, believe me, the earth never felt better under my feet.

*　　*　　*

I adored the way she talked; earnestly, intelligently, her eyes so alive and probing. She had the aura of honesty, decency and goodwill. I not only hired Shauna, I fell in love with her.

Of course, I didn't tell Bomber how I felt. When I told him I had hired our researcher, he asked, "What's his name?"

"Shauna McKinley," I said.

He paused for a moment. "Isn't that a girl's name? He's no pansy is he? I'm not keen on pansies, you know."

"He is a she," I cut him off before he got deeper into his Neanderthal prejudices.

"A she? Jesus Jenny Tod, a *she*! You hired a *girl* lawyer?"

"Woman," I corrected him.

"How old?"

"Twenty-five."

"Jesus Jenny, oh my God in heaven. I should have known you couldn't be trusted. Weren't there any men available? There must have been."

"I interviewed two b-b-boys." I said. "She was j-just so much b-b-better."

"Oh, my God!" Then he seemed to pause for reflection. "Say, you aren't sweet on her are you?"

"How could I be?" I lied. "I just met her."

"Well, get her started," he said with a sigh.

*   *   *

"We are not talking penny-ante crime here, we are talking the crime of the century. Up to about three mil a year in deaths now, isn't it?"

He winced. I wasn't sure what could be said for Don Powell at this stage, but he was sensitive to the daily disaster he helped bring about.

"You are one of the most important industrial manufacturers in the world," I said, laying it on. He shifted only slightly. "I am just a kid lawyer doing legwork. But my father is Bomber Hanson and, if you've ever read a newspaper or looked at a TV news show, I don't have to tell you who *he* is."

He gave me a small nod.

"Bomber doesn't take cases to harass people. He's a big-picture man—and where is there a bigger picture?"

"Nowhere," he muttered in agreement.

"He wants me to offer you two first-class tickets to the coast. Limousines both ways from L.A. to Angelton. You pick the time and the duration. He'd like to have an hour or two with you, but he'll settle for half that."

"What do I have to do in return?"

"Just listen to his story."

He smirked. "Like one of those condos-in-the-Bahamas scams?"

"I wouldn't know about that," I said. "This is no scam."

"You mean, if I'm not convinced, I don't have any obligation?"

You'll be convinced, I thought, but I said, "That's right."

"Besides a free vacation," he said, "what's in it for me?"

"I don't know," I said. "A clearer conscience maybe." I was throwing darts I had not intended and they were hitting the target.

"And all I have to do is sell my lifelong friends down the river," Don Powell said.

"Bomber would probably prefer to look at it as saving lives."

His head bobbed as though it were Jell-O on springs.

"But before we put either one of you to the trouble, I am obligated to get a few things straight. One thing always comes up hazy in discussions about cigarette manufacturing—at least to me. When you refine the tobacco, I understand you take all the nicotine out?"

He nodded. "Temporarily."

"Then you put it back?"

He nodded again.

"Do you sometimes put back more than you take out?"

He shrugged as though I had asked how the roast beef sandwich was. "It's possible."

"Why don't you just leave it out?"

"The taste," he said. "People don't like the taste."

"Isn't it the nicotine that makes the cigarettes addictive?"

"So they say."

"But you don't know? Is this another case of you not believing the studies because that's your employer's conceit, or do you genuinely not know?"

"I'm not a scientist." He started to say he was just a manufacturer, but I cut him off.

"And Eichman was a geneticist."

His cheek twitched. "Low blow," he said, but I didn't apologize.

"But is it so remote? You'd need a lot more gas chambers than the Nazis had to do the job you are doing."

"People smoke by choice," he said, trotting out the company wisdom. "Relaxes them. Like a drink of liquor. Booze will kill too, if you overdo it."

"So we have some three-million a year who smoke too much."

He started to nod, but he got only halfway.

"Well," I said, "it's up to you. We can call you as a friendly witness or subpoena you as a hostile witness. From my experience, when you are facing Bomber Hanson, you are much better off in the friendly category."

He stared straight ahead. No more pretense of reading

the newspaper. "I'd be finished in this town," he said. "No question. No job, no reputation, no friends. Everything gone."

"You have anything put away?" I asked, being practical.

He gave a short laugh. "I have a good pension coming, unless I screw up. I've got a lot of company stock in options and bonuses."

"Sell it," I said.

"Not so easy," he said. "I'm an officer of the company. I have to report any substantial changes. I blow the whistle, what do you think happens to my stock?"

"Hard to outguess the stock market," I offered without much conviction.

"It won't make the stock go up," he told me.

"Do you have any other assets?"

"House."

"Is it clear?"

"No, there's a small mortgage. These places aren't worth what they are in California, you know. I have about two hundred equity in the house, I guess. Of course, if you *are* successful and it starts a chain reaction, the house won't be worth anything either."

"Sell it," I said. I was full of advice.

"Think anyone would wonder why?"

"Who has to know?"

It was that hopeless snort again. "In this town, a secret lasts about five minutes until everybody knows it."

I was going to ask if he knew his wife's secret, but I refrained.

"Think about it," I said.

"I'll think about it," he said.

"Fair enough," I said, putting out my hand for a shake. "Your wife has my number."

That smirk was on his lips again.

"Everybody has your number," he said, and I watched his back shamble out of the park.

Excerpts from *The Mountain Massacres*
A Bomber Hanson Mystery
By David Champion

"Now, I believe you gave testimony that you told Mr. O'Neil he might want to get a lawyer."

"I might have."

"And did you suspect him of killing his own dogs?"

"No, I..."

"Or of any other crime?"

"Not at the time, no."

"Just so. But still you suggested a lawyer."

"Only if he wanted to file a civil action."

"Did he?" Bomber asked. Yankus looked like he didn't understand the question. "Did he bring up the civil suit, or did you?"

"I don't know. It was only a suggestion."

"A suggestion, or a put-off?"

Web was up again. "Your Honor, how much of this do we have to put up with? The officer made the report. Let him ask if he has it. What it says. We can jaw forever about this trivia. We can take this case into the next century. This is the guy who took the report. He *took* it! It's in the records. The rest is window dressing. And Mr. Hanson knows full well, he..."

"Mr. Grainger, is there an objection in there somewhere?"

"Yes, sir..."

"Sustained," the judge grumbled, adding, "sounds like a speech to me."

The D.A. sat down.

"All right," Bomber said to the witness, "you took the report?"

"Yes."

"May I just clarify the sequence of events then? Mr. O'Neil came to you at the desk of the police station on Newport Street?"

"Yes."

"He asked you to make a police report?"

"Yes. Told me his dogs were shot."

"Had a suspect?"

"Yes." Officer Yankus referred to the report. "Alf Ritchie."

"Thanks for that gratuitous answer. I didn't ask for it. Then you told him he should see a lawyer?"

"I may have."

"*Before* you made the report?"

"I don't remember."

"Is it possible?"

"I guess."

"Why would you suggest a civil action?"

"For retribution. For remuneration..."

"Not to save you writing the report?"

"Objection."

"Oh, let him answer," Judge Murdoch said.

"No, sir. I took the report."

"Eventually, you did. I just want you to know we can fill this courtroom with people who think you've discouraged them from making police reports."

"Objection, Your Honor. He doesn't have to badger this officer."

"Yes, lay off, Mr. Hanson."

"I stand corrected."

I realize, listening to Bomber go, that he has these remarkable qualities that I lack. I am more passive, like my mother. I get no thrill from besting my fellow man. I have no bloodlust. No killer instinct. I probably would have lasted two seconds in the jungle where Bomber would have been king.

But, I was satisfied. I had my music. Writing music was not combative. I could create a perfect world of sound to be reproduced by a musical ensemble where the prerequisite for participation was the ability to harmonize with each other—to work together toward a common goal. Power trips and temper tantrums were the purview of prima donnas, the conductors, the soloists. The soldiers in the pit hewed a line of their own understanding. They were the indispensable music makers.

And so was I.

"Two more questions, if I may?" Bomber said.

The judge waved his hand for Bomber to proceed.

"Is it possible Mr. O'Neil got the impression you didn't want to file the report?"

"I guess anything's possible."

"In his position: Your two collies have been shot, you think a policeman doesn't want to bother with you—might you be angry?"

"I suppose so."

"Mad as hell?"

"Maybe."

"That's *three*," Webster Grainger muttered.

"So sorry," Bomber said.

The judge waved the D.A. off.

"Okay, this is the end," Bomber said, smiling at the witness, who smiled back in obvious relief as he started to rise. Bomber put his hand up. "One more thing," he said, "if you don't mind." Yankus sat down, dejected.

I saw the zinger coming a mile away.

"Did you make any recommendations as far as hiring any particular attorney went?"

Officer Yankus smiled sheepishly. I guess he was relieved the question didn't reflect on his gold-bricking.

"I may have."

"And what did you tell him?"

"I may have told him he should hire you—if he wanted to win."

The sheepish smile was now a big grin.

"Oh my God," the D.A. groaned.

Excerpts from *The Snatch*
By David Champion

The big doors opened on the stroke of two. As though they didn't want to keep Badeye a moment longer than was necessary.

Coming toward Harry, Badeye was the cock of the walk, a man who had faced down the gas chamber for killing a cop.

When Badeye reached the corner of the city park—elevated above the detritus of its everyday life—Harry fell in behind him. Badeye turned suddenly and exclaimed, "Horseshid," and started running up the steps to the park.

He was no match for Harry, who made a religion of keeping himself in shape—he easily tackled Badeye on the grass.

As the wily con's nose sank into the moist green grass, he decided he liked the smell. Where he came from, nothing smelled like damp grass.

Harry snapped a nice new pair of handcuffs on one wrist behind Badeye's back, then the other.

Badeye wanted to put up more of a fight, but there wasn't that much fight left in him.

Holding Badeye's arm, Harry directed him to his Volkswagen Bug, sat him inside, none too gently, on his cuffed hands—then shut the door as if on a date.

In the driver's seat, he smiled at Badeye and gave him a playful wink. Badeye spoke first as Harry started the engine.

"Fukkin' sewing machine," Badeye sneered. "Fuzz on the take like you oughtta have a big-assed car."

"Now, now, Badeye, mustn't judge others like they were you."

"So what do you want, hotshot? You gonna waste me, get it over with."

"Hey, would I do that? I'm a policeman."

Badeye snorted, but seemed to relax.

Harry shifted gears and climbed the on-ramp to the

Harbor Freeway.

"This thing's a piece of shit," Badeye snorted.

"I notice you were walking," Harry said. "Let's just rap a little about the meaning of life and stuff like that. I'm speaking, of course, of the late Charlie Rubenstein–a prince, Badeye–and you will admit you are a punk–and next to Charlie your stature is something between a wart and a festering boil."

"Hey, get off my case, man, I wasn't even indicted," Badeye snorted. "Shitty police work." He seemed amused.

"Ah yes, my boy, the system." Traffic was light on the freeway. Harry was in the right lane, the speedometer needle frozen on fifty-five. "It's a system that lets a punk like you take the life of the prince of the police force and get away with it on some flimsy technicality. Now, Badeye–you boys don't seem to spend a lot of time worrying about the law of the land, and I'm just speculating on how you would handle the thing if you were in my shoes."

"Charlie was gettin' too close to the boys..."

"He was trying to show the ten- to twelve-year-olds there was more to life than killing each other. So where's the beef?"

"Not his business."

"Rather have cops on your case all the time? Better than trying to work with you–give you an alternative to the streets?"

"She-it, you don't know nothin' 'bout the street. We ain't gettin' outta here nohow. There ain't no opportunity out there for the brothers."

"Yeah? Tell that to the black mayor–tell that to the black police commissioner, tell that to all the blacks on the city council. Charlie Rubenstein wanted to help, so you killed him."

"Hey, man, I ain't had nothin' to do wid it. I mean, man, I incarcerated, or I free as a bird?"

Harry nodded vigorously, "You is free as a bird."

"Then get these goddamn cuffs offa me. They's killing me."

Harry headed the car down the Century Boulevard off-ramp. Badeye felt another twinge of relief. He was going home.

The car stopped outside an isolated deserted building that served as a warehouse in happier times. Before the brothers took it in their heads to burn the neighborhood back in '65. Though this building employed fourteen local men, the owners threw in the towel after it had been looted and burned.

"This is where we get out, Earnest," Harry said, waving his pistol in the direction of the burned-out warehouse.

"We? Hey, man, you a policeman, remember—you no executioner." Badeye's good eye was starting to twitch. "You said you wasn't gonna waste me."

They were inside the charred building, with the blackened bricks and the steel beams still intact.

"Now you just stand there, Earnest, nice and quiet like, and give me the details of how you gave it to Charlie."

Badeye stared dumbly at Harry. "You *is* gonna waste me."

"No, no, I hope not. Certainly not if you cooperate."

"Cooperate? What I gotta do?"

"Tell me about Charlie, for starters—how did you get the brainstorm to pull out his fingernails? Was that your idea—Whistler says it was—or was he really the genius behind that?"

"Stop jerking me off, Horseshid—I know my rights backwards and forwards. You get me a lawyer, you wanna ax all these personal questions."

"A lawyer? Why, what a good idea! But, geez, lawyers go with indictments, and we wouldn't want that," Harry said. "And the teeth, Earnest, you broke all his teeth with a hammer. This was the best friend your boys ever had. He was a guy who cared about them. He wasn't a cop, he was an optimistic social worker. You cut him down before he had a chance to get jaded. Hey, you know I've had a little trouble keeping partners—I never had one like Charlie. Here was a guy more interested in his duty than a free lunch. And the cuts, Earnest–the cuts all over his body and the ants–if you are in that line of work, I suppose that would be considered artful."

"I don't know nothin'."

Harry sighed.

"Now I'm walkin' outta here, man. I ain't takin' no more a your shid."

"Ah, Earnest. You wouldn't want me to have to shoot you for resisting arrest."

"Hey, man, you said you wasn't gonna waste me."

Harry was beginning to smell the perspiration. "Satisfy my curiosity," Harry said. "How did Charlie take it? I mean, was he stoic–you know, brave–or did he cry like a baby?"

"Oh, man, you know it weren't pleasant–took it a hell of a lot better'n you woulda..."

"I appreciate that, Earnest..."

"Hey, but I had nothin' to do wid it. I was just watchin'."

"Yeah, watchin'." Harry drew a breath. "Okay, Earnest, here's what I'm offering you..." He backed away from Badeye, keeping the pistol pointed at his forehead. Harry reached into his back pocket for his handkerchief, then drew another pistol from the side pocket and wiped it clean of his fingerprints.

"Here," he said, "I brought your piece from Frisco. I even put a bullet in it." He laid it on the floor a few paces from Badeye. "I thought a long time about this, Earnest. My first choice was to give you the exact treatment you gave Charlie. An eye for an eye. Then I realized Charlie would never have gone for it–woulda said we gotta treat you better 'cause we had more advantages. I never, myself, bought into that philosophy, but in Charlie's memory–I'm going to make it easy on you."

"You said you wouldn't..."

"Earnest, you got three choices. One, you run for it like a coward." Harry smacked his hand against the gun. "History. Put your prints on the piece. Two, you take yourself out like a man. Eye for an eye sort of thing." Harry stopped.

"You said three."

"Very good, Earnest. You got a good memory, and on top of that you can count as high as three." Harry shook his head. "You'da made it in the real world, Earnest. What a terrible waste. But, hey, I thought your third option was obvious. You try to get that bullet in me before I get one in you."

"How I gonna do that? You already got the piece pointed at me."

Harry smiled. "Won't be easy."

"Man, you said you wouldn't..."

Harry unlocked Badeye's cuffs, then walked around to face him, keeping his gun pointed at Badeye's gut.

Badeye looked at the gun down near his feet. The lazy mind was working, calculating his chances.

"Where's the bullet?" he asked.

"First chamber."

"How I know?"

"Pick it up an' look at it, stupid."

"You'll shoot."

"Yes, unless you shoot yourself, that's the plan."

Badeye Iler licked his lips. He had to admit he enjoyed more giving Charlie his.

Slowly, Badeye picked up the gun and gently turned it to look in the chamber. Harry told the truth, there was one bullet in the first chamber, ready to go off.

Badeye whipped the gun around, but Harry got him—Badeye's went off, but he was already on his way down.

Harry looked down at his adversary in the last throes of life. What a rip-off, he thought. An unfair trade, a sacrifice of a punk for a prince.

Badeye's eyes were open. The last thing he saw was Officer Harry Schlacter, LAPD, looking down at him. The huge, blond, lily-white policeman was crying.

Also Available from Allen A. Knoll, Publishers
Books for Intelligent People Who Read for Fun

The Snatch
By David Champion
Two cops whose methods are polar opposites—in love with the same kidnapped woman—race against time and each other to save her. From Los Angeles' lowlands to its highest mountain, *The Snatch* races at breakneck speed to a crashing climax. $19.95

The Mountain Massacres: A Bomber Hanson Mystery
By David Champion
In this riveting, edge-of-your-seat suspense drama, world-famous attorney Bomber Hanson and his engaging son Tod explore perplexing and mysterious deaths in a remote mountain community. $14.95

Nobody Roots for Goliath: A Bomber Hanson Mystery
By David Champion
Mega-lawyer Bomber Hanson and his son Tod take on the big guns—the tobacco industry. Is it responsible for killing their client? $22.95

Celebrity Trouble: A Bomber Hanson Mystery
By David Champion
Unspeakable acts of child molestation against mega-star Steven Shag prompt him to call Bomber Hanson. Courtroom theatrics abound as the nature of man unfolds in this continuation of the accalimed series. $20

Bluebeards Last Stand: A Gil Yates Private Investigator novel
By Alistair Boyle
A rich widow, a gold-digging boyfriend and a luxury cruise to New Zealand is Gil Yates's latest escapade. $20

The Unlucky Seven: A *Gil Yates Private Investigator novel*
By Alistair Boyle
Do seven powerful people rule the world? Control all of our actions? Someone thinks so, and is systematically sending bombs to kill each of these seven wealthy and influential men. Three are dead already by the time mega-priced, contingency private investigator Gil Yates arrives on the scene. $20

The Con: A *Gil Yates Private Investigator Novel*
By Alistair Boyle
Gil Yates is at it again—this time in the high-stakes art world, bringing the danger, romance and humor that Boyle's fans love. $19.95

The Missing Link: A *Gil Yates Private Investigator novel*
By Alistair Boyle
A desperate and ruthless father demands that Gil bring him his missing daughter. The game quickly turns deadly with each unburied secret, until Gil's own life hangs by a thread. $19.95

Order from your bookstore, library, or from Allen A. Knoll, Publishers at (800) 777-7623. Or send a check for the amount of the book, plus $3.00 shipping and handling for the first book, $1.50 for each additional book, (plus 7 ¾% tax for California residents) to: Allen A. Knoll, Publishers, 200 West Victoria Street, Santa Barbara, Ca 93101. Credit Cards accepted. Please call if you have any questions—
(800) 777-7623.